Book 2
TEXAS *Heart & Soul*
SERIES

His Temporary Wife

Leslie P. García

author of *Wildflower Redemption* and *Unattainable*

CRIMSON ROMANCE

F+W Media, Inc.

Published by
Crimson Romance
an imprint of F+W Media, Inc.
10151 Carver Road, Suite 200
Blue Ash, OH 45242. U.S.A.
www.crimsonromance.com

ISBN 10: 1-4405-8094-4
ISBN 13: 978-1-4405-8094-9
eISBN 10: 1-4405-8095-2
eISBN 13: 978-1-4405-8095-6

Cover art © iStockphoto.com/katielittle25

Working for minimum wage at a retail building supply store while raising children and crossing the border from Laredo into Nuevo Laredo may seem to be an adventure, but it drains a body of dreams and the energy to chase them. Fortunately, at a difficult point in my life, I met Maria Eugenia Lopez. Jeannie was bubbly and energetic, friendly—perky, even—all the things I wasn't. A gifted woman, Jeannie put herself through college and shared her music and writing with me. Most of all, she kept telling me I could. I could write. I could go to college in spite of four young children and no money. I could.

Without Jeannie I couldn't have, or wouldn't have known that I could. Jeannie, thanks for being the friend who listened to my writing, and let me listen to your songs and poems—the work we always promised each other would be published "someday." Thanks for teaching me there really was a someday, and that because of you—it's here.

Acknowledgments

We live in a world where there are at least two truths: there's an app for everything, and there's a country song for everything. *His Temporary Wife* let me indulge my passion for country music while telling the story of Esmeralda Salinas and Rafael Benton, and the very different roads that bring them together—for love or for money.

I owe special thanks to author and karaoke guru MJ Schiller. I don't do karaoke, but if I did, I'd do it like her. She taught me everything I know about the practice, and I'm grateful for that. By the way, there's a song for that—Toby Keith and Jimmy Buffet's "Too Drunk to Karaoke." A song for everything, I tell you!

I've lived in Laredo for thirty plus years, and I eat out occasionally. But not often enough or widely enough that I could decide where former Laredoans would eat if they came back for a brief visit. I can't name all my Facebook friends who commented, but want to thank Norma Y. Flores, Mary Lopez Perez, Jamie Ortiz, Lourdes Jasso, Emma Perales Gonzalez, Gina Oceguera, and Erica P. Salinas for their boisterous discussion of the nominated restaurants. To find out where "real" Laredoans would go after a lengthy absence, read on.

Without my sister Victoria M. Potter, I'd crash any book three or four times and never recover it, and that doesn't account for the times I e-mail her in the middle of the night to look something over. She's a skillful editor, a great writer—if I'd just give her the time to write—and an incredible sister.

Finally, I can't give enough credit to my Crimson Romance editors Tara Gelsomino, Julie Sturgeon, and Jess Verdi. For most of my life, I wanted to be able to say "my editors," but it was more a product of romanticized hope than an acceptance that editors are key to good writing. Tara, thanks for wanting *His Temporary Wife*. Julie, how you can keep me organized and more or less functioning on schedule, I'm not sure. And Jess—wow. Your ability to spot both the gaping holes and the missed punctuation in a story astounds. Without your help, *His Temporary Wife* would be a rough draft rather than a finished story. Thanks.

Leslie

Chapter One

Esmeralda Salinas leaned forward over the wheel of the rented pickup and peered at the road ahead. It disappeared between two sheer cuts, dotted on both sides with scrub cedar and large rocks that looked likely to fall onto the road at any minute.

In spite of the cold air blasting out of the air conditioning vents, blowing loose tendrils of hair around her forehead, beads of sweat trickled down her cheeks.

"And I thought I could drive anywhere!" she muttered and glanced momentarily into the rearview mirror, checking the horse trailer behind her, carrying all she had of her past. She couldn't see her Appaloosa mare, Domatrix, of course, but the late-model trailer seemed to be riding well and taking the curves.

She glanced at her dash and gulped air. Three, maybe four minutes more of the treacherous Hill Country back road and she'd come out on the state blacktop taking her into tiny Truth, Texas. Taking her home—if you could call a town you'd never been in, home.

Her tension eased when she turned gently onto the asphalt. She could have gone a longer way around and spared herself a lot of stress and worry for the mare's safety, but she had been in the Hill Country years ago and hadn't thought the "hills" were particularly frightening. A boyfriend had been driving then, and she couldn't say she remembered the narrow roads, the twists, or much of anything.

With relief she reached out and turned on the radio, immediately picking up a country station out of San Antonio. The station reached most of central Texas and had been her favorite back in Rose Creek.

She knew the song immediately and joined in, reveling in the music. A car on the other side of the two-lane road passed and the driver waved. She waved back, something she'd done routinely since she got off the interstate. Seemed all the drivers were friendly, even more than they'd been in Rose Creek. Maybe she could truly find a home here.

The next song blasted out, a song that had been huge for the singer Cody Benton. "Afraid for You" had rocketed up the charts to number one, and Cody was tagged as country music's next goddess. But she'd died in a drug-induced stupor, right here in Truth. Esme slowed as she coasted over a hill and passed the sign welcoming her to town. Goose bumps peppered her arms as she noticed the large billboard "In Memory of Cody Benton," and her anger pricked. She didn't remember Cody being born here or living here for much of her short life. Couldn't the town find a more tasteful salute to the woman than claiming her memory?

Still, Cody had brought Esme here in a way, so maybe she shouldn't be so judgmental. She bit her lip. She'd planned on leaving Rose Creek for some time, planned on going somewhere bigger, with women who didn't know and fear her, and men who didn't look at her with way too much interest. She'd made some poor personal choices over the years and just knew it was time to go. She'd been surprised and touched that her formal rival, Luz Wilkinson—Luz Estes now, she reminded herself, glad that it didn't hurt at all—held a small party the night before she left. Even the town veterinarian came, a clear sign of forgiveness for her trying to snag the doctor's husband for her own.

She'd chosen to come here to Truth because she'd heard her aunt was here now, and because of a late-night interview she'd seen with Cody Benton shortly before the singer's death. Cody had been vamping with the host, who'd asked her why she was spending so much time in a "one-horse town."

Cody had laughed and answered that she owned two horses herself, so that problem was solved. And then she'd winked, "If your life's been a lie, maybe you should try a little truth."

Whether or not the line had been rehearsed, Esmeralda couldn't forget it. And when she decided for sure to leave Rose Creek, she headed northwest without a moment of indecision.

Esmeralda saw her destination ahead on the right and slowed almost subconsciously. So here she was, about to drop in on the aunt she hardly knew. Tina Cervantes, her mother's sister, had visited three or four times over twenty-odd years. Once she'd gone to college, Esmeralda hadn't seen her aunt again. She could count on both hands the times they'd spoken on the phone, too. Tina had called to wish her a happy birthday about four months ago, not really near her birthday. Esmeralda didn't tell her she was two months late; she just relished the brief contact with the woman she always thought would have been a better mother than her own had been.

And now here she was, jobless and homeless, hoping to find the roots she'd struggled to cut when she'd left home back in Laredo, fleeing from cold parents and an abusive brother, heading up the I-35 corridor until she settled in Rose Creek. Gregarious and independent, Tina always insisted that Esmeralda should visit. Once, long ago, she'd offered her house, "any time, just come on over." Tina was living in Chicago then, with a man she'd never mentioned before, and Esmeralda would never have considered going. Besides, she'd been perfectly happy in Rose Creek with its proximity to San Antonio, and its easy driving distance to Laredo for those infrequent visits to her parents.

She turned carefully onto the side street running along the weathered-wood look exterior of Tía's. The neon sign outside the club was unlit, but pictured a smiling woman surrounded by an explosion of stars.

Somehow the sign sent confidence surging through her. If Tina billed herself as the town's "aunt," or *tía*, then surely she'd be delighted to have her only real niece turn up out of the blue. Right?

Apparently the business catered to an evening crowd; only two cars were in the parking lot and their proximity to the side door suggested employees, not clients. Esmeralda parked carefully, taking up a lot of space, but being sure delivery trucks or anyone cutting through the large parking lot could maneuver around the trailer. She disliked leaving the mare unattended, but couldn't see driving out to the farm where she'd found a stall for rent until she'd spoken to her aunt.

When she opened the side window, Domatrix immediately stuck her velvety nose in the opening and nickered plaintively.

"Five minutes," Esme promised. "I'll get you out of here before you know it!" Gently pushing the mare's nose back in, she fastened the panel, drew a deep breath, and headed off to find her aunt.

The front door was locked. She should have just tried the back. Esme glanced around. Across the street, a restaurant had customers going in and coming out. Probably the social hub of the town, she decided. The three—three!—bars in Truth undoubtedly catered to the cowboy and tourist crowd that wouldn't be in town until nightfall. Next to the restaurant, a neat, cheeky little salon sported a sign claiming to offer "Truth In Beauty." She smiled and retraced her steps, seeing a large pickup, dark and gleaming, slide into a nearby space.

The back door opened, letting her into a brightly lit food-preparation area. She could smell oregano-spiced *menudo* simmering on a stove and hear the sound of someone humming from somewhere unseen.

"Hello? Tina? Anyone home?" Esmeralda called, reluctant to go any deeper into this unknown place and startle someone, or set off an alarm. She moved a step or two farther along the island, and stopped short, her attention snared by the mirrored back of the door separating—she supposed—the club area from the kitchen. She brushed at the strands of hair that had come loose during the drive—light auburn hair made darker by the dampness from heat and drive-induced stress. Her breath caught suddenly in her throat as a figure loomed behind her, light glinting off almost-black hair, brown eyes spearing her own in the mirror—a formidable, unexpected stranger.

But surely this person wouldn't have just walked in if he didn't have that right. Apprehension dissipated with the logic, and she turned and held out a hand, hoping it wasn't as damp as her hair.

"Hello. I'm Esmeralda Salinas, Tina's niece." His brows went up slightly, as if her introduction surprised him. Did he know her aunt, then? He didn't look like a delivery man, in his Western shirt, creased pants, and polished boots.

Her parents had called Tina some awful names, in Spanish and English. The kindest thing Esme could remember hearing from her mother was that Tina "liked men." Could this man be her partner? The names, and the possibility of a man or men in her aunt's life, didn't bother her. Lord knew she'd been pegged, usually by other women, as everything from a tramp to a whore. None of the labels were true, but she never disclaimed them—gossips wouldn't change their minds and she didn't care. But her aunt might not appreciate her deciding to just drop by and say hello, taking her up on that long-standing invitation to come any time.

Esme ignored the misgivings. If her aunt didn't have room or time for her, she'd hang around a day or two and move on. She had a degree, a few dollars in the bank, and absolute confidence in her own abilities.

The man still hadn't answered. She arched her own brow. "And you are?" she prompted, with a tinge of sarcasm.

His head moved back slightly, almost as if he weren't used to being challenged. Then he smiled and took her hand. "Rafael Benton."

Her hand tingled under the firm pressure of his, but she ignored it. She'd come to Truth to find herself again, not a man. She'd committed a professional blunder back in Rose Creek, toying with a six-year-old's emotions because she wanted the little girl's father. One could argue that she hadn't done any real harm, but she expected more from herself. Always.

He released her hand and took a step back, but she could swear he was looking at her left hand.

Did he wonder if she was married? Was he thinking about striking up a conversation? Finding a way to ask her out? He'd better not be involved with her aunt, then. She'd been burned more than once thinking a man was free. Or giving herself free rein to pursue men who weren't available, figuring it didn't matter to her if their own women couldn't keep them from straying. Never again, she vowed.

He didn't toss her compliments or suggestive lines, though, just peered past her at the door. "You caught me by surprise. Tía never mentioned having a niece." He seemed to think that would hurt her feelings, judging from momentary awkwardness in his quick glance her way. "Not that we've spoken often."

The humming stopped and Esmeralda heard something fall, followed by a brief curse in Spanish. Then a woman emerged, her apron spattered, but her thin face changing from annoyed to pleased as she greeted Rafael.

"Rafa! How are you?" Then dark eyes turned her way and Esmeralda sensed immediate suspicion.

"Yes? May I help you?" she demanded, wiping her hands on the sides of her apron.

"I'm Esmeralda—Esme Salinas. Tina's niece."

"Her niece—oh." At least this woman, who clearly worked for her aunt, didn't seem surprised that Tina had a niece. Startled, maybe, but not surprised. She walked over to offer her hand to Esmeralda, giving her a polite nod. "I'm Angelica Morales, but your aunt calls me Angel." A slight smile lightened her expression. "Tía says a place like this in a town like Truth needs every angel it can get."

"She isn't wrong about that," Rafael Benton muttered and both women shot him a glance. He shrugged and added, "You should know, the place I live is called Witches Haven by the locals."

"Rafa," Angel scolded, her face troubled. "Why would you even repeat such gossip? Hasn't there been enough trouble in this town without helping it along?"

His lips tightened and his chin tilted, making him look angry and a little intimidating. "The trouble isn't with a house on a hill, Angel. We both know that witches had nothing to do with this town's personal slide into hell."

The bitterness and darkness of his words bothered Esmeralda more than they should. "Well, it was nice to meet both of you," she said robotically. "I'll come see Tina later. Do you think she will be in later, Ms. Morales?"

"Tía comes in every day. Mostly." She glanced at a decorative clock on the wall. "About an hour, I imagine. She always comes in to check before we open at four. You can wait—"

"No, thank you. I have a horse with me, and I need to get her unloaded. I'll drop by in a while." She nodded briefly and left.

She had her hand on the doorknob when she heard Rafael's voice, low and fierce, as he whispered to Angel, "I'll kill her.

Chapter Two

Twenty-five minutes more of twisting Hill Country roads and fingers knotted around a steering wheel brought Esmeralda to a small piece of land with a modest, well-kept home and a miniscule shed encircled by an equally tiny corral.

"It's perfectly safe, ma'am," the landowner assured her, his weathered face creased into lines of weariness. He hitched up his overalls.

"I thought you had a closed stall, Mr. Peterson," Esmeralda protested, hating the feeling that turning him down would hurt him financially, but not willing to leave her mare here in the middle of nowhere exposed to any bad weather that might blow in. She couldn't see any hazards in the corral, and the fence looked sound, but …

"Lillie Mae had her horse here after she fell," he added. "Six months. Wintered here. I closed up two sides of the shed and he was just fine."

"Yes," she said gently. "I spoke to Ms. Wilson, remember? You sent me her name as a reference?"

He looked puzzled. "Lillie Mae complained about me?"

"No. She told me you'd been wonderful, taking care of her horse for free after she broke her hip. "But—" She shrugged and waved a hand at the small area. "My mare just wouldn't have enough room or shelter here."

"Well, then, good luck to you, Miss Salinas." He scratched his chin and looked thoughtfully at the trailer. "Might find a place over at the Double Block Ranch. Not a lot of places would board a horse around here. Unless—" The sun-browned face brightened. "If you have kin—"

"I do," she acknowledged. "But my aunt Tina wouldn't have a place for a horse, I don't think."

His brow knotted. "Tina? Small town, and we know pretty much everyone here, but I don't remember ..."

"Most everyone calls her Tía, I think."

His puzzlement disappeared. "Oh, that'd be Tía Cervantes. Nice lady. But we never heard about you." He shrugged a little. "Well, if you want the truth be told, she's kind of standoffish to some of us. But I'm sure she's a nice lady anyhow."

He turned at the sound of an old sedan laboring its way along the drive, and his whole face lit up. "Connie's come home," he explained. "My wife works down at the Longhorn Bait and Wait store over at the lake."

Connie came toward them, her frame thin like her husband's, her steps a little slow, but a huge smile of welcome on her face. "Hi, there," she greeted, walking right up to Esme, pecking her cheek, and hugging her. "Y'all'd be the lady bringing the horse to stay. Emerald—" She stopped herself. "No, that's not right. It's Spanish, right? For the same thing?"

Esmeralda smiled, liking this couple who were already more accepting of her than many folks in Rose Creek had ever been. "Don't worry. It means the same thing. If you'd like, you can call me Esme."

"So, are you about to take your horse out?" Connie asked hopefully. "I love horses, but can't ride anymore. Even if we could afford to, I couldn't. Hurt my back last year, and I'm not real well."

"Ma, Esme don't want to hear all our troubles. She's changed her mind—wanted a little better place for her horse."

Connie's face fell, but she gave Esme a brave smile. "Sorry to hear that dear, but of course you want the best for your horse."

Esmeralda looked around slowly. The place wasn't luxurious, but seemed safe. Besides, if for some reason she didn't stay here ...

she breathed a little prayer under her breath that this wouldn't be a mistake. "Actually, Mr. Peterson—"

"Irving, ma'am. Call me Irving. We don't stand on formality."

"Irving, if you don't mind, I think I'll leave her until I get settled. You did hold the place for me."

Irving's face broke into a wide smile. "Well, you won't regret it. If you move her later, that's fine. And if you want her to stay, I could fix up the shed. Build up the walls so she'd be nice and warm."

"Let's wait on that, though," Esmeralda encouraged. "I need to see what my long-term plans are. I'll let her out now, if you don't mind."

"Can't wait to see her!" Connie walked over to a spot by the small corral and waited, her face full of expectation.

Esmeralda drew the pin on the trailer and let the ramp down, then eased in beside the mare and backed her out, hearing the gasps of admiration from the Petersons.

"She's beautiful! Never seen a prettier Appaloosa," Connie declared, clasping her hands together almost in applause.

Esme smiled. This must be how parents felt when their babies were complimented. Domatrix did attract attention with her stocky conformation, glossy blood bay coat, and rump-covering blanket of white, with its explosion of bay and black spots.

After unclipping the mare's lead and rubbing her ears, she watched as Domatrix inspected her new surroundings, then returned to head butt her affectionately. Connie came over, her hand held out.

"Okay if I make friends with her?" she asked, and the mare turned around and head butted her, too, then snuffed at the stranger's cheek.

"Looks like she's fine with it." Esmeralda grinned.

"What's her name?"

Right. Her name. There were times she wished she'd chosen a tamer name, that Toby, her fiancé, hadn't goaded her to choose the name she'd given her. "Domatrix."

The couple's face didn't change. "What a pretty name," Connie crooned. "I bet you call her Trixie for short, right?"

"Ummm … I usually use her whole name, but I don't mind if you call her that," Esme offered. She looked around. "I'll unload the food and get her watered. Then I need to go into town. I'll be out first thing in the morning."

The Petersons nodded absently, both busy fussing over her mare, who seemed to like the couple far more than she did most strangers.

A few minutes later, Esmeralda pulled open the door of the truck, wishing it were the Corvette she'd sold before packing up and leaving Rose Creek. At least she could leave the trailer for the moment and the sun was still high in the summer sky. Surely she'd have an easier trip back.

She hoisted a leg to swing up when she suddenly remembered the words Rafael Benton had hissed at Angela. "I'll kill her." Why the words returned so abruptly she didn't know, but she shivered slightly. Maybe she'd misheard him. And "her" could be anyone, couldn't it?

"Mr.—Irving, do you and Connie know someone named Rafael Benton?" she asked curiously.

"Hmph! Can't say I know him, but I know about him," Irving answered, face full of displeasure. "One of those rich city bigwigs come here to ruin the town."

"Irving Peterson, shame on you! Judging a man on nothing but rumors and gossip," Connie said.

"Well, he lives at Witches Haven," Irving snorted. "Can't be a godly man alive who would live there."

"Witches Haven?"

"Now don't you pay no mind to that," Connie ordered. "Just a name someone gave this house on a hill, cause it's built so secretive and so dark."

"Looks like the devil's place," Irving put in.

"Sounds weird," Esmeralda noted, climbing in and fastening her seatbelt.

"Surprised you didn't see it," Irving continued. "You drove right by it about a mile from here. It'll be on your left on the hill as you go around Death's Curve."

"Colorful," she muttered, then nodded at the Petersons and backed out.

She'd left Rose Creek after a kidnapping and fire had ended a dog-fighting ring—something she would never have expected to find in such a small town.

Yet here she was in Truth, hearing a muttered death threat from a man who lived in a place called Witches Haven. On Death Curve. *Yeah, right.* The irony amused her most of the way back to Truth, and by the time she remembered to be on the lookout for the sinister-sounding place, she'd driven right by. She shook her head and turned the radio up a little louder, blocking out everything except the music that always sustained her.

• • •

I'm crazy. Rafael Benton slouched in a plush chair in Tía's private upstairs office, and methodically closed and opened his fingers, a habit he'd had since he'd run wild on the streets of Laredo, a child without a home or hope. Sometimes he'd used those fists, often to his own disadvantage. Small and undernourished as a child, he knew he was a lot more intimidating now than he'd been then. He didn't mind; there was protection in strength, real or perceived.

But he'd been stupid, telling Angela that he'd kill Tía. He didn't mean it; he would never hurt a woman. Probably not anyone else, either; his parents had brought him up to be persistent, but not ruthless. Protective, but not violent. He smiled, seeing images of his adoptive mother and father in his mind. Good people, enormously successful. A little stubborn and set in their ways. Incredibly loved.

And he'd let them down. Irritated, he shoved himself from the chair and paced across the small, polished wood floor, his stomach churning. From up here, he could still see her life-size photo on the far wall of the club, a single candle burning there always. Cody Benton. The baby sister he'd adored. The woman he'd let die. Bile rose in his throat, and he swallowed hard. He'd had help letting her destroy herself. Tía had been chief among all those "friends," with their endless demands, pleasures, and false smiles. For every move he'd made to increase the security around his sister, Tía had managed to help Cody circumvent it.

He wouldn't hurt Tía, though, and the fact that Angela trusted him here in her boss's sanctuary proved that she knew he wasn't a threat. At least not physically. If he could cause the collapse of this damn bar around Tina Cervantes's ears, he would. She deserved to lose something; his sister had lost everything. And the destruction had started down on that stage tucked into a front corner of the bar.

He swallowed hard, trying to chase the sour taste out of his mouth. He'd been a fool to involve her in his desperate plan to provide stability and safety for Cody's now motherless son. She couldn't be trusted not to talk, though she'd sworn she could. He'd thought he could buy her silence, if not loyalty, but he wasn't sure he even had that. If she talked, his parents would find out and be crushed. And he'd endanger the only solution he'd come up with to assure his nephew's future.

His phone vibrated, and he pulled it out. The wallpaper showed a smiling little boy, chubby-cheeked with wheat colored hair and blinding blue eyes. His nephew, Justin.

The number belonged to his friend and former partner, Marc Dryer. Marc still worked out of Rafael's father's Dallas office, chasing around the globe to investigate problems within the oil company, assess threats, evaluate investments—the go-to man. A job they'd done together, before Cody launched a music career.

Wearily he clicked the phone on.

"Marc, what's up?"

"Nothing, man. Just called to see how you're doing."

"I'm good."

"Hmph. Look, you're punishing yourself. Tell your dad you want to come back to Houston. I may be flying out to the Middle East next month. I'll need you with me."

"I have some loose ends to tie up here, Marc."

They talked briefly, and then Marc said into a sudden lull, "So are you still going to do it?"

"Yes, and don't lecture me. I am."

"Man, you've got rocks in your head. Cotton brains. A …"

"Save it," Rafael snapped. "I'd do anything to make up for what I couldn't do for Cody, and you know it. Do you think I don't know how I let Mom and Dad down? And my nephew doesn't have a mother. How do I fix that?"

Marc didn't answer at first, but then he sighed heavily. "I don't know," he admitted. "But dude … I'm almost sure hiring a wife won't work."

Chapter Three

When the front door of the club swung open at four and a petite woman bustled in, Esmeralda straightened in her chair and peered at the newcomer doubtfully. If this was her aunt, her memories were faulty. The high-piled raven hair glinted under the soft lighting, and elaborate gold earrings fell almost to her shoulders. The woman wore a long, flowered skirt that stopped high enough off the ground to show delicate feet accented by the lace up heels. Esmeralda didn't remember her aunt being so petite. Even in heels, this woman was short.

The tight, low-cut top exposing a wealth of cleavage … well, she wouldn't have noticed that about her aunt on those brief moments she'd visited with her as a child, would she? When she looked carefully at Tía's face, she knew. Tía bore little resemblance to her sister Adriana; the eyes and the nose were completely different. The broad lips, though … their mouths would have been identical if Adriana had smiled more. In Esme's memories, Tía always smiled. Now, though, the woman who had come in looked serious and unhappy, and the sullen mouth clearly identified her.

Drawing a deep breath, Esmeralda rose to her feet and walked towards her aunt. "Tía Tina—TT!" The double initials were a nickname that Esme and her brother used for their aunt, apparently because at some point Beto had been unable to pronounce his aunt's formal name.

Tina stopped, utter shock freezing her face. Seconds ticked past and Esmeralda felt nerves clench in her stomach. Suddenly the faint aroma of the menudo oozing in from the kitchen made her nauseous.

Then Tina crossed over to her, and placed hands on her arms, then her face. "Esme? Esmeralda Salinas, is this really you … all

…. all ….” She wrapped Esmeralda in an enormous hug. “Where's everyone? Did Angel feed you? Has anyone given you something to drink? Angel!”

“I'm fine,” Esmeralda assured her. “It's so good to see you, TT.”

“It's … I can't believe you're here, girl! And looking like you just stepped out of one of them fashion magazines!” She pinched Esme's cheek with silver nails that sparkled. “And I don't mean beautiful, I mean you look starved!” She chortled a little. “Well, okay, you're gorgeous, too, but you seriously need to eat!”

“I'm fine,” Esme repeated. “I had a late lunch.” *And menudo would make me puke right now.*

Angel hurried in just then. “*¿Me hablaste?*”

Annoyance came and went in Tina's face. “You know I called you, and you know I don't want you to use Spanish unless there's a reason to. Did you feed my niece?”

Color tinted Angel's cheeks. “She didn't want anything, Tía. I did ask.”

“Please don't scold her, TT. She insisted, but as I told you, I'd just eaten. I really didn't want food.”

“Okay. And darling, I have a little favor to ask.” Tina turned to Esme. “Please, please, don't call me TT. Or Tina.” She smiled, not quite enough to take the emphasis off her order. “Bad for business. No one calls me anything but Tía.”

“Well, I guess I can do that. I mean, you really are my aunt.” Esmeralda grinned.

“Exactly. And all my best clients are family, too,” her aunt said. “Make them feel like family and they'll come here every time. Angel, where's Tom?”

“In the back, checking stock. We've been watching. If anyone comes in, he'll be right out.”

“Good. Can't have a bar without a bartender, can we? Go tell him it's time for him to be out here, Angel.” Tía turned back to

Esmeralda. "So, darling, exactly what brought you to the exciting town of Truth, Texas?"

"Two things," Esmeralda admitted, watching her aunt's face carefully. She reached out and caught one of Tía's hands, squeezing it. "I wanted to see you." She paused, fighting back her nervousness, and managed to smile a little. "And I decided to take you up on your invitation."

"My invitation?" Tía withdrew her hand and cocked her head a little, her glance quizzical. "What invitation, *querida mía?*"

Her aunt's endearment puzzled her a little, since she'd just told Angel not to use Spanish. But at least the tone seemed positive.

"When you were in Chicago, you told me I should just drop by whenever—that I'd always have a home. I ... I decided to drop by and see ... if you'd still have me."

Tía looked like she'd been punched in the gut. All color left her face, and one hand went to her chest, clasping the place over her heart as if she were in danger of falling over.

Esme wanted to die.

"Tía, I'm sorry. I wanted to surprise you. I should have called." She circled her hands in the air helplessly. "I'll rent a place for a few days. If you have time, we'll visit—"

"You didn't call," Tía hissed. "Moving in is a big deal, Esmeralda!"

"Of course it is," Esme acknowledged, her cheeks flaming. "I'm so sorry ... I ..."

"Never mind," Tía ordered, pulling herself together. The tight lines around her mouth eased into the grin Esme remembered so well. "I guess I did that a couple or three times, even to your Mom."

"She's your sister," Esme reminded Tía. "She ..."

"Tries to love me," Tía retorted, nodding sarcastically. "And mostly fails."

The door opened, and a couple of men walked in, choosing a table near her aunt. They were middle-aged and dressed in ranch clothes—worn shirts and boots, jeans that bore rips from riding through cedar or fighting barbed wire and losing. Not the Rose Creek kind of cowboys. Excitement pricked in Esme. Solid men, cowboys. Not these men, who probably had wives and half-grown children, but maybe she would quit looking for men and find a man. *The* man. She allowed herself a tiny smile. If the man looked anything like Rafael Benton, she could certainly live with that.

"*Hola*, Tía!" one of the men called in Anglicized Spanish. "Got Roy and me some menudo coming out yet?"

"You betcha, Chuck!" Tía turned to the bar. "Tom, take care of my boys, won't you?"

He nodded and headed off to the kitchen.

"None of my business, but … who's your friend, Tía?" The cowboy smiled at Esmeralda, "If you don't mind my asking," he added.

Esmeralda would have introduced herself, but Tía wrapped an arm around her, squeezing her. "My niece, Esmeralda. Folks call her Esme."

"Your niece!" Both men stood up and walked over, holding out hands. "Well, welcome to Truth! We didn't know our Tía here had real kin around."

Esmeralda shook their hands, returning their smiles. "Just got here a couple of hours ago," she admitted. "Nice meeting you."

Tom and Angela came out with colorfully decorated bowls of menudo and a basket heaped with steaming tortillas.

"Enjoy," Angel said, nodding at the pair as she left.

"Thanks, Angel," they answered in unison.

"Excuse us," Chuck said, nodding. "We have a date with some cow gut soup and cold beer."

"Hmph!" Tía swatted Chuck's arm playfully. "Keep insulting my native food and I won't feed you. It's not guts. It's stomach."

"That makes it all better." Roy grinned, and the two headed back to dig into the food they'd just insulted.

Tía turned back to Esmeralda. "Look, honey, things are about to get busy—for a Thursday night. We'll have our regulars, and this is tourist season. You look tired." She reached out and patted Esme's cheek, this time not pinching her with the metallic nails. "I'd be delighted to have you stay."

Esme started to protest, but her aunt shushed her. "End of discussion. My house is on Cattle Court Road. Just go back down the main street. It turns into the highway, and half a mile out of town you'll see a sign for Cattle Court Road on the left. There are only two houses there—the rest is part of a ranch, but the ranch house sits way back where you can't see it from the road. My house is on the right. No dogs, but my handyman carries a gun."

"A gun?" Esme asked.

Her aunt chuckled. "Don't worry. He pulls double duty as handyman and watchman." She fished out a cell phone. "I'll call Andy and let him know not to shoot you."

"Gee, thanks," Esme muttered, and Tía laughed again.

"Welcome to Truth, honey. Drive safe." Tía bussed her on the cheek. "Use anything you want. Probably won't see you till tomorrow. *Eat*."

"Yes, ma'am." Esme turned to the door, her legs a little weak. She hadn't eaten since breakfast, not wanting to leave Domatrix alone in the trailer on the way up, and anxiety and fatigue from the unexpectedly difficult drive and her aunt's initial reaction had taken a toll. She couldn't wait to get home. The word stopped her in mid-stride for a moment, and she almost stumbled. Home? Rose Creek hadn't been. Truth didn't feel that way. Not yet. She regained her balance, determined to give the tiny town a chance.

•••

Rafael watched the conversation going on below him, aware that nobody could have told Tía he was here yet. Otherwise, she would have stormed up here in a rage and booted him out, demanding that he speak to her downstairs. Wondering what he'd been looking for.

He frowned. The one time Angel let him wait here before had seemed proof positive to him that the woman was hiding something. Tía had been livid to find him alone in the office, and accused him of going through her desk looking for valuables. She'd fumed that strangers were never allowed here, but they hadn't been strangers. They'd met often, since he almost always accompanied Cody when she came, and given the wealth and position of his parents—and his own, for crissakes—she couldn't seriously have been worried that he'd pocket anything of hers. Clearly, the woman was overly suspicious. In his experience, that kind of alarm over something unimportant was a sign that the person had things to hide.

He hoped Tom or Angel warned her before she walked in on him not even knowing he was here.

He could see well enough to gauge some of the interaction he saw between Tía and Esmeralda. He smiled a little. The name was one of his favorites, and it certainly matched her eyes. He remembered the green gaze, reflected back to him by the mirror on the door. He remembered more, too. The cotton shirt clinging to her damply, unbuttoned a little lower than she probably realized and not nearly as low as he would have liked. *Damn, she was hot.*

Tía's expression changed from distant and annoyed to friendly. Maybe Esmeralda would even call it affectionate. How well did she know her aunt? He wouldn't call their meeting joyous, by any stretch. At one point, Esmeralda almost looked as if she'd turn and walk away.

He gritted his teeth, but it didn't help. Tía caused a lot of tears. It never seemed to bother her. He hoped Esmeralda was tough. But not tough like her aunt.

Esmeralda was leaving. What was that song about watching women leave? He remembered the lyric suddenly and smiled. Would she hate him for thinking she had a pretty nice "badonkadonk"? Almost to the door, she seemed to falter, then stumble. He reached out, his hand pressing the cold, smoked pane of glass in front of him. As if he could help.

Bitterness surged through him. As if he ever could help. *Dammit, Cody, I'm sorry. You shouldn't have counted on me to save you. You should have*—He forced the thought away. Cody hadn't been able to help herself. His parents knew that, when they asked him to become her manager, assistant, bodyguard—to be the presence he'd always been. And just as he couldn't reach through the glass to steady Esmeralda's path, he hadn't been able to reach Cody. He thought his parents truly forgave him. But he knew he'd never forgive himself. Never.

And now, Tina was jeopardizing his chance to undo at least a little of the damage. She'd promised to keep her mouth shut, and now he'd heard rumors from Lizzie Mae that she had mentioned his need for a temporary wife to her. Lizzie Mae herself wouldn't talk, but she'd warned him that trusting Tina had been stupid. He smiled. Actually, her words had been stronger than that. When he'd told the elderly woman that he planned to hire a woman to marry him in an effort to placate his parents and possibly any court considering Justin's well-being, he half-expected her to slap him silly with the ridiculously big Stetson she wore.

The door opened behind him, and he jerked away from the window.

"Having a private moment, Rafa?" Tía purred, her voice deep and gravelly as she approached him. "Watching my niece maybe and having a little fantasy?"

She'd hit too close to home, but he just shrugged. "And if I were? You didn't seem too happy to see her at first. A little interest from the cowboys there and I think you saw dollar signs flash in front of your eyes! Planning on having her come in to sing like Cody would? No one could compete with Tía's then, could they? Weren't those two Cody's first local fans? You might let her unpack before you start using her."

She gasped in rage and swung at his face, but he'd seen her like this, all false anger and indignation, and he caught her arm easily and stepped back out of her reach.

"Don't, Tía," he warned, almost whispering. "Don't you dare. You've done everything you'll ever do to hurt anyone in my family, and someone like you isn't going to hit me."

"You're trespassing," she retorted. "Go! ¡*Vete*!"

"Angel let me in."

She relented, her body visibly sagging a little as she turned away to stare across the room below. "Do you think I would ever have let harm come to Cody, if I could help it? You need to let go, Rafa! I do not believe your parents want you to suffer like this! I don't want you to hound me like this!" She spun back to him, shaking with anger. "Your sister was a grown woman! I loved her, but she didn't love herself, did she? The drugs and her damned pride killed her, not me! She didn't do anything to help herself."

"But you let them in, Tía! All of them! All those hangers-on, all those groupies who came with their little poison gifts. All those false friends, ready to give her everything she wanted. Anything she asked for, she got. Why do you think she kept coming back here? When she needed a new drummer because hers wouldn't quit trying to make her wake up and sober up, who got her a new drummer who would just keep pouring the alcohol? And you knew that bastard Harper was her biggest problem, but he was always welcome here. Always." He stopped himself. He couldn't bring Cody back by yelling at Tía, no matter what her role had been. He couldn't antagonize her any more right now, either. Not when she'd threatened to tell the entire town that he planned on hiring a woman to marry him. He closed his eyes. If word got out, candidates would come out of the woodwork. Worse, his parents would be horrified, and wouldn't trust him with Justin. Maybe not ever. His reputation would suffer. His stomach knotted. Worst of all, if Doug Harper found out before he married, he might decide to file for custody. If he was Justin's father. No matter how sickening the idea was, it was possible. Maybe even probable. He pulled out his phone and pretended to check his messages, but Justin's face—his sister's face—always gave him the strength he needed to go on.

"Tía, Lillie Mae told me you're talking about making my little plan public. You know that I can't let my parents hear talk about the marriage not being real. You and I might not understand, but they were devastated by Cody being pregnant out of wedlock."

"Your parents are uptight moralists," Tía muttered. "And you're the good little boy who wants to inherit everything someday, right?"

"My parents believe in family, and your insults don't change the situation. We had an agreement. I didn't want you to know, really. But I told the owner of the Silver Boots and Booty because he knows a lot of the locals and has connections all over Texas. I told Lillie Mae because—" He paused, thinking of the octogenarian ranch owner. Tía claimed to be Truth's communal aunt, but Lillie Mae owned the town. "Everyone answers to Lillie Mae. You were one of my sister's favorite people, Tía. She genuinely loved you, though I don't know why. So I told you. You three are the only people who know—and the only people in town who *can* know. Don't forget I covered one of your bank notes—no one else asked me for anything, Tía."

She shrugged. "You offered. I haven't said anything."

He snorted. "If I remember, the offer began with something like 'I'll scratch your back if you scratch mine.' And you said it, I didn't. I won't be blackmailed." He frowned. "And I can't loan you the money you asked for, either."

She walked over to him, her hips swaying. "Sure you could, Rafa." She ran a hand up his arm. "You just won't."

"True." He pulled her hand off his arm and dropped it unceremoniously. "You know how you said you tried to help Cody, but she couldn't help herself? That's how I see you, Tía. Scheming and manipulative and addicted to things you can't have."

She didn't answer for a moment, then simply moved past him. "I won't tell anyone about your idiotic plan," she agreed. "But we still have the deal?"

"Yes," he acknowledged, keeping his voice level in spite of the anger gnawing into his soul. "Lillie Mae and Brockton were insulted that I offered, but if you find an appropriate applicant, and she takes the job, I'll give you an additional ten thousand. As long as no one knows about it."

"No one will know. And I'm bound to think of someone. Lock my office when you leave, Rafa."

"I'm right behind you," he muttered, and followed her out.

• • •

Esme stopped at what appeared to be the only fair-sized grocery store in town, determined to provide for herself. Her aunt's initial reaction still troubled her. But then again, her mother had reacted that way when her own sister dropped in uninvited.

"You'd think Tina would realize she's another mouth to feed, not to mention more work for everyone," Adriana would mutter uncharitably. Then she'd sigh heavily and glare at her husband Eduardo as if he were to blame. "But she is family," she'd add. "We're obligated."

Her brother Beto, three years older, despised Tía, and would hurl epithets around that a child shouldn't know. Beto's behavior was never corrected, because he was the adored oldest son of the household. Some of Esme's friends complained of their brothers being favored, but Esme couldn't imagine that anyone could be as cruel and degrading as Beto was, even then. She'd been away from home for years, but thinking of Beto still made her shiver with revulsion. And remembering her mother's words about another mouth to feed seemed indelibly etched into her soul. Even now, Esmeralda preferred being her own woman, independent and in control—of finances, food, friendships—everything. So she'd buy her own food and try to make as small a footprint in her aunt's life as she could. She smiled. Maybe the problem was that she *was* her aunt, personality-wise, and Tía didn't know that yet.

By the time she finished loading up the car and arrived at her aunt's place, she found herself dragging. She drove down Cattle Court Road at a crawl, too aware of all the deer she'd seen grazing along the sides of the road. The Hill Country seemed like wilderness compared to Rose Creek's plowed and planted fields.

She pulled up to a neatly kept two-story rock house before darkness cloaked her aunt's property and spotted Andy immediately. A spry, older man was sitting on the tailgate of a battered blue truck, legs swinging with barely contained energy, his thin shoulders moving rhythmically from side to side. At first she puzzled over so much movement when he was sitting, but then she noticed the thin cord running from his waist to an ear.

She slid out of her own truck, stretching and smiling as he came over, reluctantly pulling out his device and turning it off, then putting it and the cord back in a pocket.

"Ms. Salinas," he greeted, in a voice devoid of warmth. He nodded, but didn't smile, and when Esmeralda offered her hand, he took it for the briefest of seconds.

"I unlocked the door," he told her. "If you have a lot of stuff . . ."

"I bought some groceries and have a few suitcases." She didn't wait for an offer to help, just scooped up the nearest two bags and headed up the stone walk to the house. She thought she'd have to set the bags down to try the door, but he bounded up at the last minute and pulled the door open. "Kitchen's to the right, just go through the dining room. And your room's the one at the end of the upstairs hall." And he was gone, leaving her to haul the rest of her stuff in alone. So the handyman/watchman didn't like her? She refused to worry. At least he'd kept his gun in his pocket. She yawned into her arm and shuffled into the kitchen to get rid of the bags. She was on her way out to the truck for the next load when she realized that in most small, tranquil communities, even business owners didn't need armed guards.

• • •

There were no pictures of family on the walls or mantel in the living room, the dining room, or the spacious room Andy told her would be hers. Her aunt moved a lot, and she'd never been close to her sister. Esme toweled her hair as she walked around the room and wondered about the lack of photographs.

How deep had the rift between sisters been? Would she and her aunt get along? Did Tina even want her here, or had she just asked out of some sense of duty? Worried, she tossed the towel aside and padded out in the hall, decided to get a bottle of water, chug it down, and go to sleep. Somehow.

On her way down, Esme paused suddenly, glancing at the door nearest the stair landing. Was it her aunt's room? Tía's closed at two and it was only one-thirty, so she doubted Tina would be home yet. Feeling guilty, but almost possessed by the need to peek into the room, Esme gently opened the door.

The room was huge, painted in soft peach shades. A four-poster bed dominated one corner, and a nearby door opened, she supposed, onto the tiny balcony she remembered seeing as she drove up. A mammoth dresser took up most of one wall, with a desk and chair against the other. And over the desk, there were the photos. The memories of a life.

A life spent with others, not family. There were men, with their arms wrapped around a young, smiling Tía. Other women, clearly friends and companions, sharing drinks or hugs, laughing at the camera, forever young and perfectly groomed.

And then—Esme's heart thudded. Her aunt stood next to a young woman, smiling up at her as if she were flesh and blood, one hand on the younger woman's cheek in a caress the camera hadn't missed. The tall, blond woman in the low-cut, high-slit gown was Cody Benton. And on her other side, head bent slightly as if listening to something, devastatingly handsome in a tailored tuxedo, stood Rafael Benton.

She stared at the picture for a long time before the last names hit her: Benton. Cody and Rafael ... were married? Somehow, she couldn't remember anything at all about Cody's family. Her presence on the country stage had been explosively successful and tragically short. Try as Esme might, she couldn't pull anything out of her memory about husbands, parents—anyone.

But she knew one thing: Cody Benton was dead. No matter what her relationship to Rafael, the last man she'd actively gone after had been a widow, grieving for a wife. She wouldn't make that mistake again. She spun around and choked back a startled scream. Angel stood just inside the door, watching her with wary eyes.

"You startled me, Angel!" Esme swept a hand around the room. "Hope you and Tina don't mind that I wandered into her room ..."

"My room." Angela came into the room, moving a little stiffly, and patted her arm as she passed and went to sit on the bed. "You're always welcome in my room, Esmeralda."

"I'm embarrassed," Esme admitted, coloring slightly. "If I'd known it was your room ..." She waved at the walls. "I just felt drawn to come in, and when I saw the pictures, I assumed it was my aunt's room."

"No. Your aunt insisted I live with her when she gave me a job, back in Chicago. I'm … I guess you'd say I'm her assistant. Or companion." She shrugged. "Sometimes we hate each other. Sometimes it's love. But she's always generous. Her room is much smaller than this."

"I'm a little ashamed to tell you this, Angel, but I don't know Tía very well. I grew up having this image of her as the most exciting, most beautiful woman in the world. I wanted to live with her since I was little. My mother and father always hated it when she came to visit, though." Esmeralda looked around the room again. "You have so many pictures of her and her friends."

"Your …" Angel seemed to hesitate for a second, then continued, her tone weary. "Your aunt dislikes pictures. Clutter, she calls them, and she always says an uncluttered life is a free life." Angel shook her head. "Well, she says that. Most of these pictures are hers, but she told me I should take care of them for her. She's not easy to figure out, I'll tell you that."

"But freedom is important to her, isn't it?" Esme folded her arms against her chest, warding off the chill of the air-conditioning humming softly in the background. "Even as a child, I remember she'd never stay."

Angel nodded. "I've known her for over ten years now. She doesn't stay anywhere. But she claims the club is her last stop."

"Is she here, too?"

"No. She stayed talking to some customers who left a little late." Angel pushed herself off the bed and walked over to place an oversized purse on the desk. "Her room is downstairs, the room Cody had built on to the original structure. Down the hall, beyond a study and bath. Cody always said a downstairs room was easier to get into and out of without being seen. Tía will probably come in and go straight to sleep. Don't count on seeing her for breakfast, Esme. Anything else?"

Esme cast a final glance at the picture of her aunt with Cody and Rafael Benton. "Just ... were they married?" she asked, indicating the picture with a gesture.

"Married? Heavens no, child! Rafael is—was—Cody's brother."

Stunned, Esme said goodnight and went back to her own room.

Chapter Four

The aroma of coffee percolated through the house, and Esmeralda's eyes, heavy-lidded and unwilling, fought slowly open. Sighing, she pushed herself up on one elbow and glanced at the clock, surprised that she was up before nine after yesterday's trials.

She wondered if Angel took care of her aunt's needs in the morning, too. Apparently the woman was something more than an employee but less than a respected companion. She forced herself into action, determined not to slouch around if her aunt were actually up and busy so early.

Twenty minutes later she hurried downstairs, invigorated by a shower, her hair still damp, but caught up neatly in a ponytail. Maybe she could bring her visit up to her aunt and be sure she was welcome here, not just a relative who had to be taken in.

When she got to the kitchen however, Andy, not Angel, turned from the stove and nodded curtly.

"Your aunt said I should feed you," he told her with hostility, shoveling eggs and sausage links onto a plate, then picking up a biscuit with his fingers and putting it on the side. "Sit down."

"Andy, you clearly don't want to feed me. After today, don't bother. Today, I'll eat this to save you and my aunt from any unpleasantness." She walked over and snatched the plate away, leaving him gaping and scuffing the toe of his boot against the tiled floor as she sat down at the table, facing him.

"Andy, how dare you?" Tina's voice crackled into the silence, and Andy straightened so quickly he backed into the stove. Esme dropped her forkful of eggs back to the plate.

"I expect courtesy to my guests, Andy. You understand that, right?"

The older man mumbled and left the room, and Esmeralda pushed her chair and stood up to greet her aunt.

"I really didn't mind. He probably isn't used to fixing breakfast for strangers." Hesitantly, Esme kissed her aunt on the cheek, the greeting her mother would expect. She wasn't sure Tina would appreciate it. She bit back a sigh, feeling more unsure than she had in years. But she accepted responsibility for the awkwardness, aware that she should have called. Surprises weren't always the best options for family reunions.

Tina accepted the kiss without comment, and moved toward the stove, but Esme stopped her.

"I'll get your plate, Tía," she offered, carefully using the name she'd been told to use. "Juice or coffee?" she asked, as she spooned food onto the plate and set it in front of her aunt.

"Andy can't make coffee. Just juice, and I'll pick up coffee in town."

Once Esme sat down again, Tina reached over suddenly and patted her wrist. "Might not be so bad having you here."

"Tía, I don't have to stay here. I can rent a place until I decide what my plans are," Esme offered, again feeling that she wasn't truly wanted as a houseguest. "We've spent so little time together. We can visit, if you want. I have a horse, and I want to figure out if I'm staying or not before I move her again."

They ate in silence a few minutes. The ornate clock on the kitchen wall ticked off the day in loud increments.

Finally, her aunt lowered her fork and impaled Esme with a hard gaze. "Girl, are you running from something? From someone?"

"No!" Esme set her coffee cup down so hard some of the coffee sloshed over. She wiped it up with her napkin and frowned at her aunt. "Why would you think that?"

Her aunt shrugged and gave Esme a half smile. "I ran a lot. Almost always from bill collectors or men." Her smile faded completely. "Usually I'd wind up at your mother's, and I suppose I shouldn't have been surprised I was never welcome."

"You can't think …" Esme struggled to defend her mother, but as always, found it a difficult task. "You two are sisters. She might not have always approved of you, but … she loves you."

"You don't even say it like you mean it," Tina countered dryly. "But that's not what I want, empty assurances from you. Adriana and I can hash out our own differences." She reached across the table and caught Esme's wrist unexpectedly. "So, there's no husband? No boyfriend? No lover in your life right now?"

None of your business. The questions rankled—they sounded too much like an inquisition from her mother or brother. Cr assorted acquaintances who called themselves friends and tried to dig up whatever dirt might lurk hidden under the surface of a very routine life. "No, no one."

Her aunt's fingers tightened slightly. "You're sure? Because I just had this brilliant idea, but it only works if it doesn't cause either of us any grief."

She took a deep breath. "So, what's up?"

Instead of answering, Tina released her wrist and shoved her chair away from the table and walked over to the sink to peer out the window. When she turned back, her eyes glittered with unshed tears.

"I might lose the club," she said. "So long I wanted something to call my own, I had visions of just what I wanted to offer. But between the downturn in tourism here and the competition from that new bar, I'm not making it. Just a little sales boost and I could hold on until things pick up again."

Esme stood up, too, hugging herself, wanting to reach out to her aunt, but feeling too awkward and unsure of what her aunt wanted. What she expected. "How can I help you?" she asked.

Tina rubbed one hand across her face, and lifted her chin. "Do you still sing?"

The question came out of left field, so totally not what she expected that she gaped and didn't answer immediately. A request for a loan, a suggestion that she find somewhere else to live made sense, but this?

She tilted her head? "Sing, Tía? I don't sing, except with the radio."

"Nonsense!" Tina walked over to her, this time catching both Esme's hands and swinging them. "One of the times I was there, you won that singing contest, remember? And you could sing anything you wanted to. Your mom kept scolding you for making anyone who came to the house listen to you." She arched her eyebrows. "In fact, didn't you tell me you wanted to be a singer when you grew up?"

"I have a degree in child psychology, Tía. I never really considered music."

"Probably just on account of your mother," Tina muttered, letting her hands go and cupping her chin. "Come sing karaoke tonight. Tomorrow, too, if it goes well tonight."

"How would that help you?"

Again, Tina shrugged emphatically. "The main thing is, how could it hurt? Do you know who Cody Benton was?"

"Of course." To her annoyance, Esme felt goose bumps pebble her arms, and she forced herself not to shiver. "I loved her music. Too bad she's gone, Tía, but ..."

"You should have seen my place when she dropped in," her aunt continued, her gaze losing focus as she looked at something over Esme's head. "She'd do karaoke or sing with some of the local musicians. Stay all night. No one could touch us when she'd drop in. She was golden." Her eyes refocused on Esme, losing their far-off expression. "You can be golden."

What? Singing karaoke? Esme shook her head. "Look, Tía, I wouldn't mind singing if others were, but ... it's a stretch to think I can generate business."

"You can be a hostess," Tina went on, ignoring her protests. She grinned wickedly. "Fresh meat—the lifeline of any small town bar. Or small town, for that matter."

Tina's proposition seemed more bizarre by the minute. Esme frowned. She'd never considered herself either an introvert or a prude. But something about her aunt's tone of voice made her uneasy. Why on earth would Tina expect her to be much help one way or another, if the club was really in trouble? Coupled with the questions about her love life, in fact, her aunt's tone was almost offensive.

"I couldn't pay you of course," Tina added. "But you have a roof over your head and food on the table. And if folks come in—"

"Just what kind of hostess do you want me to be?" Esme asked slowly. "You seemed to think it was important that I wasn't dating or involved with anyone."

Tía waved a hand. "Just be my niece," she scoffed. "I'm the real hostess. You'd just smile, look pretty, and sing a couple songs. Just for a night or two. Customers come in, you get 'em moving around, dancing a little—they drink more, have fun—that's really good for the bottom line."

Stealing her aunt's gesture, Esme shrugged. "Okay. Tell me the time and where to sign up."

"Eight's kind of early, but it's about right for what I need," Tina said, then beamed at Esme. "Eight'll let word get out before ..."

"Before what?"

Tía's smile broadened. "Truth is just where you need to be this weekend, girl. You'll help me for an hour or two now and then, and I'll help you."

"Help me?" Esme prodded, interested. "By giving me an unpaid job singing in a club to cowboy wannabes?" She tossed the words out lightly, though, careful to make sure her aunt wouldn't be offended.

"Oh, yes. Help you." Tía's wicked grin reappeared, and her eyes sparked dark fire. "There's a job opening in town and it's got real specific requirements. Unreal money for a temporary position—set you up for a long time. But to apply, you have to be single. Uninvolved."

"Wow." Esme fell silent for a minute, thinking, then shook off the surprise. "But those are pretty weird qualifications, aren't they? Besides, I have a job—or at least, I have a career. I planned on looking for counseling positions ..."

"Hmph." Tina snorted dismissively. "You can open your own clinic with what you'd make in six or seven weeks."

"I'd be lying if I said that doesn't sound interesting," Esme admitted, and her aunt chuckled, and then gave her a wink.

"The money's not the best part, either."

"Really? What's the best part, then?" Esme asked.

"You'd be working for the devil, but most women in Truth wouldn't mind that a bit. *El diablo tiene las suyas*—he has his own charms, and his own followers."

"I thought we were talking about a job offer. Now you're suggesting I take up devil worship?" Esme challenged, her words tinged with sarcasm. "Who is this irresistible devil you want me to work for?"

"Rafael Benton," Tina answered. "Of course."

• • •

Esmeralda stood in a corner of the small stage, half-hidden by a huge television and a small jumble of mismatched stools and chairs, and tried to catch her breath. The crush of people, the catcalls and applause when she sang, her aunt's broad smile and encouragement sent her spirits rocketing. If being helpful to Tina Cervantes was this much fun, she could do it forever.

Although, clearly, her relatively quiet life of late wasn't keeping her fit enough for line dancing to Alan Jackson's "Good Time," belting out a little Reba, and helping the waitresses deliver a few rounds of beers at one particularly chaotic point when she was "on break."

"You know everyone's looking for you, right?" Tía asked in her ear, startling her.

"I'm just breathing," Esme assured her, shooting her a teasing glance. "I do get to breathe, don't I?"

"Can you do it while you sing?" her aunt retorted. "Knew you'd be something else if you'd sing a couple songs for me! I've got an eye for talent, you know. Just look at Cody …"

Hearing the singer's name tempered Esme's exhilaration. Almost involuntarily, her eyes glanced at the picture across from where she stood. Again she felt the slight irritation she'd felt when she drove into Truth and found the town claiming Cody as its own. Her aunt seemed to imply that she herself had figured into Cody's success, but she'd always heard the woman was a product of Nashville.

She shook aside the irritation. "I'm hardly Cody Benton, but I'm having a lot of fun. Besides, men can't paw me if I'm up here singing."

"One drunk and you're complaining. Really!" Tía looked at her watch and shook her head. "You have time for one more before you call it a night, girl. Just one!"

"But if you don't close until two …"

"Just one more," Tía repeated, looking around the room almost apprehensively.

"You're the boss," Esme conceded.

A couple passing by noticed her. "Hey, you're great," the woman shouted, and her partner nodded. "And pants-dropping gorgeous," he added, laughing when the woman elbowed him and pretended to drag him away.

Esme watched them go, feeling successful. And sexy. How long had she been ignored and avoided in Rose Creek when she let herself feel like this?

"Hey, Tom," she said as the bartender fiddled with the karaoke machine. "You got Carrie Underwood's "Cowboy Casanova"?"

Tom's eyebrow with its decorative skull ring shot up and he grinned slowly. "Oh, yeah," he told her.

Moments later, Esme stood in front of a cheering crowd, belting out the song about a bad boy/cowboy—weren't those the same? She moved as much as she could without losing track of the music. She felt the song course through her like fever, heat her like a lover's touch—but hers wasn't a blue-eyed cowboy, she realized. Darkly intense eyes, broad-shouldered, lean-hipped, whispering threatening words like caresses … she could almost see him on the stage, moving toward her as the music built to its climax.

"Esme! Stop! *¡Para!*"

She could hear her aunt's frantic whisper. But she could see the crowd listening, feeling the song—she didn't want to stop.

So she didn't, pouring out the last of the music and acknowledging the tumultuous cheers and shouts from the crowd with more satisfaction than embarrassment. She was amazed by the response, although, she reminded herself, her aunt had explained her charm early on. What had she said back at the house when she asked for help? *New meat.* Better not get too full of herself just yet.

"Esmeralda Salinas, get off the stage," her aunt hissed, looking around as if worried by something. Or someone.

She waved a final time and headed for the side steps. "What's wrong?" she whispered, aware that her aunt seemed genuinely upset.

"You idiot!" she spat. "When I say something here at the club, I expect you to do it. I told you to stop! And of all the songs you had to be singing—"

Esmeralda straightened and glared at her aunt. "Don't you ever, ever insult me again, Aunt Tina," she whispered. "Because I'm nobody's idiot."

Tina's face flushed with anger, but her tone was level when she answered. "If you lost what you might have gotten, *querida*—let's see what you call yourself! You should not have been up on that stage singing *that* song when Rafael Benton walked in." She reached out and snared Esme's wrist, the metallic nails carelessly pressing into her skin. "He hates karaoke. He especially hates that song—and there you were."

And with those parting words, she stalked away, engulfed immediately by the crowd of people that seemed to materialize around her.

• • •

Rafael sat in his usual chair, nursing a beer and wishing he were somewhere else. This place was poison and had been since Cody died in an upstairs room. Poison or drug; he was addicted to the sadness, apparently. A young woman walked past, showing off her jean-sheathed rear, putting a little extra wiggle in and turning her head enough to wink at him. Nice, but no.

He sighed heavily and downed the remainder of the beer in a gulp. No point in hanging around here, listening to music that just kept punching him in the gut. Although … his eyes scanned the crowd, finding her immediately. He'd come in as she finished a pulsing rendition of a Carrie Underwood song Cody used to sing for Harper and he'd more or less eyeballed her ever since. Even though he didn't want to. Too bad she was Tina Cervantes's niece. He wouldn't have minded throwing his hat in the ring with the other yelling, stomping jerks in the room. He could compete for her, and he would win.

He allowed himself the luxury of a smile. Confidence had come easily to him in the past. Even as an unwanted kid shuffled from strangers to shelters to street corners, he'd believed he'd win. He liked to think his confidence—or brashness, depending on who was describing him—was the quality that the Bentons couldn't resist in a ten-year-old street kid. The quality that compelled the wealthy couple to adopt him and love him as fiercely and unconditionally as any mother and father ever could love their children.

He drew in a breath and stood up. The game warden, Prince Jackson, still in his tan uniform with its wildlife insignia on the sleeve, walked by and paused to shake his hand. He'd learned right from the start that there were good guys and bad guys in Truth, and PJ, his preferred handle, was one of the good guys. Too bad the game warden was just arriving; he was leaving. He'd have enjoyed drinking a beer with the man and chatting about his job protecting the native wildlife—anything but the loss of his sister.

"Leaving so soon?" Tía purred beside him.

He knew that voice, the false honey dripping out of words meant to deceive. "Yes," he answered curtly, trying to step away from her, but she moved in front of him and shook her head at him.

"You've spent four years trying to step around me, Rafa. Why don't you get it? You and I don't have to like each other to use each other. To profit from each other."

"The way you used Cody? The way you profited from her? Look, I don't need this. I don't need you—"

"What if I told you I have the perfect candidate for you?" She batted heavily shadowed eyes at him and reached out a hand to stop him from escaping. Her nails glinted silver in the lights. He frowned. More like expensive talons than nails.

"Tell me tomorrow."

"Okay." She lifted a shoulder indifferently. "You were the one who said there wasn't much time. And tomorrow might be too late, because the candidate has other job offers."

He stared at her, considering. He wished he hadn't included her, but he knew that she had contacts outside Truth, tarnished as many of them were. He couldn't stomach any of the hangers-on he'd known in Cody's last troubled days. Surely she wouldn't dare suggest any of them.

"You know someone who meets all my qualifications? A serious prospect?"

"A perfect prospect." Tía winked. "Ready to lose a small fortune?"

"You make this sound like you're pimping someone," he gritted. "You shouldn't be so eager for a payoff, Tía. I'd be a lot more inclined to listen to Lillie Mae or to Brockton."

Tía snorted and turned away.

"Who?" he asked, knowing that he had few choices and time really was running out. If he were going to be happily married—or at least legally married—before his parents returned, he had to find an acceptable wife. Chris and Alice would see right through him if he married in front of them.

Tía faced him again, triumphant. "My niece," she said. "Esmeralda."

Chapter Five

After the third time she hurled aside an outfit and looked for something else, Esmeralda had to admit to herself that she was nervous. Which infuriated her, because nothing unnerved her. She hadn't felt so jittery and apprehensive since ... since her mother found out about her first serious boyfriend, Toby. She pressed her eyes closed momentarily. Old news, Toby, and the pain no longer bit, but in a way, their doomed relationship had become the foundation of the life she'd lived ever since.

Defiantly, she went to the closet and jerked out a celery-colored sheath with a plunging neckline and shimmied into it. An hour until she had to present herself at this place called Witches Haven on Death Curve, and damned if she'd be late—or nervous. She'd met Rafael Benton and if he'd uttered a threat, real or imagined, she didn't see how it could have been directed at her.

In spite of her aunt's insistence that the opportunity of a lifetime was just ahead, she also didn't see how she could work for a man she'd much rather have a fling with and forget. He'd unnerved her, those dark eyes boring into hers in the mirror at Tía's. He'd loomed so large, his presence so close, that she'd thought at first he would slide his hands over her shoulders and pull her back against him. Not the behavior she'd expect, but there'd been a daredevil air about him, a hardness and recklessness that ...

"Esmeralda Salinas, you're full of it!" she hissed at herself, looking into the mirror, glad that Rafael didn't lurk there to feed her lunatic fantasies. The man got under her skin and made her want him, but there was nothing other-worldly about that. And she'd be very unlikely to wind up with whatever job he was trying to fill, so ... screw everything.

She put on her favorite earrings and dawdled over a necklace. She fingered her prettiest, a delicate gold chain holding an ornate cross with emeralds. A present from her mother on her fifteenth birthday, she seldom wore it, because she knew her life wasn't what her mother had intended when she gave the necklace. Sometimes she thought of the chain as a curse, meant to embarrass and shame her whenever she stepped over the thin line her mother tried to draw in the sands of moral behavior.

Laughing at herself, she snatched up her favorite necklace, a clunky fashion piece with oversized amber and brown beads pieced together with leather. The colors went well enough with green, she supposed, and the gift from an ex-student she'd counseled always boosted her spirits.

She snatched up her purse and hurried downstairs.

Andy sat in a rocking chair on the porch, ear bud attaching him to his ever-present music, and shot her an indifferent glance as she passed.

"Off to the devil's lair?" he asked as she reached the bottom step.

"The devil's lair?"

"Oh, I know the townsfolk call it Witches Haven," he said, nodding sagely. "The man who built it—twenty years ago or more, I guess—called it that." He smiled and winked. "The parties, you know? But that dude that owns it now, he's no witch. The devil, that one. Mad as hell about what happened to his baby sister. You might want to be careful, Esmeralda Salinas." The words issued out in a strange tone that raised the hair on her arms.

"Why should I be careful, Andy?" Esme demanded, aware that Andy still would rather see her gone than here, although she didn't know why he disliked her.

"I hear Benton wants your aunt gone—or dead," the watchman said, still rocking the chair and swinging a foot. "I bet she's glad

I decided to come down here from Chicago with her. Good luck with the devil," he added, and closed his eyes in dismissal.

•••

Even in the broad daylight and looking for the place, Esmeralda could see how she'd missed it those times before. Death Curve started out as an innocuous bend, although there were speed warning signs with their contorted arrows. But the steepness and the "s" part of the curve took a driver by surprise, and strangers undoubtedly would keep their eyes glued to the turns. Up on her left, a hill loomed, a little higher than most in the immediate area.

Untrimmed cedar, so predominant in the Hill Country, stormed up the hill, quilting in dull green with patches of brown where weather or disease had claimed a tree. The growth was so dense that the hill itself seemed dark and unwelcoming.

The house on the hill—not at the front of the summit, but set back, with a dark rock fence shielding part of the view—was even darker. Unlike so many of the rock homes in the area, the house appeared built of very dark timber, treated perhaps to prevent decay, but providing a fort-like façade that made no effort to be inviting.

The drive itself began several hundred yards beyond what seemed to be the front of the property and Esme almost missed it, having to brake sharply and then wait as an annoyed biker scooted around her, scowling her way.

"Sorry," she muttered, not any happier than he apparently was about the poor design of this place.

The drive climbed the hill gradually, the view on both sides consisting only of cedar and underbrush, and then she broke out near the top, onto a gentle, terraced slope dotted with neatly tended rock gardens and ornamental plantings. Off to one side, an intricate path of rock led into a series of fish ponds and gardens, all created from the abundant Hill Country stone, and she could see benches scattered around among the pools, with water lilies blooming in the sun in the nearest ones.

The change in scenery couldn't have been greater, and she slipped carefully out of the truck cab and walked a few steps closer to take it all in.

Bet it's something else in the spring, she thought, imagining the bluebonnets covering all the cleared acreage and lining the edges of the walk.

In the sunlight, with flowers all around, the hulking structure lost its air of malevolence. By the time she approached the steps again, she was the same professional woman who had never been rejected after a job interview. She might not accept, but she knew she could make Rafael Benton offer her his job, whatever it was.

She put one foot on the bottom step and stopped short at the boom of thunder announcing her arrival. In synchronized majesty, two fawn Great Danes rose from their places in the sun and turned dark, curious gazes her way. Apparently these were not killer watch dogs; they stood like stones after sounding the initial warning. But they were *big,* and just marching up to the door seemed a little foolish.

Before she could muster her nerve and do just that, the door swung open and an attractive woman, a few years older than her, peered out. "Luc! Chief!" she scolded, and the two dogs wagged their tails and retreated a few steps.

The door opened, and the woman walked out, holding out a hand and offering a smile that bordered on annoyed.

"You must be Ms. Salinas," she noted. "I'm Marie Thompson, and I run Witches Haven for Mr. Benton, who is waiting for you."

Esmeralda frowned at the curt, overly proficient brunette, wearing jeans and a clingy top that made her look emaciated. "Waiting? My appointment isn't until—"

"Twelve," Marie finished. "I know. Perhaps I should say he is 'expecting' you, then, but he'll be glad that you came early." She smiled mirthlessly. "Always better to get business over with, that's Mr. Benton's motto."

Well, don't I just feel welcome. Esme followed the woman's hand-wave into the house and looked around the cavernous living room as a prickle of apprehension came back. The woman wasn't friendly—was she involved with her boss? Esmeralda had encountered the veiled hostility often enough in the past when someone was worried about a man straying. She'd gotten tired of it, in fact, and given up trying to reassure women who disliked her on sight.

"Please follow me," Marie ordered crisply, keeping Esmeralda from trekking over to an ornate rock fireplace, with a mantel holding a collection of trophies, awards, and pictures of Cody Benton.

They climbed a winding staircase that took them to a second floor and went along a marble hall to the last door. Marie knocked, opened the door as slightly as she had opened the front door, and said into the crack, "Ms. Salinas is here to see you, Rafa."

A muffled voice answered, and the door swung open. "Go on in, honey," the brunette said, suddenly catty.

Thank you, sweetie. Esmeralda ignored the dig.

Across the room, behind a huge mahogany desk, Rafael rose gracefully, smiling, and she walked toward him, remembering again all the unease and dark feelings she'd had since running into him in the club kitchen.

He held out a hand, nodding at her as she arrived, and greeted her politely. "Ms. Salinas! Thanks for coming. Please, sit down."

He sat after she did, and seemed momentarily at a loss for words. After a brief pause, though, he gestured at a nearby bar full of bottles and cut glass decanters. "Something to drink? Tea? Water?"

"No, thank you. Mr. Benton, my aunt asked me to come here to interview for some job she thinks I might be interested in. I'll be honest—I have a profession, and I hadn't planned on working this summer. I don't think I'm interested in anything you could offer."

Sparks danced in his eyes, *chispitas* of fire that burned. "Nothing?" he asked, dimples slashing his bronze cheeks. Then he shrugged and the slow-burning fire died away as the businessman he had to be took over.

"I don't know that you'd meet the qualifications, either, but perhaps we should both look at the situation. I'm not offering a common job, and I don't expect the applicant to accept a common salary. Because of the extremely complicated situation, I'm offering a salary—with expenses covered—which could close in on two hundred thousand. For six, seven weeks—maybe two months, tops."

She stared at him, shocked. "You're serious?"

He nodded somberly.

"Wow." Disbelief still clutched her. "This isn't a joke? I don't have to hurt or kill or destroy someone?"

This time he shook his head, just as serious.

"Wow," she said again, and just stared at him for a long time.

What kind of temporary position was worth more money than she could make in three years as a school counselor? For two months? She ran a hand through her hair, mussing it and not caring, then clutched the clunky necklace as if it could answer her questions.

What would she even do with close to a quarter million dollars? Unbidden the thought came: *I could save Tía's. Couldn't I?* But ..

"I guess you'll have tons of candidates to sift through," she said at last. Why did she pretend she could win a job with that kind of salary? It couldn't be clerical, could it? She could do correspondence and she was trained to deal with upset parents and children. She'd had training in suicide prevention and CPR. On a purely practical level, she didn't consider herself worth a six-figure income for secretarial work. So what did the man want?

"I'm going to break all the rules and tell you you're the only candidate I've considered so far." He leaned back and locked his hands behind his head, watching her intently. "The job I need filled isn't one I can advertise for."

He might have seen something change in her expression, because he leaned forward again so abruptly he startled her. "Just to be clear, I don't necessarily think you're the best candidate. I'd need a lot more information. But I promised your aunt I'd at least consider you." He paused again, then sighed. "Your aunt's recommendation doesn't help you. You should know that, too. I … we … detest each other. Unfortunately, sometimes that's not reason enough not to deal with each other."

She shrugged and shifted in her chair, crossing her legs. "I'm a big girl, Mr. Benton. I don't expect family to get me jobs. I never have."

He rubbed a hand over his chin, and she thought he suddenly looked tired. Or sad. She couldn't imagine why he would, though, and so she lifted her eyebrows and gave him a tight smile. "Before I give you any additional information, Mr. Benton, shouldn't you tell me what this very lucrative position is? Because there are things I'm sure your money can't buy."

"I wish that were true," he said, more to himself than her, his eyes fixed on his cell phone, though she hadn't heard it ring or vibrate. Then he tossed it aside, straightened, and speared her with hard, dark eyes.

"My money needs to buy *you*," he told her flatly. "I need to hire a temporary wife."

●●●

I could have handled that better. Duh. He sighed and retrieved his cell phone, checking that nothing cracked when he'd tossed it. He skimmed the switch, and Justin's innocent face peered up at him.

"Sorry, *chiquito*. That was about as dumb as it gets," he muttered, standing and pushing the phone into his pocket. He walked over to stare out the window, looking out, seeing her pick-up disappear into the part of the drive hidden by cedars. She'd made her escape.

Damn. He leaned his forehead against the air-conditioned glass, hoping the smooth, icy surface would help him recover his composure. He wanted to buy her? Sure as hell not what most women wanted to hear from a complete stranger. He'd let his distrust—and dislike—of her aunt color his words. His father and mother would be horrified if they had heard him. Of course, they were the reasons for this subterfuge, this whole desperate shot at repairing Justin's broken life. His parents and Doug Harper, he amended. Hadn't that s.o.b. done enough damage without starting to bare his damn fangs and mutter he was Justin's father and wanted custody? Parasitic, blood-sucking creep. The phone almost flew again, but he settled for slamming the desk with his fist, hard enough that it hurt. He could blow things so easily, not just as far as being awarded custody himself, but even endangering the temporary rights extended to his parents. If Harper was Justin's father and found out that Rafael had entered a marriage primarily to look better in a custody dispute—and to placate his own parents—it would be easy to twist his motives to hell and back. Harper could claim that Rafael's own parents didn't trust him with Justin. That a man who would pay a woman to be his wife, wasn't fit to be a father. And then his parents would face the attacks in social media and some business circles when their relentless belief in marriage before parenthood became a controversy again.

Cody had faced questions over that when news of her pregnancy first broke. A disgruntled Benton employee had accepted a settlement after suing the Bentons for creating a hostile work environment by actively encouraging marriage at company functions. A particularly vicious gossip reporter even had the nerve to bring the Bentons's well-known views on marriage up as one of the reasons Cody embarked on her path to self-destruction. The Bentons had embraced their first grandchild and gone on loving Cody, even without a husband in the picture. Sure, they'd made offers to help the father if he married her, and sure, they wished Cody's choices were different. But he still could hardly believe the attack they'd suffered over their own personal belief in marriage. He could give them the comfort of a traditional marriage for Justin until the danger of predatory "fathers" claiming the child faded away. And someday he would marry for real. His birth parents hadn't married, hadn't wanted him—hadn't even known him. Every child deserved better, and he could take the first steps to ensure that Justin had a solid future.

That meant he needed to set things right. He doubted Esmeralda would be interested in the position, and he didn't blame her. But she was one more person who knew whatever woman stepped into the small town spotlight of Truth, Texas, would be an actress, a woman pretending to be his life partner. He couldn't afford to have her spoil everything, especially given the danger to his plans her aunt already represented. He sighed heavily, feeling a grinding weariness that hadn't bothered him in years.

He tapped a button and spoke into the intercom. "Marie, I need to know where to find Ms. Salinas. Let me know right away."

He thought Marie huffed, but maybe he imagined it. He sighed. Marie was efficient and she needed the job desperately. She supported two aging parents. But sometimes he worried that she thought because there was no one permanent woman in his life, he was actively looking. She was the least of his problems, but a temporary marriage might even help assure that Marie knew he wasn't available—at least not to her.

He shoved his hands into his pockets, and walked over to look out the window. Roses and bougainvillea were a riot in the stone-ringed gardens below. The Hill Country weather wasn't optimal for the decorative plants, but given his gardener's devotion and skill, they flourished. The bright gardens lightened the house's dark mood, and he couldn't say he minded that. When he'd followed his sister here, the house already had its damning name, Witches Haven. But he supposed he hadn't exactly helped soothe the locals' distaste for the property.

Marie knocked on the door instead of using the intercom, which he would have preferred. "She's not at her aunt's house, which is where she's living, according to the man who answered the phone there. He thought she might have gone to Tía's, or maybe she stopped at Irving Peterson's to see her horse."

"Thanks, Marie."

"My pleasure," she murmured. "Anything else you want, boss?"

He shook his head. "No. You may go."

She shrugged and slid out, closing the door a little loudly between them.

He picked up his keys and his phone and headed out to find Esmeralda Salinas.

• • •

She wasn't dressed for visiting Domatrix. The Petersons' car and truck weren't in the drive, but they'd told her she could just go down to see her horse anytime she wanted. She trekked carefully across the uneven ground, a little afraid of stumbling on a rock and twisting an ankle. Heels weren't a good idea over Hill Country terrain, unless they were shorter and stubbier and on a pair of boots.

She stopped halfway and glanced at the truck, parked back near the house. Maybe she'd just go home and change.

But she couldn't, because Domatrix suddenly appeared from behind the wall of her shelter and whinnied pitifully. And loudly. Then she trotted back and forth along the fence line in desperation, stopping again after a moment to stomp the ground and whinny again.

Laughing, Esme discarded any idea of leaving and went to pet the mare.

"You big baby," she scolded. "I dropped by yesterday. And Connie told me she gives you home-baked cookies every day, which you've never gotten in your life. In fact, my friend, at your age you should be careful of sweets." She stroked a hand down the sleek neck, glad that there were few signs of the mare's seventeen years. Constant care and gentle use worked wonders for horses, apparently.

Domatrix snorted and snuffed, reaching out to blow against her cheek.

"Look, let me go change and I'll come back and ride you. How's that?"

Domatrix's head went up suddenly and her ears pricked.

Clearly she wasn't alone any longer. Careful not to dig a heel into the rocky ground and trip herself, she turned to find Rafael there, even though she hadn't heard him pull in.

The man who'd offered to buy her had followed her here? She frowned, anger flaring through her.

"Stalking me, Mr. Benton? I believe I refused your kind 'job' offer!"

He stopped where he was, and held out his arms, palms outward, as if to reassure her. Or fight her off if she lunged at him, which she was sorely tempted to do. The click of a heel against a rock stopped her, though, so she just glared at him, her hands knotting into fists again as she fought her own temper.

"I didn't follow you here. I'm not a stalker."

She snorted. "You just showed up at this shed in a mud field by chance? Please! How stupid do you think I am? Wait—don't answer. You mistook me for a whore, so you're pretty stupid!"

He looked … shocked. Appalled, maybe. His mouth opened slightly, wordlessly, and then he pressed his lips together, ignored her, and walked over to the fence.

"Hey, pretty girl," he crooned, and the usually finicky mare went right up to him.

Traitor. First Connie, and now you're in love with this … this. "Do you have some reason to be here?" She kept her tone neutral this time, though, not willing to show how furious—and uneasy—his coming here made her.

He half-turned toward her, leaning on the fence, and Domatrix leaned her head over his shoulder, looking like she, too, was waiting for his answer.

"You need to know that I was—am—offering someone a very legitimate position, Esmeralda." He gently pushed the mare's head away and stepped a little closer. "Look—I spoke stupidly. Agreed. But it wasn't how I meant to say it, and …" He shrugged. "I'd love to go some place you choose and explain myself."

"We don't need to go anywhere. I got the gist—you're offering me money to go to bed with you. Does calling it a 'temporary marriage' make it any cleaner or more proper than calling it 'hooking up' or 'shacking up' or …"

"You're the one who brought up sex," he pointed out. "Makes me wonder …" He shook his head, chasing away whatever he was apparently thinking. "I offered marriage." He waggled his bare ring finger at her. "Gold ring, pre-nuptial agreement, license in the courthouse, marriage at church if you want … marriage."

"And just why would you be doing that, Mr. Benton? And how is that not paying for sex?"

The sounds of tires crunching down the drive kept him from answering. The Petersons were pulling up to the house. Connie slid out first, then waited until her husband came around the truck to grasp her arm and pat her shoulder, leaning close to say something that made her nod. Together they walked over, never letting each other go.

Now that's marriage. Esme smiled as the two reached them, stepping forward to kiss Connie's cheek.

"Hi. Just dropped in to tell Domatrix I'd come ride a little later. Do you all know Rafael Benton?"

"Phillip Irving," Connie's husband introduced himself. "And this …"

"Is Connie, right?" Rafael shook Irving's hand, but smiled warmly at Connie. "You work over at the Bait and Wait, right? You've sold me bait the last couple of times I decided to waste a day on those legendary big mouths in the lake!"

Connie flushed, but looked pleased he knew her name. "There are fish there, but I don't deny they're tricky ones. You gotta fish years to catch a good 'un!"

"Is that where the 'Wait' part of the name comes in?"

Connie laughed. "That, and the owner's wife Ellen used to have snit fits every once in a while. Wouldn't wait on anyone she didn't cotton to."

"So … should I ask where Ellen is now?" Rafael asked.

"She's okay—hasn't run off or passed, if that's what you didn't want to find out," Connie chortled. "She's found being a grandma's more fun than being a worm saleswoman."

Everyone laughed at Connie's tale and for a moment, the tension eased. Then lines of worry filled the older woman's face. "Guess I should say I worked there, Esme, Mr. Benton. They let me go today."

"Why?"

Irving shook his head and patted his wife's arm again. "Told my Connie not to worry. Times are hard, and the owner said he can't afford help—just not many people stopping by and his oldest boy don't have a job, so he's fillin' in for his pa." He shrugged weary shoulders. "It's what should be, families helpin' their own."

"I don't begrudge 'em," Connie added. "They gave an old woman a job when lots of folks wouldn't. It'll just take getting used to." She forced a smile. "Why don't y'all come have some sweet tea? I've got some nice and cold, just waitin'."

"No, thanks," Esme and Rafael chorused together, drawing a look of speculation from the elderly couple.

"I'm not dressed … I … had a business appointment," Esme explained, not looking at Rafael. "I'm going to go home and change, then I'll come ride, if that's okay." She smiled. "I'll have a glass of tea then, if you've still got some."

"I have to go, too," Rafael put in, and Esme knew he'd shot her a glance before addressing the Petersons. "Nice to meet you, Irving. Connie. Hope things work out for you both."

"Ms. Salinas, wait …" She turned as he fished a business card and pen from a pocket and jotted something down. "Here." He extended the card, and she reluctantly reached out to take it. No point in making the Petersons part of this whole charade.

"That might help you with the questions you had about jobs around here," he added smoothly, then nodded again to the Petersons and left. When he started backing out, she said goodbye again and walked to her truck, buckling in and checking the rearview mirror before curiosity got the best of her and she glanced at the card again.

Lillie Mae. Silver Boot and Booty. Ask her.

Lillie Mae. She'd spoken to the woman weeks ago, when she checked out the Irvings before considering their place to board Domatrix. She'd only been in town a couple of days, but she'd heard the name everywhere. An old woman, from what little she knew, whom everyone in Truth seemed to adore. And she knew the Silver Boot and Booty—the newest bar in town, right next to the traditionally named Silver Dollar, which she supposed had been the first building in town. But why she was supposed to go talk to a strange old lady in some bar that represented a real economic threat to her aunt?

She backed out faster than she should and hit the asphalt with every intention of going home, changing, and coming back. She didn't know when she changed her mind, but she knew when she passed Cattle Guard Road that she was going into town. And talking to an eighty-year-old woman about Rafael's proposition. Crazy. She couldn't think of another description for what she was about to do. The fact that she laughed out loud in the empty cab of her own truck didn't worry her nearly as much as it should have.

Chapter Six

There was a longhorn steer wearing a saddle, tied to the hitching post outside the Silver Boot and Booty. There was a golf cart parked next to the longhorn. And the few people walking along the sidewalks in front of the buildings weren't even glancing at them. Esme shook her head. Rose Creek had been as small—maybe marginally smaller—than Truth. There had been eccentrics there, too, but nobody rode longhorns and parked golf carts outside saloons. Either she'd fallen into a rabbit hole, the whole town was crazy or—hope flared—someone was shooting a music video. She'd seen lots of weird stuff in country music videos. In fact, hadn't Cody been photographed somewhere on a longhorn that looked a lot like this one?

Holding on to that fragile hope, Esme grasped the rail running alongside the steep, enclosed stairs and descended into the Silver Boot and Booty, Truth's newest bar. The rock exterior and deep stairwell were at odds with the garish neon sign, but the interior was as bright and gaudy as the neon. Light gleamed on a polished hardwood floor. The bar took up most of the front of the establishment—high, polished wood that reflected almost as much light as the floor. The tables scattered around were along the sides and towards the back, leaving most of the inside space for dancing. Not as cluttered as her aunt's place, or as dark.

"Hey, there!" a friendly voice called from behind the bar. A cheerful woman with steel gray hair nodded at her. "We're really not open, but if I can help you with something …"

"You're not open?" Esme questioned, waving her hand at a table near the front, but not the one nearest the bar. A man in western garb sat there, a glass of something in front of him, and a half-finished bottle of beer beside him, near a high-crowned cowboy hat.

Before the woman at the bar could answer, an elderly woman came out of the hall beneath the large sign pointing to the restrooms. Western shirt and jeans, boots with ornate embroidery. Hair the color of mountain snow, framing a face that showed age, but was still striking.

Esmeralda had never seen the woman, but she knew. "Lillie Mae. Hi," she said in greeting. "I'm …"

"Tina's niece, Esmeralda." The lady nodded with assurance. Of course you are." She closed the distance and held her hand out. Fringe dangled down the sleeves of her long-sleeved shirt and tickled Esme's hand as her own was pumped energetically. She must have flinched away from the spidery-tickling sensation, because Lillie Mae laughed and let her go.

"My Sunday duds are a mite annoying," she said. "And don't tell me what day it is, 'cause I know." She leaned her head forwards and lowered her voice. "I just ain't washed my workday clothes yet." She winked and grinned. "Asides which, tourists would rather see the Sunday me." She waved a hand at the table. "Join me for a bit?"

"But … it's not open …"

Lillie Mae snorted. "It's open to me and my guests. Kind of like my office, this place. Come on, sit with me."

"Sure." *Isn't that the plan?* As the women reached the table, the man stood, removing his hat and holding out a hand.

"Hondo, ma'am. You'd be Tina Cervantes's little girl?"

"Uh … her niece," Esme corrected. "I'm sorry … Hondo? Didn't I drive through Hondo on the way here?"

"Yes ma'am. I'm named after the town, or maybe just the river that runs through it. Didn't ever ask." He grinned affably. "Figured one of the reasons I used to get chosen a lot to play extras in cowboy movies was the name."

"Hondo, would you go check on Babe? Can't be too careful these days. Someone might just try to lift him, even though everyone in the Hill Country would recognize that worthless old critter on the spot. Almost as famous at the UT longhorn, Babe is."

He nodded at both of them, then replaced the hat. "Nice to meet you, Miss Esme. Lillie Mae, I think I'll hitch ol' Babe on the cart and run by the feed store. He gets a kick out of it 'n' so do I."

Lillie Mae didn't really reply, just watched as he wandered away. "Good man, Hondo," she said eventually. "Just wish he got it—this boat's sailed. Buried four husbands and there ain't gonna be a fifth, but he keeps tryin'. Sit down, girl. I bend a little slow these days."

Esme sat.

"So, spill it. What brought you here?"

"Didn't you ... isn't it ... part of Rafael Benton's plan? Didn't he send you here to meet me?"

"Now, see, a few years ago, if I'd seen Rafael, I wouldn't have been talkin' about any ships sailin' 'less he was right there on it." Lillie Mae chortled, and Esme smiled a little in spite of herself. This woman was something else, for sure. But she didn't know what, or why Rafael Benton—the devil, according to Andy—had sent her here after he propositioned her. Then the mirth left Lillie Mae's face and she lifted her beer bottle, finished it in a gulp, and pointed it at Esme. "Nobody sends me here. I come sit a spell here every day. Sort of my office, you could say. Now—what you do for a livin', girl?"

Lillie Mae's question caught her off guard, and for a moment, she just stared in surprise.

"Come on, girl, that ain't one of the hard questions." The older woman giggled, and Esme's anger started building. This was "dear" Lillie Mae? "Sweet" Lillie Mae? She drew herself up and breathed deeply.

Before she could answer, though, Lillie Mae did. "You're one of them counselor workers. For a school."

"I am a counselor," Esme said coolly. "I have a certificate and might open a clinic, or I might go back to work at a school."

"So you're a counselor? You give advice?" Lillie Mae repeated.

"Yes."

"Then why the hell are you here talkin' to an old lady you don't know? Shame on you, girl. You gotta make your own mind up about this job Rafael's offering."

Derision crept into Esme's voice. "Job? What do you suppose the qualifications for a job as a 'temporary wife' are?"

Lillie Mae leaned back a little in her chair and narrowed her eyes, then straightened again. "Hey, Freddie!" she called at the woman behind the bar. "Bring me a water and … what would you like, Esmeralda?"

Esmeralda hesitated. She seldom drank so early in the day and she really did want time to ride. But a tiny part of her didn't want to give Lillie Mae reason to think she didn't make her own rules. "Got screwdrivers?" she called past Lillie Mae, not letting the older woman order it for her, and got an affirmative nod from the woman behind the bar.

Freddie hustled over with their drinks and Esme smiled at her energy. "Bet you can hold your own when the place is open."

Freddie laughed. "Well, I don't usually tend the bar, just haul drinks. But when I'm alone … old habits die hard, I guess. I've always worked as a waitress of one kind or other."

Freddie left them and went back to dusting and arranging barware and bottles, and Esme downed a large portion of the drink and turned her attention to Lillie Mae again. "So, you were telling me I should make up my mind about Rafael's 'job?' What are the chances he'll walk in any minute, Lillie Mae?"

The older woman just stared at her for a moment, then snorted, a sound between insult and laughter. "You got some woman *cajones*," she noted. "No one in town would've asked me that if they'd only known me a couple minutes." She reached over and patted Esme's hand, her fringe tickling again. "And that's fine, if you're showin' 'em for the right reason. I'm no enemy, girl. Just someone drawn into a predicament and wantin' to help."

Esme considered the words, then shrugged. "What kind of predicament could make a decent man propose marriage—temporary marriage—to a complete stranger?"

Lillie Mae's eyebrows shot up. "He proposed? So quick?"

So the old lady knew more than she was admitting? No point in getting her dander up if she could get her to talk, though. "He didn't exactly propose," Esme admitted neutrally. "He told me he needed to hire someone, that he didn't like my aunt, and that I was the only person he'd approached."

Lillie Mae nodded thoughtfully, but didn't say anything. She fished in her pockets and drew out a bright red cell phone, checking her messages, then placed the device on the table. "I still bring ol' Babe into town out of habit," she confided, "but these modern contraptions sure do beat the old ones to heck." She picked up the phone and waved it at Esme. "'Specially this. But there's one thing that's even faster than this in a town like Truth—"

"Gossip?" Esme suggested, remembering Rose Creek, and even her teen years in Laredo, which wasn't really a small town.

"You got it. And see, that's what Rafael's up against—waggin' tongues. He confided in you, and if you won't listen and see what he says, I hope you at least don't talk."

"You seem to be defending him."

"He's got a name in this town. But he didn't earn it—at least, he don't deserve it." Her fingers drummed an irregular beat on the table. "How'd you hear about it? He look you up?"

"My aunt asked me to talk to him—set up the interview, I guess. She didn't give me a clue what kind of job I was applying for."

Something changed in Lillie Mae's face, almost imperceptibly. "You don't like my aunt, either?"

"No, girl, I don't. But one thing everyone in this town respects is family. We don't choose 'em, but we honor 'em to the grave and beyond. Don't you mind what you hear about your aunt any more than what you hear about Rafael Benton."

"I have to tell you that I wouldn't have even gone to ask about the job if my aunt had told me what it was." Esme took a bit more of the orange juice and vodka, more slowly, thinking, but not understanding. "Lillie Mae, I don't get it," she admitted. "Why did Rafael tell me to come here? What do you have to do with anything?"

"Well, a couple things, I guess. Look, I ain't gonna tell you I think Rafael's doing the right thing, but you oughta hear him out, 'specially since he might not even choose you anyway."

Gee, thanks.

"You'd be helpin' some good folks, if his crazy idea works. I told him he was crazy when he came to me, but he knows I'd never lie for him if I thought he was twistin' the truth or tryin' to do something wrong. And I won't tell you why he's so set on this fool plan of his, 'cept that it's for family, and family's sacred—to me and him both. I believe one-hundred percent his job offer's just that—the strangest damned job a woman could get rich doing."

"Any other reason you're in this?"

"Well, I'm gonna sound full of myself, but ain't nobody gonna believe a marriage here in Truth is legit if I'm not right there in the weddin' party. Last couple that got hitched here had me and Babe drive 'em to the bus stop to take off on their honeymoon. Made the front page of the Truth Trumpet."

Esme nodded. "So—and I'm not asking advice, because like you said, I'm a big girl with a counseling degree—I should talk to Rafael Benton one more time? Give him a chance to explain this … weird predicament."

Lillie Mae beamed. "Knew you were a smart girl." She winked. "When you're as old as me, dumb's just plain easy to see."

Esme smiled slightly in spite of herself. Truth be known, she often told herself something similar. "So I just have one last question," she added.

"Hit me," Lillie Mae invited.

"What's up with the stupid steer? I mean, okay, the Hill Country, tourists, Texas state large mammal, but …"

Lillie Mae drew herself up. "Don't never insult one of my longhorns," she warned. "My ma and pa raised 'em afore me. They're family." She finished her water without lowering the glass, then set it down. "Besides," she said, conspiratorially, "they're our only claim to fame. Bandera is older and claimed the 'Cowboy Capital of the World' title long ago. So we have to do more to attract attention. They have longhorns all over, but ours are more public. We had Cody, for awhile. And we're lookin' for the next big thing. Meanwhile, I bring Babe to town most every day."

"For this little one horse town?"

"One bull town," Lillie Mae amended, then laughed out loud. "Okay, not quite a bull, but close. Lots of tourists don't ask or know where to look. And honey, this town? I love it. I'd do anything to keep it from dryin' up the way so many do."

Esme fished a bill out of her wallet and stood, laying the bill on the table. "Nice to meet you, Lillie Mae. Take care." She bit back an urge to tell the old woman she'd talk to Rafael Benton again. She would, but it wasn't anyone's business but hers.

• • •

The dogs weren't on the porch and Rafael's flashy pickup wasn't anywhere to be seen. *I'm batting a thousand. First I don't call my aunt Tina, now I don't call Rafael Benton.* She glanced at her truck. Her cell phone was in the cup holder of the console, and her aunt had given her his number. Or, she could march up the stairs and ask the snotty Ms. Thompson where she could find him. Marie didn't like her, and that knowledge alone stiffened her resolve. She'd spent her lifetime confronting dislike, only occasionally from anything she'd done. *Oh, give me a break. I do occasionally flaunt my pride just a little. And that's when I'm being the lovable me.* She was grinning a little at the self admission when the door opened and Marie stepped out, not even faking a smile.

"Ms. Salinas. Mr. Benton didn't tell me you were coming back."

"He didn't know. Where can I find him?"

"He isn't here." The woman cast a glance around almost as if expecting him to appear suddenly and steal her control. "I'll take a message—"

"Where can I find him?" Esme repeated. "Because I left my phone in my truck and I can call him, but since he invited me ..."

Marie colored a little, not missing the emphasis on who had called whom. "He's down at the river," she said, sweeping a glance over Esme's still unchanged attire. "But it's steep and dirty there. You probably should wait. I'll call him."

"I can do that. I'm sure he'll give me directions."

Marie's face grew redder and tighter. "You follow the trail there—it runs across the pasture and into the tree line. Just follow it until you find him." She spat the words out with a drumming cadence meant to intimidate. "This ranch has livestock, Ms. Salinas. If you open a gate, close it. And don't run over the dogs."

"Yes, ma'am," Esme said, and Marie stared at her a moment more before slamming back into the house.

Esme was still grinning by the time the truck jolted over another root-filled crevice in the path down to the river and she saw Rafael's truck parked at an angle where the path ended. She pulled the truck up beside it and slid out, pulling her skirt down and casting a dubious glance at her heels. She'd be amazed if they held up to much more hiking around over stones, exposed roots, and ...

A lizard skittered over her foot, and she shrieked and kicked, startled, and somehow wound up on her butt in the dirt by the truck. Out of the corner of her eyes she saw a flash of gold and heard barking that sounded more like rolling thunder. She hadn't seen Rafael, but she'd certainly found his dogs. Or they'd found her. They were standing, splay-legged, heads down, clearly being protective of someone. She'd never thought of Danes as dangerous, but from her position, they were sooo big.

What were their names? Luc and—

"Good boys. Good Luc ..."

One of the dogs stopped barking and tilted his head.

"Chief, Luc. Stop!" She heard Rafael before she saw him. The dogs heard him, too, and immediately came up to her, tails wagging, now completely willing to be friendly. She raised an arm to fend it off, but one of the Danes managed a quick slap of its tongue across her face.

"Yuck!" she muttered, dragging her arm over her mouth. "Idiot dog!" The dogs didn't look abashed, though, and she heard Rafael laughing.

"I'm sorry." He chuckled as he pushed the Danes away and reached down to help her up. "I couldn't help remembering that little girl in the *Peanuts* cartoon—the one who hated it when the dog kissed her."

In spite of herself, Esmeralda smiled a little, remembering the ongoing gag. When Rafael's hand closed around hers and eased her up, she tried to ignore the warmth and strength of his fingers locking hers inside his hand, or the way he reached out with his other hand to support her arm as she stood, setting off tiny sparks of heat where his skin met hers.

"Marie should have let me know you were coming," he said, noting her disheveled clothing. "I'd have made sure the dogs behaved. Are you okay? You didn't ... sit down too hard?" In spite of the concern in his eyes, she saw his dimples appear and heard a note of amusement in his voice.

"I sat down plenty hard. I'm not sure how you judge too hard," she retorted. "Marie gave me directions. Guess she decided you'd figure it out when you saw me."

"I'll have to talk to her. So, what brought you here?" He indicated the thick growth on banks sloping down to an unseen body of water.

Without answering immediately, she carefully walked over the rough terrain until she could see what the growth and distance hid.

"Y'all call that a river?" she asked, sarcastically.

"We all weren't born long side the Rio Grande," Rafael retorted, moving up behind her to look down at the small stream gurgling over small stones. "Although, actually, I guess we both were."

That surprised her. Esme turned a little, careful not to catch a heel and fall on her behind again. "Really? You? I didn't know the Bentons were ever there."

"They—we—have been there. But I was born there. I'm adopted."

She turned to face him then, surprised. "So Cody ..."

"Was my little sister," he answered. "Period."

"Okay." She fell silent, not knowing where she wanted the conversation to go. He didn't say anything else for a while, just stared out over the landscape. Then he sighed and waved a hand at the truck.

"Luc, Chief, in, boys."

The dogs, apparently somewhere nearby, materialized out of the undergrowth and jumped easily up into the bed of the pickup. Those were the rambunctious mutts who'd threatened her?

"Nice," she muttered. "They listen remarkably well when they're not knocking someone off their feet."

"I didn't see you coming," he explained. "Again … I'll speak to Marie. I'm sorry about your dress."

"What's wrong with my dress?" she demanded, smoothing her hands over the sides and glancing down at the front.

His eyes followed the path of her hands and something sparked in his dark eyes. Something hot and enticing. Not to be encouraged, she reminded herself. This was the man who'd offered to "buy" her.

"You … um … sat down hard enough the dirt kind of . . clung." He started out searching carefully for words, then suddenly shrugged and flashed her a grin. "You've got a nice print of your ass on the back of your skirt."

"Shoot!" She ran her hands over the unseen print, feeling the dampness and grit. "It's probably wrecked."

"I'll replace it. The dogs …"

She couldn't let him blame the dogs; she'd fallen before they arrived. She suddenly wished one of her promises to herself back in Rose Creek hadn't been to be as honest as possible. Taking advantage of any situation had been a strength of hers up until a few short months ago.

"They didn't knock me down. I'd already tripped and fallen."

"Still. You must have come here to find me. Did Lillie Mae have anything to do with this?"

"Lillie Mae!" She shook her head slightly. "Cantankerous old woman. Yet from everything I've heard, she's like the town conscience or something."

"Something," he agreed, smiling again. "She can make or break you here in Truth."

"Why did you tell me to go see her? She took my head off for being stupid enough to need advice. She knew I was a counselor. Did you know that?"

"Everyone in Truth knows that. Didn't you say you came here from a small town?"

"Yes, but ..."

"Everyone knows. But I figured she'd at least assure you I'm not some depraved sex fiend trying to buy you for a summer of ... whatever depraved sex fiends do."

She looked around at the deserted surroundings. She didn't feel threatened, not at all. But she didn't want to sit on a tailgate in the middle of nowhere in a dirty dress and discuss Rafael Benton's insane job offer. Before she could say that, though, his phone rang.

He pulled it out of his pocket, checked the number, and declined it. "Not important," he explained. "Look, Esmeralda, let me show you something. Then maybe we can go back to the house and talk. Here."

He handed her the phone. She looked at it blankly. The phone screen was of a cute kid with blue eyes and dimples. His? She blinked.

"So?" she asked.

"That's my nephew, Justin. Cody's little boy." He paused, let her look again at the picture, then gently retrieved his phone. "He's why I need a wife."

• • •

They wound up in the covered gazebo in a garden behind the gloomy house. The garden was walled on three sides with the white and gray rock so common in the area, and like the other gardens she'd spotted when she came the first time, had a mixture of flowers she recognized, from canna lilies to roses. Hummingbirds darted around, additional bits of color, iridescent sparks in the sun.

"If it's too hot, we can go in," Rafael suggested. "Your dress really isn't a problem. I don't obsess over the furnishings or anything."

"Hmpf. Out here's fine." *Nothing you can say will actually interest me. I'm just here ... because I'm curious. Nosy. That's why I'm here.*

Glum-faced Marie must have been chastised when Rafael stopped by the house, because when she brought out a pitcher of tea and bottles of water she greeted Esmeralda formally, put down the drinks, and left.

Serves her right for thinking I'm after the boss. "So, tell me what your nephew has do with this really strange nonsense you're spouting," Esme said, after sipping some of the tea Rafael handed her. "Not that I think anything you say will convince me you're not ..."

"Crazy? My best friend thinks I might be. But at least he knows my mom and dad, and what happened with Cody."

"Where's Justin now?"

"At my folks's home outside Dallas. They had a business trip to Europe planned for some time and couldn't take him."

"But they didn't leave him with you?" she pressed gently.

"No." He stared off for a moment at the horizon, then drew in a deep breath and faced her. "He stayed with my Nana Ellen. She's the woman who took care of me when my parents had to travel and I was in school."

"But you're here and they're not?"

"He's used to the house there and they didn't want to move him." He stood up and walked to the far side of the gazebo, distancing himself, and then turned to add, "I don't know that they trust me with him. Yet."

He didn't sound agitated, but Esmeralda noticed the faint tightening of his lips and his hands knotted against his hips. She didn't want to press, but she wanted to know more. "Why would you think that? I don't understand ..."

"I didn't keep Cody safe for them. My one job and I couldn't do it." Now the defeat in his voice was unmistakable. Strangely, she felt sudden empathy for this man she didn't know at all. How could parents blame one child for the death of another from a drug overdose, especially when both were adults? Her parents condemnation of her relationship with Toby had inflicted wounds that never quite seemed to go away. They'd done everything they could to drive Toby away, even filing police reports and threatening to send her to live with her father's family in Michigan. Toby had caved, joining the Army to prove he was responsible and willing to support Esmeralda. He had died, just as Cody had, and she still blamed herself sometimes. And her parents. But how unfair of his parents if they truly blamed him for Cody's death. And how unbearable would it be to have your sister's child kept from you because of her own mistakes?

"Rafael …"

He raised a hand. "That probably sounded defensive. I don't mean it to be. I blame myself for what happened, probably more than they do. My parents are great people, Esmeralda. They picked me up—pretty much literally—off the street when I was a ten-year-old. Full of hate and anger. I don't remember everything, but I know Dad and Mom met me when I was breaking the windows out of their Cadillac."

"They must be really good-hearted, if they wanted you after you ruined their car," she observed, wanting to hear more, unable to imagine the successful man across from her had ever been poor. She could believe the anger, though; she had heard anger in his voice when he muttered that he'd kill someone.

She should remember the Rafael who claimed he'd been full of hate and dismiss the thoughts that kept teasing her senses. About how good he looked in the perfectly fit jeans and snug T-shirt. About how he'd stolen her breath when he came up behind her in the mirror that day at her aunt's.

"They're the best people in the world," he said, and came over to sit down again, leaning toward her, sincerity clear in his voice. "But they believe what they believe, and no one can make them compromise their principles. They're business people and they built an empire from nothing, so it's not like they're these rigid monsters who can't work with others."

She thought she could figure out why he was telling her that, but …

"My mom has worked with children from broken homes for thirty years. When she's at home, she's volunteering. And she and Dad believe absolutely that children should have two parents—they believe in marriage." He smiled fondly. "They're working on forty years and they love each other like crazy. Guess they can't see past their own love for each other."

"But, today …"

"They accept that not everyone will be married. Not all marriages are happy. They get that. But they fight it. Dad offers marriage counseling to his employees who want to try it. He has single mothers who work for him. He and Mom are fine with that, except for occasional subtle efforts to match lonely souls." He smiled a little. "They haven't had a lot of success with that, from what I've heard. In fact, there has been the occasional bad publicity or lawsuit. But they mean well and mostly, everyone understands that about them. They were raised by poor parents who had very little, but who loved their families beyond anything, and that's what they want for Justin. And for me."

The tenderness and conviction in his voice almost brought tears to her eyes. Her mother Adriana and father Eduardo had celebrated their thirty-fifth anniversary last year. They were still together, but the happiness and joy seemed to be missing—always had, really. They professed to love their children and each other, but the atmosphere had been so constrained, so lacking in excitement or enthusiasm. She straightened a little, though, reminding herself not to judge on what he said. He was, after all, trying to paint his own picture. She had no idea if he was being truthful.

"Which is why …"

"I decided I need to hire a wife. Temporarily." He said it quickly, almost as if that would make it more acceptable. "My parents would be reassured that I'm ready to settle down and not go running all over the world with Marc."

"Marc?"

"My best friend. He works for my dad, too. It's mostly for them, Esmeralda, but not only. Now that Cody's will has been probated and news leaked out that Justin inherited everything, we're afraid that fathers will suddenly come out of every swamp or hole to be found."

"Fathers?" Esme asked in disbelief. She'd dealt with cases at school of mothers whose children all had different fathers. She'd even counseled two students who were half-brothers but didn't know it. Difficult situations. But if Cody Benton was the daughter of such wonderful parents, and such a big star to boot … no. She wouldn't judge Cody Benton. Lord knew her parents and high school friends had assumed the worst of her.

"She didn't know. There were men in her life who were … in and out." He shrugged and looked away again. "It's hard to admit that we don't know who Justin's dad is," he said eventually. "And that of the men who might be the father, not one of them's worth squat."

"You love Justin," she noted quietly.

"I do. I adore him. He's so little, and happy—he looks so much like Cody. But he's lost his mother, and we—my parents and I—can't lose him. We just can't."

"How would marriage have anything to do with that, though?" She stood up to stretch, fingering the necklace thoughtfully. "I wouldn't think anyone would even consider marital status anymore. I mean, think of all the living arrangements, and break-ups, and blends and … why?"

"Courts still have to act in the best interest of the child, and there are still some very conservative courts. My parents are in good health, but they're not young. My job involved a lot of traveling, until Cody broke into music. Even then, but it was different: I was with her. We usually were on buses and in the States. Slightly more kid-friendly than my previous life, when Marc and I would go flying off at a moment's notice. We'd be in the Middle East one day and South America the next." He smiled, remembering. "We had fun, even if there were a few scrapes along the way. Right before Cody got serious about music, Marc and I noticed Dad was sending us to much safer places on sort of made-up work. Like studying the fracking process in North Dakota, when we both knew he'd already committed to an operation in Texas." The smile faded. "When Cody started calling Truth home, Mom and Dad asked me to stay. Now that she's gone, family—a wife—would give me more reason to settle down."

"So you'd lie to a court?"

"No. Not really. In the first place, I'm talking about a legal marriage. And I won't be leaving after the divorce. I'll be here in Truth with Justin when and if my Mom and Dad decide to give up custody. He was born here." He stood again, too, eyes intense as he continued. "I didn't have a home for the first ten years of my life. Justin will never go through what I did. He'll always know where he was born, where home is, and who his family is."

She didn't have an answer for that; she couldn't blame someone who'd apparently had a tough childhood for wanting to protect his nephew. But marriage for parents and a child that really wasn't yours? Not to mention the other obvious problem with this crazy plan of his. Not that she was considering it. But still …

"You seem to be overlooking one major problem. It would be a problem for me, anyway, and I'm sure many others."

"Problem?"

"Call it what you want, temporary wife, a job … but how is money for sex not asking a woman to be a whore?" She chose the vulgarity deliberately, wanting to make him see the insult his misguided offer could inflict.

He looked a little taken aback at her question, but only briefly, then shrugged it off.

"Esmeralda Salinas, get your mind out of the gutter. I have no intention of having sex with you or anyone else while I'm married."

Chapter Seven

Esmeralda's mouth fell open. He'd heard the expression "jaw dropping," but he wasn't sure he'd ever seen such surprise on such a lovely face. Or any face.

When he realized how his answer sounded, he sort of understood. He'd either implied she wouldn't interest him sexually for possibly up to two months in an intimate environment, or that he personally could abstain from sex for some infinite period. Neither of those were what he meant. Looking at her close her mouth slowly and then moisten her lips with her tongue was torture, even standing several feet away from her. He didn't want to think of the temptations they'd encounter sharing a room, even one as large as his upstairs suite.

But he might only put his foot in his mouth again if he tried to correct any of her false assumptions, and clearly, she wasn't going to accept the job anyway. In a way he regretted that. Besides being beautiful, she was a counselor and had nerve. Her training in helping young children would have let her interact safely with Justin—helping him without becoming too attached to him. Or letting him become too attached to her. And her nerve—he took a step away from her, turning, pretending to be engrossed in watching a deer who had wandered out of the trees encircling the house and started to munch on the flowers in one of the gardens.

Luc appeared out of nowhere, walking over to the deer with a wagging tail. The two touched noses and then the doe went back to her food, and Luc sprawled where he was, watching her feed.

Wasn't there a song about everyone having someone? He just couldn't remember with the multitude of country songs he'd been surrounded with for the past three years who sang it or the exact words. And here he was, seeking a temporary wife—a make-believe wife—when many men his age were settling down happily. Marc was right. He was being stupid.

Behind him, he heard Esmeralda shuffle slightly, and reluctantly turned back.

"Look, Rafael." She seemed softer now, less condemning of him. "Some of what you say is sweet. I don't think it makes sense, but you know the situation and I don't." She hesitated, then held out a hand. "Good luck."

He realized as he took her hand he didn't want someone else as his wife—not even his temporary wife. "So you won't consider letting me give you more details?"

She shook her head. "Find someone else if you think you have to go through with this."

He released her hand. "Esmeralda, can I ask a favor? Would you mind keeping this quiet? I mean, your aunt knows, but only she, Lillie Mae, and one other person knows. It's not the kind of thing I want everyone in Truth gossiping about, or I'd never be able to make it work. My parents should be here in about three weeks."

"I won't say a word," she promised, and he believed her. She took a step toward the door, then stopped and shot him a glance over her shoulder. "Too bad you'll be a married man soon," she said.

He raised an eyebrow. "Why?"

The smile she shot him sizzled through him with the sting of a bare electrical wire. "We could have had a good summer. But I don't date married men."

He watched her go, the stain on her skirt less noticeable but still hypnotizing, and her words playing over in his head like the chorus of one of Cody's songs.

•••

By the time she pulled into her aunt's drive fifteen minutes later, Esmeralda's head was pounding and she wished she could just sit in a dark corner and forget everything for a few minutes. Just a few minutes. What kind of man was Rafael Benton? His idea was insane. Her attraction to him was insane. She needed to remember that she'd almost wrecked her own life pursuing men she couldn't or shouldn't want. Rafael fell in that category, without question. She could still see the passion in his eyes, the love, when he spoke of his parents and nephew.

She hadn't had much luck with family. Her parents had fed and clothed her, and hadn't been abusive, really, not beyond letting Beto insult and harass her without any consequences. They had been harsh and cold occasionally, but she knew others who had fared so much worse. If she hadn't fallen in love with a high school boy—so madly in love that she willingly committed to him heart, soul, and body—her parents wouldn't have been so disappointed in her.

She tried to shrug the past off, knowing her head would only hurt worse and nothing would change. Toby would still be gone; he'd gone into the military right after graduation, to support her. To prove to her parents he wasn't a no-good kid interested only in a girl who would defy anyone to have sex with him. Even when he went to Afghanistan—even when he died there—her parents never forgave her for having a sexual relationship outside marriage. They never understood she was just a kid in love—in love with only one man. The sex had been bright and new, but she had loved Toby. She didn't plan on finding someone to replace him. Yet they started watching her day and night, taking her to and from school, making her life hell. Using the same words for her some of the high school crowd did. Until she had found the strength to leave home for Toby.

No one was around, and she was glad. Angel must have gone in to work already. Not seeing Andy around was always a good thing; they didn't like each other. She had no idea whether or not Tía was down the hall in her room, but didn't want to make any noise just in case. She fished a bottle of diet tea out of the refrigerator and headed upstairs to shower and change. With the sun out so late, she might still have time to ride for a while, if she could just shake the headache.

An hour and a hot shower later, she felt ready to face anything again. She put on her favorite riding jeans, boots, and the lightest long-sleeved blouse she could find. The heat was prohibitive, but if she ventured onto paths through cedar, she'd need to keep from being swatted and scratched by untrimmed boughs.

She resisted the urge to hurry down on the stairs, afraid that if Tía hadn't left for her club yet, noise would bother her. As she reached the next to last step, she suddenly heard her aunt's voice off to her right, coming from behind the door.

"You'll regret that! Keep your stupid money and threats! No one needs you!"

Silence followed, and she tried to be even quieter as she hit the floor and headed as quickly as she could do the door, afraid that her aunt would be more upset if she thought she'd been overheard.

Her hand was on the doorknob when Tina's voice behind her froze her in place. "Esmeralda! You're leaving again? Come visit a minute."

I am never going to see Domatrix again. Let alone get to ride her.

Esme pasted on a smile and turned around. "Tía!" She glanced at her watch. "You're going in a little late." Her aunt turned and walked to the kitchen and she followed, sitting down without comment in her usual place.

Her aunt fished in the fridge and pulled out two wine coolers. Mild stuff, really, but Esme had already had one drink more than usual. "If you don't mind, I'll get myself a water."

"Don't be a baby," her aunt muttered, setting the bottle on the table with a thump and sitting down across from her. "And I'm not going in to the club, either. That's why I pay people."

She'd seen little of her aunt since moving in, but she'd never seen her so angry and upset. She wished she knew more about Tina, more about how to calm her, to make her feel better.

Since she didn't, she tried for the neutral, non-judgmental face she used to approach troubled students with. "Anything I can help with? Are you feeling okay, or … "

Tina jerked her hands across her face and through her hair, then breathed deeply. With fingers that shook, she opened the bottle and downed half of the beverage in a gulp. Then she pushed it aside and blotted her mouth with the back of her hand. "I'm fine."

"Seriously, if I can help …"

"Just the money problems I mentioned before. Things'll turn around." She smiled at Esme. "How did your job interview with the gorgeous Rafael Benton go?"

"I spoke to him twice, and neither one went well." Esme got up, carried the cooler back to the refrigerator, and sat down again. "Tía, why on earth would you think I'd be interested? How could you …"

"You weren't?" Tía's eyebrows shot up. "A woman not interested in spending two months pretending to be Rafa's wife?"

"Rafa?"

"Oh, come, *niña*. Aren't all Rafaels 'Rafa' to their friends?" Her aunt smiled tightly. "If you were a little smarter, dear, you could be calling him Rafa yourself." Esme bit back her protest over Tina's dig. The fact that her aunt used the common nickname for Rafael made her wonder how well they knew each other. Rafael claimed not to like her, but her aunt seemed on good terms with him. She couldn't really ask, though. Nothing her aunt said right now would be rational: clearly she was having some sort of meltdown.

"Seriously, Tía, why did you even mention the job to me? Has my mom convinced you I'm so worthless, so … cheap that I'd marry a man for money?"

"Quit with the drama and the outrage, dear. You said you wanted to be like me? That you thought I'd be a better mother to you than my sister is? Please!" Tina reached across the table and clasped Esme's wrist. "I would marry Rafael Benton for eight weeks for much less than I expect he's offering. And dear, just for the record—he told the three of us who know about his little proposition that he's not paying for sex." She released Esme and shrugged emphatically. "You'd be set for years, for a few weeks' work pretending to be a devoted wife."

"Women aren't property anymore, Tía! We don't have to marry. No one marries for convenience anymore. No one!"

"Bull." Tía shoved her chair back and went over to the counter, rummaging around and finding a pre-measured container of coffee, which she poured into her single serving coffee maker with hands that were still unsteady. "You know better," she continued, not even looking back. "Men, women—especially women—lots of marriages are all about the moolah, and you know it!" She turned and glared then. "Tell me that's not true! Tell me you don't know women—friends of yours—who stay in bad marriages for the money. Or tell me you haven't heard of someone—or talked about someone—you knew didn't really marry for love!"

Esmeralda couldn't deny any of that. Maybe she hadn't had close friends, but she'd had acquaintances who clearly weren't in relationships for love. She fidgeted with her water. Sex for pleasure's sake, short-term relationships both parties agreed to, that was one thing. But marriage—she shook her head slowly.

"Maybe it happens," she admitted to her aunt, "but it's not something I'd feel right about."

"You'd understand why he's trying to do it if you knew his parents," Tina told her, filling her mug with the freshly brewed coffee and coming back to stand by the table, blowing on the coffee. "Stubborn as mules and just as stupid."

"From what I hear, they're very successful."

"And kind and loving," Tina added, in a childishly sing-song voice that raised the hair on Esme's arms. Did her aunt need mental help? Were her problems driving her to some invisible cliff? Again, she wished she'd known her better. She remembered her aunt as fun—a laughing free spirit who hadn't come around often, but made her childhood sparkle with hope and possibility when she did. Not as the sometimes hard and bitter woman mocking the parents of a man she apparently knew fairly well. Rafael Benton had confided in her aunt, and that had to mean something.

Didn't it?

"Well, if his parents are so traditional and difficult, all the more reason to say no," Esme pointed out. "The reason my parents and I had problems is how set they were on their way or no way at all."

"And yet you would have married a horny teenager who didn't have the proverbial pot to pee in before you were even of age?"

Esme's hand tightened around the bottle, but she kept her voice level, trying hard to think of her aunt as an emotionally distraught parent. Someone hitting out because of a lack of coping skills. "I loved Toby. I would have married him … if he had come back from Afghanistan."

Something in the flatness of her answer must have gotten through to Tina. She suddenly slumped into the chair and looked at Esme with watery eyes.

"I'm sorry. I didn't mean to be so … sarcastic and petty. I'm just worried about my situation, and wishing you could have everything I can't have." She shrugged again, less forcefully, and tried to smile.

"Aunt Tin—Tía—would you get anything out of me marrying Rafael Benton?"

"No. What could I possibly get?" The scowl returned to Tía's face. "Why do you ask?"

"No reason. You were close to Cody, though, right?"

Her aunt's smile was instant and genuine. "She was the daughter I always wanted. We bonded the day we met." Just as quickly, the smile disappeared. "Which is why Rafael hates me. Or says he does. He couldn't stand not being the most important person in his sister's life. She'd always looked up to him, and he was jealous when she stopped. Cody had grown up and he never has."

Her aunt's odd mixture of rants and raves threatened to give her a headache again. Or emotional whiplash. *Cody had been a daughter to her? I could have been.* "I'm sure he doesn't hate you, Tía. And—thank you for thinking maybe I'd be the right person for this … strange job offer. But I'm not." She walked around the table and rested a hand on her aunt's shoulder briefly. "I need to go check on my horse. Do you need anything before I go? Or maybe I could bring dinner back."

"Don't bother."

Esme wished her voice didn't hold so much indifference, such emptiness. "Hey, even if you're not going into town, I could run by Tía's. I'll even sing if you think it would help—though I still don't know why me doing karaoke would help anything."

"You're a big girl, Esmeralda," Tía said, unwittingly echoing Lillie Mae. "Do what you want." She blew in her coffee again, and with a final pat on her shoulder, Esme left.

• • •

There weren't a lot of cars outside Tía's, but Rafael pulled in anyway. He'd spent a couple of hours over at the Silver Boot and Booty, talking business with Jade Brockton, the owner. He smiled. Brockton was a son of privilege; he'd probably choked on a silver spoon somewhere along the way, because he hated his father—one of the richest men around, apparently—with a passion. But he liked Brockton's straight-shooting demeanor and the plans he had for his own ranch, the Double Block. And he didn't mind at all that the Silver Boot and Booty had probably three times the vehicles when he left than Tía's had now. Weeknight or not, if Brockton's bar put Tina Cervantes out of business, he wouldn't mind. Not at all.

He saw Esmeralda's pickup immediately, parked near the edge of the parking lot, so she must have come in fairly late. He was surprised at his sudden eagerness to see her again. Her fault. Why had she teased him about having wanted to spend the summer with him? That she knew he planned on being married in a couple of weeks made it easy for her to flirt and still keep her distance.

Damn. Was he as crazy as Lillie Mae and Marc both thought? Marc knew his parents and claimed to understand the idea—he just didn't think anyone could fool Chris and Alice Benton. Lillie Mae—he smiled at the dressing down she'd given him. She thought he was crazy, period. But he didn't mind her scolding him. Marc should have his back, though. What were best friends—and best men—for?

He paused a moment outside the door, surprised at the lack of voices filtering out into the night. He didn't hear drunken laughter, the jukebox—just silence. When he opened it, though, he knew why.

Esme was sitting on a stool on the stage, feet resting on the brace, crooning into a microphone. Low and haunting, he knew the music only because his Mom and Dad loved classic country and had played this one over and over. The sadness and mystery in the song had attracted his attention, but he'd forgotten the words since he'd embarked on all those constant travels, first for his dad's energy conglomerate, then with Cody.

He sank into the first empty seat, watching her sing with fascination. She was just singing karaoke, but her voice was beautiful and captured the feeling of the song so well. Cody's voice could do that when she was on, but toward the end, she'd just belted out songs without the emotional impact of her earlier vocalizations. Lost in the power of adulation and quick success, Cody had lost the love for the music that had propelled her so high, so fast.

Esmeralda. He closed his eyes for a minute. Just as well she'd turned him down. No way in hell could they pull off a platonic marriage, even though he couldn't afford sexual involvement with the woman he married. Sex complicated everything, no matter what anyone claimed. He didn't want to hurt the woman who would be his wife for a few very public weeks. And he couldn't afford to become attached to anyone, either. Not after the disaster of the one serious relationship he'd had, when he'd been played with, used, and discarded. He still couldn't believe how blind he'd been, or how dearly his parents had paid—emotionally and financially. No, the pre-nuptial arrangement his lawyers had drawn up couldn't prohibit consummating the marriage for obvious reasons, so he'd have to be very clear with the woman— his wife—who would share his life for a summer.

He frowned. Except for the impossibility of being around her and not wanting her, he couldn't imagine a better candidate than Esme. He'd need to know a lot more, of course, but she was educated, single, so confident.

She clearly enjoyed attention a little too much. She finished the last notes of the song, her voice trailing away into husky sorrow, then silence, and the small crowd went berserk, cheering, stomping feet, clapping, and hollering. He applauded briefly, knowing his attitude sucked, but unable, as always, not to think of Cody, and how quickly innocence and talent had fallen in the onslaught of attention and the descent into pride, then selfishness and indulgence.

And then death.

He stood, thinking he'd just sneak out without being seen, but Esme stepped off the stage and saw him immediately.

"Rafael!" she called across the room.

At least she wasn't as furious with him as she'd been off and on earlier today. Today? He glanced at his watch and smiled mirthlessly. Yesterday. And she looked just as fresh and fine as she had when she walked into his study for the first interview. His smile broadened as he remembered the dirt stain on her skirt. Okay, she looked fresher than that.

She looked good.

"Last song I thought I'd hear tonight was 'Ode to Billie Joe,'" he told her. "You killed it."

"Thanks." She looked a little abashed. "I hadn't done it in years, but I used to love hearing it." She grinned. "This town must be starved for entertainment if folks'll listen to me sing old country I've half forgotten! You'd think they'd never heard a singer."

He saw the sudden horror as she realized what she'd said and her face turned red in embarrassment.

"Don't apologize," he said gently. "You didn't mean anything. And you were great." He sighed. "Can I buy you a drink?"

"No."

He hadn't expected her to agree, but wished she had. He really didn't want to walk out the door and leave her here.

Before he could say good night, though, she stepped close and lowered her voice.

"Rafael, can you take me somewhere? Somewhere you can tell me about this job offer again."

He couldn't believe what he'd heard.

"You …"

"I want you to convince me I'm the right person for your job," she said. "I want you to convince me that I can marry you for money."

Chapter Eight

Esmeralda heard her own words echo in her head. So matter of fact and so … crass. She hadn't promised to agree, she reminded herself. After the blow up with her aunt and her long ride through the low hills around the Petersons, she'd decided to listen to him again. She wanted to believe in marriage, that it was special. Sacred. But she'd had to admit, on her trail ride, that she'd known few happy marriages. She hadn't been wildly popular in Rose Creek, and she'd tried to steal a married man and a man in love with someone else. No wonder she hadn't been invited to many homes to consider the blessings of marriages.

If his proposition was as cut and dried as she'd just made it sound—maybe. She still might not think so, but if she did, she might be able to help her aunt. Her parents were well-established, not wealthy, but she didn't think they needed anything. A brief pang shot through her at how distant she'd become from them. Maybe she could build a relationship with her aunt, and then work on cutting through all the old anger directed at her parents. As for her brother, there was no room for a relationship with him. In fact, her loathing for Beto probably had much to do with the lack of love her parents showed her. After all, Toby had been gone for a long time now, but they still treated her as if they'd walked into the house and found Toby asleep in her bed. Undoubtedly Beto kept her parents' contempt for Toby well nurtured.

Rafael wasn't answering, though, and his smile was gone. Had he changed his mind? He'd told her that he didn't particularly want her because of his relationship with Tía. He'd said that his parents were coming in a few weeks. Did he plan on being married by then, or marrying when they came? Either way, if he actually went through with the madness, he didn't have much time to look.

"Rafael?" she prompted, not wanting others to notice—or get close enough to hear their discussion.

"You caught me off guard." He flexed his arms. "Let me walk you to your truck. I saw it when I came in and it's way in the back."

She nodded and waved goodbye to Angel and Tom, who were standing near the bar, talking.

"You don't have a purse?"

"Didn't need it. License in the truck, keys in my pocket. I travel light."

"I guess that's a good thing. You're okay to drive?" he asked, as she clicked the fob to turn on the truck and unlock the doors.

"Why wouldn't I be? I haven't had a drink since Lillie Mae sort of dared me to."

He chuckled. "I bet she didn't say 'dare you,' though, right? She just sat there and drank her morning beer and you figured you needed to make her blink."

"Smart ass," she muttered. "So … are you still interested in me taking the job, or have you decided to move on?"

"It's one in the morning and I know we've both been up since at least ten, Esme. You're not at all tired?"

"I am, but …"

He maneuvered around her to pull her door open, passing so close that he brushed her, although she didn't think he meant to. "Let's call it a night," he suggested matter-of-factly. "We'll probably both think better tomorrow."

"You're assuming a lot," she retorted. "Tomorrow I might not be living on adrenaline and thinking I can do anything." *That sounds a lot like the old Esmeralda. Not who I planned on becoming when I left Rose Creek.* She lifted herself into the seat and closed the door, then rolled the window down. "When and where would you like to meet?" she asked.

"Do you fish?"

"Excuse me?"

"Fish? We could go to the lake, spend some time trying to catch a fish. I never have, there, but we could try. And we could talk."

She leaned her head out the door to gauge his expression. "Is this a test?"

"Why would you think that?" His face fell a little. "You don't fish, do you?"

"No, not recently. But I can go watch you fish."

"Good. It's peaceful there, Esme. There's this shady spot with boulders. We can talk without anyone interrupting."

"How do I get there? I'm new in town, remember?"

"Why don't you go over to Witches Haven around nine and we'll just take one truck?"

He frowned at her hesitation.

"Sure," she said, finally. "Why not? Bring food, water, and the dogs. Oh, and whatever you need to fish with." She grinned and put the truck in gear. "Oh, and move," she added. "Just in case I run over your feet or anything."

He laughed, but moved back anyway, making a show of checking his feet.

"Idiot," she murmured, glancing in the side mirror and seeing he was still standing there, watching her leave. But then she thought of the immediate surge of desire she'd felt at the sound of his throaty chuckle, and knew she was the idiot.

• • •

Esme couldn't help smiling a little when she saw the back seat of Rafael's truck. He'd covered both seats with sheets, and the dogs took up the entire space. The bed of the truck held all the things the cab couldn't—fishing gear, ice chest, folding chairs, a canvas heap he told her was for shade—enough stuff, she thought, to survive being lost in the woods for a week.

Not that that would happen, she reminded herself. But she thought she'd moved fewer belongings from Rose Creek to Truth than he was taking for a few hours fishing.

And interviewing her, she reminded herself.

He saw her grin at the overload and smiled, too. "You wouldn't believe I'm an accomplished world traveler, would you?" he admitted.

"Why do you need all this?" she asked, careful not to actually link herself to him or anything he had planned. Just business, that's what today was.

"Honestly?" He slanted a glance at the truck. "You're the one who said to bring the dogs and food. The fishing gear—well, we needed that, right? Besides," he added, with a slight shrug, "I'm practicing for when Justin comes. You're supposed to over-pack for kids, right?"

"I don't have kids," she reminded him. "Packing for them usually doesn't come up in my line of work."

"Right. We're late. The fish get up a lot earlier than we did. Let's go."

They climbed in to the cab, and when both Danes reached over to greet them, Rafael reprimanded them. They obediently turned away to their respective windows, and Esmeralda couldn't help being relieved. She really didn't know why she'd told him to bring the dogs; they were gorgeous, but they'd already started drooling. At least with them along, he'd have to watch them and his fishing. Less time to focus on her. She, on the other hand, could ask him the questions for which she needed answers.

The road to the lake was like the road she'd come into Truth on: narrow and dug between high banks of clay and rock, with trees perched awkwardly sometimes. When she wasn't driving a horse trailer, they didn't seem nearly as formidable, though a car careening around a curve partially in their lane elicited a curse from Rafael as he swerved farther toward the shoulder to avoid it.

"I'd been going to suggest you talk, but maybe not," she murmured. "Does everybody come back from the lake in that big a hurry?"

"Not everyone. The scary ones are towing boats, though. Twice the chance of getting hit." He didn't say it with real concern, though, so she relaxed against the seat.

"I don't know why I said we should talk again," she said. "I still don't think …"

"You still think I'm crazy," he finished for her, and she saw his dimples slash across his cheek. "Maybe I am, but if it's crazy for my family, it doesn't embarrass me. You're not seeing anyone?"

The question caught her off guard and she blinked, but answered levelly enough. "We'd established that, hadn't we? I wouldn't be talking to you if I were."

"There's a reason I asked again, Esme. If you were … wouldn't your parents prefer you married, or would they be okay without the formalities?"

"My parents." She fell silent briefly. "Yes. They'd prefer marriage. But they've pretty much given up on me."

He turned to look at her, surprised, and this time an oncoming driver leaned on the horn as he moved too near the middle of the road. "Are you close to them?"

"We talk. I visit now and then. But …" She didn't finish. "One of my plans when I moved here was to start mending fences. Thought as I spent some time with my aunt, I'd find out more about my mother." She looked out the window at the wall of rock, clay, and cedar crawling past as Rafael braked for a sharp curve. "I've never understood why my mom and aunt aren't closer than they are. I've always wished I had a sister."

"I was lucky," he said, as they suddenly came out on a cleared parking area overlooking the lake. "I have parents who never gave up on me. And when I had a sister, she and I were close." He parked and turned to her. "Let's get set up down by the lake, and then we can talk."

He opened his door and slid out, then turned back to grin at her. "Quietly. We will talk quietly, or I'll never catch anything here!"

The dogs bounded out the moment he opened the door, but stopped obediently and waited while he clipped leashes on them. Then he handed her the leashes with a grin. "You wanted them. You babysit."

Drat. That hadn't been in her plans.

"And I can control these things?"

"You can control a horse, right?"

"Mostly. And one at a time."

"Quit whining," he ordered good-naturedly. "If they try to run into the water, though, don't let them. We don't want to scare—"

"The fish away. Got it." She headed down toward the water's edge, comfortable that her tennis shoes wouldn't slip, but a little uneasy about actually controlling the dogs if they decided to chase something. Sure, Domatrix was bigger, but she was usually calm and well-mannered. These giants could drag her half a mile before she got them stopped.

They behaved halfway down to the water, walking so obediently that she dismissed her worries and relaxed her hold on their leashes. Only, Rafael clearly hadn't been joking about their love of the water. A few yards away from the edge, both dogs suddenly bolted, catching her completely off guard, and raced straight for the calm water.

She shrieked, startled, then hung on for a step or two, but the vision of winding up face-down in the lake and spending the morning around Rafael in a wet T-shirt made her let go of both leashes, flinging them away from her just as one of her feet went under water. Unrestrained, the dogs bounded about, barking and splashing. Their joy was contagious, and she laughed at them.

"Oh, no!" Rafael said. "They're in the water."

"Surely you can get them out," she reassured him, then looked at him. "So … how long it does take for the fish to calm down?"

"You're serious, aren't you?" he asked. "Fish don't 'calm down.' You've really never gone fishing?"

She looked out over the lake. She didn't want to answer, but she'd come to talk, hadn't she? "My fiancé and I went fishing at South Padre right before he left Laredo for the Army." She managed a faint smile. "We never got to the beach."

He made a noncommittal sound and unfolded an expensive chair, with cup-holders and a padded seat. Then he whistled the dogs out of the water and removed their wet leashes. While he was working, he asked, "Did you ever marry?"

He couldn't see her, because he was still trying to untangle fishing line that had tangled around a leash, but she shook her head. "No. He never came home from Afghanistan. The trip to South Padre was the last time we were together."

That brought his head up. "I'm so sorry. Are you still in love with him? Is he why you never married?"

"How do you know I never married?"

"Well, you're not married, not dating …" He carried the tangle of line over and tossed it in a trashcan, then came back. "I just assume he must be the reason."

Esme stopped searching through her beach bag for her iPad and tilted her chin. "Just for the record, I loved Toby, but I went through hell for that. From the first time Toby got me home late, I was called a tramp, a slut, a whore. Since I got labeled anyway, I don't think you could say I've been carrying a flame for Toby. When I think of him, I'm sad that he lost his life. Maybe we would still be together, but really, who is? There have been a lot of men in my life since Toby. A lot. And I enjoyed them. I'm not apologizing for that, got it?"

"Yes, ma'am," he said immediately, picking up a fishing pole. "Do you know how to cast this?"

"Cast means throw, right?" When he turned, startled, she laughed. "No, I don't know how to cast, and yes, I know what the word means."

"Look. Hold it like this—one-handed. You can steady the line and hook if it distracts you," he added, noticing the face she was making at the synthetic worm hanging off the hook. "Then draw it back and to the side, depending on where you want the lure to go, and just let it rip."

Let it rip? Esme watched attentively, but only thought to look where the lure landed when she heard the splash and saw water ripple near a stand of reeds growing a fair distance away from them. She'd been entirely too captivated by the taut muscles under his shirt—the movement from his shoulder outward along one muscled arm stole her breath and her attention. *Show me again?*

She dug a heel into the damp ground and bit her lower lip. She couldn't be caught swooning over someone she'd just told about her abilities in bed, could she? She'd exaggerated, but the gist was, she had enjoyed the men she'd dated. Women who disliked her on sight and some of the men she had refused to date created an image and a reputation she didn't try to correct: a woman unafraid to be sensual. Unafraid to seduce and move on.

"Here." Rafael handed her the pole, and picked up another, this lure fish-shaped and glittering in the sun. "Variety's the key," he said innocently enough, and cast his line out beyond hers. "When we pull them in, we'll have to be careful. Otherwise, there'll be a tangled mess."

Again, the play of his muscles working so easily under the thin shirt mesmerized her. They stood there quietly for a moment, if not in silence. The big dogs panting nearby, the shrill scream of some distant birds, and the far-off hum of a motorboat or Jetski filled the day with its own kind of music.

"So, you named your horse?"

The question came out of the blue and the pole slipped a little in her hands.

"Uh … yes. Yes I did. Problems with the name?"

"No." He jerked on his line suddenly, then began reeling it in. "I just don't know what Domatrix means."

"You're kidding, right?" This time, the pole slipped completely out of her hands. "You're a man, for starters, educated, you travel, and even if your mom and dad are the nicest, tamest people in the world …" She broke off, shaking her head, but staring at him in disbelief.

"Domatrix was a present from Toby when he left Laredo. He had a car a friend of his really wanted. He knew I wouldn't go home after I'd run away to be with him. So he sold the car and bought Domatrix for me." She sighed, remembering. "Not a great gift since I was working a few hours at the mall and going to school. But one of my friends agreed to keep her if she could ride her now and then."

"So the name?"

"Well, you saw her. Those long black stockings." She'd never told anyone where her horse's name came from before, although she used it once or twice as innuendo when she was trying to impress someone. She shrugged and said with a slight twinge of embarrassment she rarely felt, "We were … kind of crazy then. He said she'd always remind us of how it was … and that anyway, she would always control who rode her."

"And Toby named her?"

"Yes." She hesitated. "I really didn't know. He had to tell me what the name meant."

He laughed out loud, with such amusement that the dogs picked up their heads and stared, and a water bird flapped out of its hiding place and flew away.

"So much for the fish! Just what is so funny?"

"Well, from your explanation, I suspect you named your horse the wrong thing. Toby probably either said—or meant to say—Dominatrix. You speak Spanish, Esmeralda. "*Domina*—to control—and then the English 'tricks,' but the French spelled it wrong—and there you have what you thought you named your mare!"

"We named her the wrong thing?" Esme asked, a little put out by how funny he found that. As he tried to control his laughter, though, she couldn't help smiling. "No wonder no one ever got my little jokes, even when I knew they couldn't be that naïve." She finally laughed, too, remembering how she'd told Connie just to call the Appaloosa Trixie, imagining how embarrassing that conversation might have been if Connie had understood the intended name.

"You'd make one heck of a language teacher," she teased. "*Domina* from the Spanish and the English 'tricks'—misspelled by the French? What kind of explanation is that?"

"Hey, words are everything. You'd be surprised what I've gotten with a few right words."

Her smile faded. No, she wouldn't. Good-looking men with a talent for words usually could get whatever they wanted. Why would his boast, made even in jest, surprise her? She'd come here with every intention of considering his proposal again. His job offer. It didn't matter, because he was right. He probably could have sold her on anything—all with the power of his words.

"Why don't you pick up your rod and try casting it?"

She bit back a comment and lifted the rod. Then she maneuvered it just as he had done, and heard a yelp of pain and muttered curse. Surprised, she whirled around, involuntarily jerking the pole.

"Don't move, dammit! You hooked me!"

Esmeralda stared in horror at the hook caught on the side of his neck, a thin trickle of blood beginning as he grappled to remove the barbed metal. "I am so sorry—"

"No biggie," he reassured her, but then cursed again when his fingers slipped. She watched sickly as he tried to ease the hook out of his skin.

"There!" he said finally, and let the hook go, before catching it between his thumb and index finger and steadying it. "This isn't the first time I've seen this happen. Now try again." He winked. "But this time, aim for the water." He let go and raised his hand. "Wait while I just walk over here by the dogs."

She watched him scoot away from her with a smile. The man wasn't just gorgeous, he was fun to be with. She hadn't had a lot of fun the last two times she'd been out with men—they'd had their women on their minds. As far as she knew, Rafael Benton wasn't taken.

As far as she knew. She cast her reel and watched the lifelike worm drop into the lake. She glanced over his shoulder, hoping he'd noticed, but he was smearing something on the wound. She cranked the reel around once the way she'd seen Rafael do, and wondered why they were here playing games. Had he made his job offer in good faith? Would he play by those rules of not making physical demands? Could she?

It was time to stop fishing and decide once and for all if his job interested her. She started retrieving the line, winding the reel slowly as she tried to make sense of her tangled emotions and doubts. Suddenly, the line went taut, and then the rod bent double as the line ran out.

"Pull it up a little. I think you've got one!" Rafael cupped his hands around hers, helping her give a quick upward tug on the line. The line cut crazy patterns in the water, and whatever was on the other end seemed perfectly capable of pulling Esme in after it. Adrenaline coursed through her, and as she fought the fish closer to shore, eager to see it, she suddenly was acutely aware that Rafael stood so close behind her that she could feel his heat, his own excitement. Before she could decipher what kind of excitement surged between them, though, there was a flash of silver as a fish broke the surface and dived again.

"Keep reeling," he ordered. "I'll go get it."

"I can catch my own fish!"

"Not if it breaks the line," he explained, and went crashing merrily into the water, net at the ready. "Try to get it up a little again … there! Got it!"

He thrashed out of the water, the jeans clinging to him wetly, extending the net toward her. "Your first, right?"

She forced her eyes to the fish that was flopping frantically, gills gasping, and forgot the tight jeans in a sudden feeling of guilt.

"Whatever it is, let it go," she pleaded. "I can't stand to see it like that."

"It's a smallmouth bass, but it's too small to keep anyway" he agreed, pulling it out of the net. "It'll be okay for a minute. It's your first fish." He handed the fish, still on her line, to her, then pulled his phone out of his shirt pocket and snapped a quick picture.

With quick, skillful movements, he freed the fish, holding it up one final time. "Sure you don't want to stuff it?"

"I thought I'd caught something worthwhile. It fought so hard."

"Which is why fishermen love bass." He waded into the water and leaned over, holding the bass in the water for a moment, then stepping back. Within seconds, the fish seemed to realize that it was free. With a final splash of silver and water, it was gone.

He waded out of the water, smiling broadly. "Haven't had this much fun fishing in a while," he said, patting the bandage he'd put over the ointment. "In spite of everything. We'll have to do it again sometime."

"I was just thinking I'll never do this again," she retorted, then grinned, remembering the line of a song about giving up love for fishing. "Of course, if I'd brought my guitar, I probably could write a country song."

The smile faded and the dimples disappeared. She wanted to kick herself and opened her mouth to apologize, but he shook his head and touched her cheek with a gentle finger. "Cody will always be there, *la espina de una rosa*, and that thorn may always hurt, but it isn't your problem." Then, after a moment, he asked, folding the chair he'd set out for her, "Do I pick good first dates, or what?"

She shouldered him aside and picked up the folded chair, handing him the fishing pole instead. "There's no way I'm carrying this to the truck. Who knows what I'd catch."

He nodded, but she couldn't miss the aura of sadness closing in around him. She didn't want it to, but it tugged at her heart. She could remember losing Toby, and how the pain lingered for years after. And the chasm separating her from her parents still haunted her at times, making her wonder what she could have done differently. Cody hadn't been gone long, and she didn't want him to think he had to pretend for her sake.

"Let's go," she said gently. "But we still need to talk somewhere."

"We will," he promised.

She stowed the chair in the bed of the truck and climbed into the cab, letting him settle the dogs and check for forgotten items.

Finally he climbed in and shifted in the seat to face her. "So, where to? Fishing just didn't bring us the right mood."

"What's the right mood to propose marriage to someone you don't know? For money?"

He ignored the jab as he backed out, pushing Luc's head out of his way as he turned to look behind them. "Why don't we just go back to Witches Haven and talk there?"

"Didn't work too well last time," Esme pointed out. "And your secretary doesn't like me."

"Marie's my assistant. She hates to be called a secretary. And she's usually … fine." He made the tight turn onto the road leading to Truth and on through to Witches Haven and grinned at her. "You already sound like a wife."

They drove along and as they neared the hidden drive up to the dark house, he suddenly pointed. "Look! Haven't seen wild turkeys in a while."

She watched the three birds flap awkwardly into cover, a little amused at his enthusiasm. He said he'd traveled the world, but Rafael Benton was clearly a nature boy at heart. She didn't dislike animals and she loved horses, but she couldn't see herself being so excited over wild birds, no matter how big, ugly, and apparently uncommon they were.

"What are you smiling about?" Rafael asked curiously.

"Hummingbirds. The ones in your yard are a lot prettier than the turkeys we just saw."

"When I first started coming here, turkeys weren't something you saw constantly, but at certain times of day, you'd see them. Now, not so much. I think it's sad to think of animals dying off or leaving an area, that's all."

Luc and Chief, quiet and well behaved for most of the ride, were excited to be home, and Esmeralda found herself ducking and bobbing to keep out of their way as they crowded her window. As soon as they stopped, Esmeralda threw off the seatbelt and jumped out, running both hands over her hair. "Dog slobber," she complained. "And I thought having one lick my face was disgusting."

Rafael didn't say anything, just grinned as he opened the door and let the Danes hurtle from the truck and bound away. Then he leaned an arm against the truck and held out a handkerchief. "I have this," he offered. "But it's got a little blood on it. Someone tried to rip my neck open with a fish hook."

"Oh, all right," she muttered, following the dogs toward the air-conditioned house. "We're even. But you don't play fair."

Chapter Nine

You don't play fair. Her words stopped him in his tracks. She didn't have a clue how right her words were. She could marry him and never have cause to complain. The draft contract he'd had written up as soon as he'd had this monumental idea would protect them both, financially. And he would be sure the relationship would remain platonic, as he promised.

Sure, women sold their virginity online these days, and "reality" shows delved into the most intimate of moments. But he knew, somehow, that as liberated as she claimed to be, even consensual sex with him while they were under contract would trouble her. And him, too.

He walked after her slowly, wondering how he could make her understand the need for his plan while exposing his own life as little as possible. He'd never liked talking about the pain of his childhood, or the mistakes he'd made moving from unwanted street child to the son his parents doted on. He'd been honest—mostly. His parents' stance on marriage—undoubtedly grown from their own love for each other as well as their upbringing, their faith, and their work with troubled youth—was unpopular and sometimes hard to explain. But he loved them for their commitment to each other, and a temporary marriage to give happiness to two of the only three people who had ever loved him was a small price to pay—regardless of dollar amount. Money didn't matter in the face of their happiness and approval. He'd hurt them so often over the years. The marriage would make them incredibly happy. A divorce would hurt them, but it would be amicable. Something they'd accept as better than waiting until it became bitter and complicated. At least, he hoped they'd accept it. He shook his head slightly, then touched the bandage as he felt a slight twinge of pain. A little too early to worry about a divorce when he hadn't convinced anyone to marry him yet.

She'd stopped on the porch, obviously waiting for him, probably not wanting to face Marie. He'd have to talk to them both, if she agreed to take his offer.

And thinking of Marie made him think of Tina Cervantes. He wouldn't deliberately destroy her, because vengeance wouldn't bring Cody back. He tried to think rationally, but the bile rose and soured his throat, and his fists clenched. Or maybe he would, and that's why Esme's words needled him. If he found out that Tina was still harboring Harper—maybe even encouraging his claims of being Justin's father—then there wasn't a power play in the world he wouldn't use to stop them both. Destroy them both. Play fair? Tía's bar was already teetering on the edge of financial ruin, and he'd heard around town that she wasn't even coming in every day. She was drinking more, and alienating some of her suppliers. He smiled grimly. She'd better not know where Harper was. He'd seen ruthless business deals over the last ten or twelve years, and participated in a few. Pushing a failing bar over the edge into oblivion wouldn't be hard. And no one would deserve it more than Tía.

Esme must have heard the low, snarling oath that forced itself out of his throat, because she faced him in surprise.

"Did you say something else? I didn't hear—"

Good. "No, not really." He opened the door for her. "Let's sneak up to the office before we're seen. We can talk there." They walked together to the stairs, and about halfway up, he noticed the dampness where one of the dogs had covered her with drool. "Heck, if you want, you can borrow the shower to wash off."

I shouldn't have said that. Or thought it. Images of her reaching up to lather her hair, her hands sliding over her body as she covered herself in soap … he stubbed his toes on the next step because he couldn't see anything but her. *Don't let her turn around and find me drooling like one of the damn dogs.*

She did, though, and raised her eyebrows. "Sneaking upstairs and a shower? Sounds more like funny business than legitimate business to me."

She wasn't helping.

"I only thought … but if your hair doesn't bother you, then never mind."

She reached up and patted the side of her head, and drew her hand away with a look of disgust. "Gross. I shouldn't have checked. Point me to a towel and the shower."

He led her down the tall, opening a closet on the way, exposing an array of neatly folded towels in a rainbow of vibrant colors. "Grab something you like and follow me."

She grabbed the top towel and shook it out as she followed him through his bedroom. He opened the door and stepped aside, then saw the towel she'd chosen. An oversized bath sheet with a lifelike, nearly life size picture of Cody.

"This day couldn't get weirder if it tried," he muttered. "Look for me in the study when you're ready, and uh … if you need anything."

"Thanks, Rafa." She patted his cheek as she moved by him. She'd never used his nickname before, but before he could comment on it, the door closed between them and moments later, water blasted against the shower walls.

The urge to turn the handle and see if she'd locked the door almost overwhelmed him. He beat it back. Why would he want to know if the door was open? He'd offered the shower and promised a hands-off relationship even if they shared a bedroom for a few weeks.

What he should want to know was just what would happen if she married him and he couldn't keep his crazy promise about not wanting her in his shower every night. With the door open.

•••

Esmeralda stood under the pounding spray and dropped her head, letting the water massage her neck and shoulders. She should turn off the faucet and get out. But she wasn't ready to sit down next to Rafael Benton and discuss marriage, even a mock marriage. Stripping her clothes off and stepping into his shower seemed the most daring thing she'd done recently. He was sitting in his study waiting for her. Had he been thinking about her, here? Naked? A shiver of desire coursed through her. Probably. When she'd turned the water on, she'd had a delicious image of him in the stall, water sliding over his remarkable body … and of his eyes, burning dark fire, focused on her. She smiled as she stepped out and started to towel herself dry. She'd promised herself in Rose Creek not to pursue momentary relationships that were high risk and low emotion. Rafael had taken himself out of the running, and that was smart. She couldn't see herself sleeping with a man when money was involved. But fantasizing about him? That couldn't possibly be wrong. And sometimes fantasy was better than the real thing anyway.

He was working at a laptop when she went in, frowning over some numbers. "I'll be right with you. The Houston office sent me a report they didn't think looked right."

She watched, mesmerized, while his fingers flicked over keys and his expression seemed to change constantly in relation to the severity of whatever it was that he was correcting. She knew he had money and hadn't really thought he'd had to work for it. But clearly he knew what he was doing, and enjoyed it. She smiled to herself, thinking that he attacked this task with the same enthusiasm as he did fishing—probably with better results, too.

He finished and logged off, then stood and stretched and managed to half hide a yawn behind his forearm. "Late night," he explained, with a wink. "First I got trapped into buying dinner for half the town at Rosita's. Don't ever let anyone there talk you into playing that game where they draw straws, because I haven't won yet, and the loser buys dinner for everyone in the game. Then some redhead singing old country brought the house down around my ears and marches up to demand that I marry her."

"Really?" Esmeralda stood and closed the distance between them. "What I heard," she whispered throatily, "is that this smart-mouth little rich boy who thinks he's all that tried to pick up this naïve karaoke singer …"

"I'll buy the naïve," he answered gravely, but laughter tinged his voice anyway, and the dimples were there again. "I mean, this naïve karaoke singer couldn't even name her horse after the simplest kinky fetish."

Esme stepped closer and rested a palm on his chest. She could feel the slight tensing, the rhythm of his heart. She'd meant to stop his teasing about Domatrix, but she knew her own fingers quivered slightly in response to his reaction to her touch. And they were going to share living quarters and not touch for how long? She couldn't give in, though, needed to make him understand that she controlled the relationships she was in.

"You know how you said you don't always play fair? Well …" Her fingers trailed down slightly, lingering on his taught stomach and stopping there. "I'm not naïve, Rafael. You'd do well to remember that."

He raised an eyebrow, and lifted a hand to cup her chin. "You'd be surprised at how well I remember things, Esme. Take the first time I saw you, in the mirror—your hair wild, those green eyes." His voice went still lower. "Your blouse half unbuttoned."

She closed her eyes. Oh, she remembered. The memory sparked fire low in her belly and made her feel a little shaky. She could reach out, pull him close …

"Oh, excuse me." The reproach cut through the room and the moment, and Esme let her hand drop, but refused to move away from Rafael. Marie was his secretary. And his watchdog, apparently. Let him deal with her.

"Yes, Marie?" The question was bland and professional, and there was some satisfaction that he didn't immediately move away from her.

"I'm very sorry to interrupt."

Yeah, right.

"It's just that Missy from Angel Wings called to ask if you had room for a few more things. She wanted them to go to the Children's Home in Nuevo Laredo."

"Call her back and ask if I can swing by later tonight to pick everything up. I'll find a way to fit everything in."

"Right." Marie nodded curtly and left, and Esmeralda glanced at her watch. "Tonight's going to happen before you know it, and we haven't talked." She took advantage of the broken mood to return to her chair and sit down. "You've got one last chance to convince me, Benton," she finished.

"All right." He walked over and propped a hip on the corner of his desk. "What do I need to tell you?"

"Why you're doing it. I still can't wrap my mind around having to marry someone in this day and age for your parents. I mean, couldn't you just pretend?"

He rubbed his chin, shook his head, and sighed. "I wish it were that easy. If you meet them, I think you'll understand. I made the mistake of pretending once, Esme. I had a girlfriend in college. Serious, I thought. Paulette."

"And?"

"I knew how my mom and dad felt even then. I was sure Paulette and I belonged together, even though none of my friends liked her. They all warned me she was with me for money, not love, but I blew them off."

"What happened?"

"I took her home to meet Cody and the folks. Cody hated her, but I just thought Cody wasn't ready to see her big brother—her only brother—with someone else. She was used to being the center of attention, and I thought she was jealous of Paulette. But I didn't want Mom and Dad to think badly of Paulette or lecture her on how marriages create foundations for unbreakable families. So I told them we'd married secretly in college. Stopped on the way home from UT to buy her a ring. She didn't mind playing along at all."

"But she didn't love you? Maybe—"

"No. Trust me. She didn't. I spent several months playing husband to a woman who only wanted more. More money, more attention, more things. She kept going to my mom with complaints about how she'd given up her life for me. She kept asking my dad for money for this and that, saying that I'd told her we needed to be responsible and not take advantage of my parents. I was studying business then and not really working for my dad yet, except during the summer. I didn't have my own income. I didn't know she was telling them we were having all kinds of financial problems."

Esme could remember all the years she'd spent trying to please her parents. Apparently he'd done more than she had to keep their affection; he'd toed the same line that she'd been so intent on crossing all those years ago. There was irony in that, and a little sadness. But she didn't say anything, and when he didn't go on, she prodded him, needing to hear how the story ended.

"And after that?"

"Eventually my mom had suspicions—not about the marriage, but about Paulette loving me. I caught Paulette in lies and knew something was wrong. But it came to a head when my mom visited her family out of town. She came back earlier than she expected and found Paulette in their bedroom—in their bed—hoping my father would walk in. She actually thought she could take him away from my mother."

"But at least you hadn't really married her."

He laughed derisively. "You won't believe this, but apparently it would have been smarter to do that! My folks paid a fortune in legal fees, because I'd passed her off everywhere as my wife. Common law, and she had some experience taking money from jerks." He shrugged. "That's when my mom and dad asked me to show them a pre-nuptial agreement before I married again. They said they needed to protect themselves and Cody, but I know they want to protect me. I guess they think I'd fall for that kind of woman again."

"Would you?"

"No."

She hesitated, but he'd asked about Toby. Besides, if they were going to be married, they'd obviously need to know about the exes—at least the important ones. "I know you're angry, but ... do you still love her?"

"No. I don't even like to think about her, let alone discuss her. But you did ask."

"I thought I should know."

"Sure." He pushed himself up and moved to the chair behind his desk, pulling open a drawer and taking out a folder. "These are the terms my lawyers drew up. Certain settlements are provided after short increments of time—to cover the salary I mentioned. By the end of the summer, if not sooner, Mom and Dad will have made their decision. Hopefully, if that bastard Harper or any other make-believe father comes forward, we'll have been able to debunk their stories and be sure Justin isn't taken away."

"And we all live happily ever?" Esme asked.

He cocked his head. "That's the plan. Why wouldn't we?"

She shrugged. "Plans don't always work, Rafael. What if the woman you marry decides to hang on to you?"

"She won't. At least, she shouldn't, and I'll make that very clear. Whoever I choose will need to be able to take the money and run."

"It is a lot of money for a few weeks' work. But you're worth a lot more. I can see someone not being willing to go. I assume the longer you're married, the more a woman could get."

"Yes, but the pre-nuptial limits the money for two years. I thought that would be safer. She wouldn't have to agree to leave me in order for me to file for divorce."

"And there's no sex, no wild passionate love?"

He grinned. "Should make leaving a little easier, shouldn't it?"

Oh, yeah. "Your method has madness. Good." She nodded. "So, a hands-off marriage. Is that written in the contract?"

"Of course not! That would be stupid," he retorted. "My mom and dad aren't going to look at a pre-nuptial that says, 'no physical contact of any kind allowed' and believe it's a real marriage, are they? I mean, most pre-nuptials set amounts of money for the time spent married. The way mine is written specifies the two hundred thousand and expenses for up to two years as a settlement amount. In other words, if the marriage lasts for a period from one month to two years, the two hundred thousand is what my wife would be entitled to—she couldn't try to collect more money from me. Amounts after two years would have to be agreed upon by both parties, with stipulations about things like children and length of time the marriage lasts. But since I'll file for divorce at the end of the summer, there won't be any long-term implications. And in addition to the pre-nup, I've drawn up an employment contract for a summer assistant's job, where the two hundred thousand is listed as a salary. Of course, my parents would never see that contract."

"Why are you so sure the marriage will be hands-off?" she pushed. "What if whoever marries you can't keep her hands off you, or vice versa?"

"Obviously we're not going to be able to avoid everything. A kiss, holding hands—we'll have to go through the motions."

"And what if going through the motions gets out of hand? Because in my experience—and I do have experience, Rafael—a little hand-holding and a few kisses can lead to more. A lot more. In no time at all."

He drummed his fingers on the desk, apparently considering his answer, then sighed. "Why does everything sound like a dare with you?"

"Surely you've thought about it."

"Yeah." His lips twitched. "And considering your self-proclaimed experience, I'm sure you'd consider it a sacrifice. I'm not saying it will be a great marriage. But it's a terrific job for the right woman. Are you interested, Esme?"

She laced her fingers together. She could help her aunt. Maybe with money problems put to rest, Tina would be more approachable. Maybe she could develop the relationship with her aunt that she'd coveted as a teenager. She unlocked her fingers and stood.

"Before I can tell you that, I need to know one last thing."

He leaned back in his chair. "Hit me."

"The day we met, at Tia's, you said something to Angel as I left."

"Okay. What's your question?"

"Who did you swear to kill, Rafael? My aunt—or me?"

• • •

She'd heard? Damn. He knew when he uttered the words that he shouldn't have. In fact he'd worried about Angel not letting him in and out of Tía's office the next time he asked her. And he hadn't imagined Esmeralda could have heard him.

"Why the hell would I want to kill you?" he asked, stalling.

"Why would you want to kill anyone? You didn't sound like you were kidding. You meant it."

He stood and walked around the desk, but stopped several feet away.

"No, I wasn't kidding. I also wasn't serious about doing it."

Esme stood there, so close, clearly suspicious. Her lips were pursed and she stared at him, unblinking.

"You said when we talked the first time that my aunt's recommendation wouldn't help me. What did she do to Cody?"

What didn't she do? Used her, lied to her, gave access to the scum who would make sure she never could beat the demons of music, drugs and fame . . . He didn't think Esmeralda had a clue about her aunt's manipulative, uncaring character. What if he was wrong? Tía had sent her to him. But he couldn't tell her that. He'd have to talk about Cody, and he didn't want to. Not right now. Maybe never. Guilt haunted him, cold fury threatened to undo him every time he went there. So he'd just believe that Tía's only interest was the finder's fee she'd insisted he pay if he chose her candidate. He wondered what Esme would think knowing that her aunt had bartered for her. If sex were involved—which he would not let happen—he might be crass enough to say the older woman had pimped her niece.

He tried to temper his hostility when he spoke again. None of this was Esme's fault, unless he was judging yet another woman wrong. There was no reason to hurt her. And she could be so perfect with Justin, able to relate with him without letting him become too attached. A few weeks, limited encounters—Justin would be fine. He'd manage.

"Your aunt knew that Doug Harper—an off and on boyfriend— and others were destroying Cody. The drugs and alcohol—Tía's. Cody was her own woman, though, legally old enough to be there and choose her friends. I couldn't find a way to stop her. Sometimes I'd distract her, then your aunt or Harper would call, and off she'd go." He didn't want to continue, but Esmeralda's unflinching stare told him he hadn't said enough.

"Since I couldn't talk any sense into her, I made a deal with your aunt. I hired security—guards, a bouncer, I put in a security system—all at my expense. But security doesn't work when the bad guy runs it. Doug Harper and Cody's other so-called friends kept getting in with the drugs. The booze." He shrugged. "That was pretty simple. It was already there, just waiting. Your aunt claimed to love Cody, but she wouldn't lift a finger to help save her. Just gave and gave—every damn thing my sister shouldn't have had."

"And weren't there authorities—people who could have intervened?" She looked upset, as if hearing the hard truth about her aunt had shocked her. He was relieved to think that she didn't seem to know the real Tina Cervantes, but also a little worried. About her.

"The sheriff dropped in a couple of times, but didn't find anything he could act on. Besides, I didn't want to hurt Cody and my mom and dad even worse than they already had been. That's one reason I blame myself along with your aunt. Maybe I should have pressed for more police action of some sort, but I let it slide. For them, I told myself."

"Lots of people wouldn't turn in a family member," Esme said, her expression sympathetic.

He opened his mouth to tell her he couldn't talk more about Cody, but Esmeralda's stomach rumbled loudly. She glanced down, startled, then blushed furiously. "Sorry," she muttered, then lifted her eyes to glare at him. "It's all your fault. I asked you to take food."

"I took food. We just had too much fun fishing to take a break." He picked his phone up and glanced at the time. "Would you like to run into town?"

"We could just eat whatever you packed so it won't go to waste."

"But no one will see us," he protested.

"And that's a bad thing? Who do we want to run into, anyway? Lillie Mae?"

He grinned. "Yes, actually. If we wind up married, we have to date once or twice, don't you think?"

"Rafael, have we actually gotten anywhere? We keep talking, but I don't know how serious you are about whether I'm your first choice. And if I am, what do we still need to do?"

Her persistence might be a problem. He couldn't seem to escape from cold, hard facts with her. Usually he liked that in a woman, especially if she were going to work for Benton Energy Resources. But when you were planning a temporary marriage that had to work perfectly, persistence was just a pain in the ass.

"You're my only choice, which puts me in a bad spot if you say no." He let himself lay it on the line for her, making it clear that she held all the cards. "Look, Esme, this isn't one of those jobs with specific duties and hours."

She grinned a little. "Well, seeing as how the primary wifely duty is out, I just wonder what takes its place. I only wash my own dishes, and I only cook if I'm in the mood. For cooking," she clarified. Then her humor faded again. "Seriously—you have to expect something for that much money."

"Of course. When my mom and dad come, you'll have to be the world's best actress. You'll have to make them comfortable that you're my wife because you care about me, not money. You'll have to show an interest in Justin." He hesitated, not sure how she'd take his next demand. "You're not going to be able to sing karaoke at your aunt's. And you have to promise never to sing 'Cowboy Casanova' again."

She looked surprised. "You didn't like it?" she asked, disbelief in her voice. "That song is my best—"

"That song is the one she'd sing to Doug Harper whenever he came around. The one he used to help draw attention to himself when he decided he could sing."

"Oh. I didn't know."

"So … could you give up everything? I mean, you wouldn't have to give up riding …"

"My aunt probably won't let me sing if she knows you don't want me to," she muttered. "Look, I'm not sure I want to give up Tía. My whole reason for coming to Truth was to get to know her. And to be honest, if I take this … gig … it's to help her."

He frowned, not missing the slight emphasis on the gig word, nor the stubborn set of her chin when she refused to stop seeing her aunt. "This whole job is about family," he reminded her curtly. "I'm trying to save mine. You don't have to sacrifice yours. But you do have to put me first once we're married, in front of the public, at least."

He went to his desk and opened the drawer again, pulling out a single sheet of paper with the BER logo. He felt uncomfortable asking her for her personal information, and if she asked, he'd have to admit he'd run a background check on her. He'd hired an employee once with few references and a couple of questionable incidents in his past. The company's personnel director had tried to override him, but ultimately, he'd used his position to insist. Doug Harper had come on board, and a month or so later, he himself had introduced the country singer wannabe to his sister. To Cody. Never again.

"I'd need you to fill this out. I'm going to handle the job application outside the company, but I need to check references and be sure there aren't any criminal complaints."

He'd expected some sharp remark about lack of trust. Or about the damned experience she kept bringing up constantly.

Instead she took the paper, glanced at it, and looked at him. "Got a pen?" she asked.

Chapter Ten

Esme walked around the screened back porch with its comfortable furnishings and bright flower arrangements, admiring the artwork on the walls. She didn't recognize the artist's name, but the paintings were beautiful. She lingered in front of one depicting an old gray mare knee deep in bluebonnets, a scene she'd seen from time to time over the years. She thought Cody might have chosen it, because it seemed too dainty for Rafael, in spite of his usual good nature.

He'd gotten a call from his parents just as they were leaving to go eat, and told her he'd be down in a few minutes. Maybe he was right about them being able to keep a safe distance from each other. He seemed to be interrupted by business fairly often.

She heard the door open, but Marie came across the room, her heels clicking loudly on the tiles. In spite of herself, Esme couldn't help but compliment the shoes: tall, elegant heels in a popular taupe color. "Really pretty shoes, Marie," she offered. Didn't all the advice books say to make friends with your husband's secretary? That thought almost made her snort, which probably wouldn't have helped patch things up with the woman. But even if she wound up married, he wouldn't be her husband, just her boss.

"Thank you," Marie said, pleased. "I came to see if you wanted something to drink while you waited for Rafael."

"No, I'm good."

Marie nodded. "Okay. I'm in the library downstairs if you need me. Through the living room and back at the end of the hall." She hesitated a moment, then asked, "Are you going down to Laredo with Rafa?"

"No." Esme shook her head. "Well, I don't think so. He hasn't mentioned it."

"Hmm. Well, he's had this trip planned for weeks," the assistant volunteered, walking over to arrange the throw cushions on the wicker sofa. "You should ask him to take you."

"I'm from there. It wouldn't be a pleasure trip," Esme assured her.

Marie smiled. "All the more reason. He's from there, too. Look at the time you'd have alone together. To talk. Or whatever."

"Maybe he'll ask. We're going out to eat."

"He probably won't," she disagreed. "He's always loved to drive off somewhere alone. I guess you'll be trying to change those habits." She gave another smile, this one clearly forced. "Besides, he's used to making plans and not changing them. He won't think to ask you himself."

She made another slight adjustment to a coffee table book on birds sitting on a glass table, then nodded again. "Have a nice evening."

Rafael didn't come down for another five or six minutes, so Esme kept running the pros and cons of asking to go to Laredo with him. Her only argument against was that she wouldn't get to spend any time with Domatrix. The pros were the four or five hours alone with him. He'd be forced to talk.

He might expect her to talk, too. That wouldn't matter. She'd told him about Toby, the most important part of her past. She really didn't have to discuss any of her other life experiences with him.

"Have you fainted from lack of food yet?" Rafael had changed into a knit shirt and slacks, and she looked down at her T-shirt and jeans with a frown.

"I should have gone home to change."

"You look fine." He smiled. "Did you know that the Truth city council voted unanimously to name T-shirts and jeans Truth's official clothing?"

"You're kidding me. We couldn't even wear jeans at school unless we were taking field trips to a farm."

"Well, here, they're welcome everywhere. Although there was an amendment; jeans cannot 'ride low enough to expose objectionable parts of the buttocks to public display.'"

"You *are* kidding me, right?" she insisted as he escorted her outside.

"No, really. That's the official language. Marc and I were there because the council had a complaint about Witches Haven, and Cody was out of town. When we heard that, we cracked up. He finally got escorted outside to wait for me. Now and then I get a picture of somebody's butt labeled 'Code Violation.'"

She laughed. "Small towns are something else, aren't they?"

"Yeah, but generally the people are as good as they come."

"Did you grow up in a city? After your parents adopted you?" They paused by the trucks.

"Houston, yeah. Crazy big city. There's a lot there, but I always wanted to leave. Coming here has been like coming home, even though I had never lived here."

He opened the door to her truck. "Meet me at Rosita's? I thought we might as well take our own vehicles so you wouldn't have to drive back so late."

"Okay. I'll just run home and change."

"You look fine," he repeated. "You might not make it back if you go home. Hey, let's stop at Elrod's Western. They're a block away from the restaurant."

"I've seen them from Tía's. But—"

"I did say I'd cover expenses," he reminded her. "Our dinners out to attract attention should be covered expenses."

"We can argue about that later, if it comes up again." Esme jerked her door open and climbed in. "An hour?"

"Don't be late, though. I'm starving. If I get through at the bank first, I'll save you a place."

In the end, with only an hour, she decided to do just what Rafael had suggested, except that she paid for the filmy, off the shoulder dress she changed into at the store. "Thanks," she called to the middle-aged woman at the cash register. "I didn't want to have to go home and come back!"

The woman dismissed the gesture. "No problem. See you around, honey."

She had parked across the street at Tía's, and walked over to drop off her T-shirt. Two pick-ups and a delivery truck dotted the parking lot. Even for a weeknight, business was bad. She went back to the restaurant, hoping customers would come later on. She hated to see what the financial worries were doing to her aunt.

Rafael's empty truck was at the last space on the corner of the block, so he'd apparently beaten her. She walked in and looked around, almost deafened momentarily from the clamor around her. The rough paneled walls sported all kinds of memorabilia ranging from high school and pro sports uniforms to hundreds of pictures of actors and faded movie posters. A high wood counter ran most of the length of the structure, separating it into two eating areas. Well-worn saddles straddled the counter, some of them looking as if they might belong in museums rather than this noisy place.

The food smelled wonderful, though. It took her a minute to find Rafael, who had claimed a booth at the back of the second room, and waded through diners heading to the salad bar to meet her.

"Thought you might have stood me up," he greeted her, taking her arm to guide her to their place. "Beautiful change, by the way."

"Thanks." She slid into the booth, and watched as he did the same. A very young waitress hurried up, introduced herself as Jenny, and provided them with water, menus, and silverware, promising to come back for their orders soon.

"So, Esme," Rafael said, leaning forward so he could be heard without raising his voice. "You gave me your application. Have you had any second thoughts? Are you ready to accept my job offer?"

"Yes," she said, without hesitation, memories of her aunt's hysteria still vivid.

"And when you answered that you were available immediately, you meant that?"

She laughed. "Yes, but I don't see a justice of the peace or preacher anywhere around. Tonight may be a little too immediate."

"No, I don't think so." He reached across the table, catching her hand. "Esmeralda, will you marry me?"

• • •

The words shouldn't have surprised her. Her breath shouldn't have caught in her throat, making it impossible for her to speak. Then she reminded herself that it was just a job offer, a formality. He'd caught her off guard, but shouldn't have. He'd made it clear earlier that he wanted the marriage to look real.

"Yes. Yes, I'll marry you," she managed, just as Jenny returned carrying the drinks.

"OMG! OMG! How romantic!" Jenny squealed, almost dropping Esmeralda's tea. "Folks, they just got engaged!"

Diners looked their way and clapped or called out congratulations.

"This is worse than those birthday songs when friends out you at a restaurant," Rafael murmured and Esme nodded, unwilling to admit she'd never had a birthday surrounded by friends.

She found herself feeling even more uncomfortable when diners would spontaneously get up and come over to kiss her cheek and shake Rafael's hand. By the fifth or sixth well-wisher, apprehension over the whole affair had begun building again.

When their food arrived, she wondered if she'd be able to eat it at all, as constricted as her chest felt.

"What's wrong?" Rafael whispered as soon as Jenny scampered away. "You look pale. Or as if something hurts."

"This hurts," she mouthed, keeping her voice as low as she could so no one could hear. "This is the biggest lie I've ever told. I can't—"

"Did I hear someone's gone and gotten engaged?" Lillie Mae appeared suddenly at their table, wearing yet another fringed shirt, and jeans that sparkled with rhinestones. "Well, congratulations!" Both Rafael and Esme stood, and Lillie Mae hugged Rafael first, kissing him on the cheek, then turning to embrace her.

"You did good," the matriarch announced in her ear, but loudly enough that everyone in the room could undoubtedly hear her words. "Got yourself a king of a man, and you're doing a good thing."

Lillie Mae knew about the lie and didn't care. She sounded as sincere as if the wedding would be one between childhood lovers, and her stamp of approval made Esme feel a little better.

"So, did you bring Babe?" Rafael asked, when Lillie Mae waved them back into their seats.

"No, not this time. I'm here in my pickup truck, since Hondo didn't mind drivin' it tonight." She patted Rafael on the shoulder. "You treat this woman right. Treat her like she's doing you a huge favor, marrying you."

Was Lillie Mae about to ruin everything? Rafael looked concerned, too, Esme thought, and placed his hand over hers.

"'Cause the truth is … when someone marries an ugly ol' dog like you, well that's a testament to love and it's one Texas-sized favor to boot!" And then she broke into her distinctive laughter, and suddenly everyone around them was laughing, too.

"See y'all. Let me know when you have a date set." And she turned and left, hugging and patting her way to her seat in the front room.

"She's something else." Rafael grinned. "But you passed the first test with flying colors, Esme. Lillie loves you!"

"Hmm." Esme couldn't really answer, because the first bite of the restaurant's famed enchiladas reminded her that she was starving. They concentrated on the food and for a long time, neither spoke.

Rafael finished first. "Could you come over to Witches Haven on Friday? We have some plans we need to put into place."

"Why not tomorrow?" she asked, draining her iced tea and waving the glass at Jenny, who came rushing over with a pitcher.

"I'm not going to be here. I—"

"That's true. You're going to Laredo."

He nodded, but didn't invite her. She shifted in her seat, remembering Marie's observation about how valuable their time together could be in implementing *his* plan. She tapped her foot restlessly on the floor, waiting for him to invite her. *He did just propose marriage, even if it was make-believe.* But when he merely sat there and continued to eat, she gave up. "I'd like to go, if it's all right."

He put the potato he'd been about to eat down and looked at her in surprise. "Well, I usually don't take anyone."

She smiled. "But I'm your fiancée."

He sighed. "I'm doomed, aren't I? Never a free minute again in my life?"

"In your life for eight weeks," she reminded him. "In August, when it's a hundred thirteen in the shade, you can go by yourself."

"It's June, and it's a hundred nine. I can go by myself."

She leaned across the table and placed her palm on his cheek. "But why would you want to?"

"Look, the thing is …"

An idea occurred to her, not a good idea since she shouldn't have her hand on his cheek. Their relationship was hands-off. She jerked her hand back, hoping it looked more like outrage than sudden wariness about the physical hunger burning inside her when she watched him.

"Headed to Boys Town?" she crooned sweetly.

Mention of the infamous zone of prostitution in Nuevo Laredo made him widen his eyes and straighten in his chair. "No!" He shook his head.

She stretched her leg and her foot bumped his.

"Look, you can go."

"Why don't you want me to?" she asked curiously.

He didn't answer at first, just finished his food and pushed his plate away as Jenny came hurrying up.

"Drinks? Coffee? Desert?" she asked breathlessly.

Esme felt sorry for the young woman. The place was still packed, the noise level rising and falling as people received their orders and began eating, or newcomers went around greeting friends and then sat down and tried to talk over the other conversations going on around them. Surprisingly, no one here seemed glued to a phone, and everyone knew everyone. She'd seldom eaten at the one diner in Rose Creek, preferring the short drive into San Antonio, but she liked the hominess all around her.

"I don't want anything, thank you," Esme told her, and watched as she gave the bill to Rafael.

"I'll pay at the register," he told her, and grinned at Jenny as someone in the front yelled her name impatiently. "Save you a trip."

She nodded at him and headed toward the annoyed party almost at a run.

"I do not know how people survive waiting tables," Esme murmured. "I did it once and the tips were fine, but I quit a week and a half after I started." He put a tip on the table and they stood.

"Thanks, Jenny," they both chorused as she rushed past en route to somewhere else.

"Have a great night," she called, not stopping. "Oh, and congratulations again!"

Getting to the cash register seemed to take forever. Rafael knew almost everyone, and introduced her to diners she didn't know. She thought Rose Creek residents were close to each other, but clearly Truth could outdo them without a second thought. She waited while he paid, then they stepped out onto the sidewalk. Daylight was dimming, but hadn't gone, and looking across the street at the trio of bars with their lights already on seemed a little strange.

"Something wrong?" Rafael asked behind her.

"You could get a beer in Rose Creek, but we didn't have three bars that opened before the sun went down. About the closest it got was Bob's Garage, where folks would go to drink and watch sports together. I guess I'm just amazed three bars can survive here."

"Couldn't without the tourist trade, and it's way down."

"It's just the dude ranches around here, right? I really don't know the Hill Country very well."

"Mainly the dude ranches. There are also golf courses, lakes, exotic game ranches—which are mostly pay-to-hunt—and a few well-known restaurants, although most of those are a little farther north. I hear the roads around here are popular for motorcycle clubs."

"Hmmm."

"Where are you parked, Esmeralda? I'll walk you to your truck."

"No, don't bother. I'm going to Tía's for a bit."

"Are you going to sing?" he asked.

"Probably not." She thought he looked relieved, even though she hadn't agreed not to. At least she wouldn't sing "Cowboy Casanova." Maybe no Underwood at all—surely that would be safe. He had come in the night she sang "Ode to Billie Joe" and hadn't seemed upset. "Are you telling me not to?"

"I don't have a say in whether you do or don't," he answered, shrugging. "Yet."

Yet? Did he think he'd have a say after they signed a marriage license? She thought they'd agreed that wasn't settled. She straightened a little and nodded curtly. "Goodnight, Rafael."

He caught her arm before she could leave. "Two things," he said. "One, I'll pick you up at eight tomorrow. We'll be there in time for breakfast, and I'll have a chance to meet your family."

He certainly seemed sure of himself suddenly. He wouldn't meet her family until long after this pretend relationship ended. Not if she could help it.

She didn't argue the point, though. No point letting him get a head start on manipulating the situation.

"And the second?" she challenged.

"We're engaged. This is how we say goodnight."

He drew her close and lowered his lips to hers.

She froze for a moment, surprised, then slid her hands up to cup his face, urging him closer, returning his kiss, trying to stifle a moan as his hands caressed her back and slid down to rest on her hips, holding her against him.

The blare of a car horn and a blast of derisive laughter made them jerk away from each other.

"We're in trouble if this is hands-off," she muttered. He started to say something, but she held up a hand. "I've signed the contract. We're going to have to find other ways to lie to this stupid town for two months. Pick me up on time." She turned and stalked off, not giving him a chance to speak.

Chapter Eleven

Esme didn't sing. Angel, Tom, and a handful of customers greeted her warmly when she came in, but she asked Tom for a handful of quarters and went to the jukebox. She'd always said you could tell anyone's life with country songs. She put on a lot of Rascal Flatts, including a song that always made her remember her brief time with Toby. "What Hurts the Most" could still make her cry, but she vowed not to let it affect her tonight. She punched in a number of songs, ending with another Flatts tune. "God Bless the Broken Road"—where had that come from? She'd been following broken roads all life, and none of them had led her anywhere. Certainly not to love, and even if she'd found Truth, she couldn't say it was much different than any other place she'd stopped. She wanted it to be home, but she just wasn't feeling that yet.

After filling the jukebox for a selfishly long time, she chose a table by the window and slowly sipped a margarita, occasionally glancing out the window. Night had come on while she tuned everything out and listened to the music, and most of the people walking around arm-in-arm or hurrying by on worn boots with hats pulled low were people she hadn't met. Apparently the other two bars had far more weeknight traffic than her aunt. She puzzled over that briefly, wondering what could help Tía. Advertising in this tiny town didn't make sense, and really, neither did the almost nightly karaoke sessions, if there just weren't any warm bodies to come in.

The Silver Booty and Boots had that horrible, almost sinister descent into the bar, but it was spacious and friendly—nicer, she thought, after meeting Lillie Mae there, than her aunt's club. That establishment seemed, from the cars she saw parked there and comments she'd heard, to be the most popular of Truth's watering holes. She hadn't been in the Silver Dollar. She'd heard it was "old" country—sawdust on the floor, beer being passed around from patrons to the live bands who played there sometimes, and the infamous honky-tonk women. She grinned. They wouldn't appreciate her thinking of them that way, with the reputation she had in places where people knew her. Her claims were overstated, but she did have a horse misnamed Domatrix. She giggled, not meaning to, but a couple of nearby customers turned and looked at her curiously. She'd have to be careful, or Tom and Angel would be trying to cut off her alcohol, knowing that the route home was full of curves.

She looked around, noticing for the first time that Tina wasn't down here mingling with the clients and playing her role as town aunt. She could be up in the office; the smoked glass wouldn't let light through, but the blinds were drawn. Esme had never even seen that there were blinds before. Worried, she walked over to where Angel was rearranging some bowls of nuts she'd just filled.

"Hey, Angel, is Tía here?"

"No." Angel stopped what she was doing and sighed. "She's been coming in late when she comes. I hope everything's okay."

"I hope so, too. Do you think I should go home and check?"

"That's up to you," Angel said, "but if it were me, I wouldn't. She wouldn't thank you for it, and if she's drinking she can be really *pi*—" she broke off the Spanish vulgarity, flushing. "I'm sorry. I forget myself sometimes."

"Angel, I've heard my aunt treat you pretty badly," Esmeralda admitted, keeping her voice low. "Why do you stay with her?"

"I owe your aunt." Angel moved away to take and refill a mug from someone Esme recognized as a regular. When she came back, she moved even closer to Esme. "I got in trouble when I was younger. Bad choices." Emotion clouded her face for a moment. "I had a record. No one else would give me a job."

"Well, she should still respect you." She'd felt her aunt's sharp rebukes several times; they were as bad as her mother's, worse if being gouged by metallic finger nails counted. "I wish I knew how to help her. She's not who I remember."

"You didn't spend a lot of time with her, though, did you?"

Esme must have shown her surprise, because Angel patted her hand. "I've been with her about thirteen years, and she mentioned you once or twice, but you never visited." The older woman took an order and turned to hand it off to Tom. "So, I guess you didn't."

"No. You're right." She glanced off toward the windows for a moment. A tall man in a cowboy hat, western garb, and boots passed by slowly. He glanced in, apparently noticed her, and waved a hand. Not a local, probably, Esme decided. She'd found the quaint practice of tipping hats an endearing Truth custom. Waves just weren't as … western. She nodded anyway and turned back to Angel.

"You remind me a little of Tía," Angel added. "Sometimes."

"Me? How? I don't even look like my parents, although my dad's tall."

"Not so much the looks, but you're outspoken. Confident. Those are good things when you don't become overbearing with them."

"I guess. Thanks, Angel. I want to know more about my aunt. I used to wish she were my mother instead of my aunt. Is that terrible to admit?"

Angel's thin shoulders shrugged. "It happens." She paused, then said solemnly, "My only daughter doesn't claim me. My sister raised her and now … we don't have a future. My fault."

"Hey, looks like a funeral," Chuck said, passing by and shooting them a wink. "You should just get up there and sing, Miss Esme!"

"Go leave us be with our girl talk," Angel told him and he nodded agreeably.

"Go easy on us cowboys," he called as he continued back to his table of friends.

"I didn't mean to make you feel bad," Esme apologized.

"Truth is what it is, and I'm not talking about this town, either!"

"You like Rafael, though?"

Angel's face lit up. "If I'd had a boy, I'd want him to be Rafael. Or a lot like him."

"Why?"

"He's got a good heart," she answered with absolute conviction. "He's nobody's fool, but you can't make him hurt you unless you're hurting somebody else."

"The day I met you, he came in right after me."

"I remember."

"As I left him, I heard him say he'd kill someone. Yesterday, he told me he was threatening my aunt."

"He didn't mean it. He's furious that she let some really rotten lowlifes come and go as they wanted. He blames them for his sister's death, to some extent."

"Who does he think is most responsible? Does he understand it's ultimately Cody's fault?"

"No." Angel glanced at the picture of the singer and shook her head. When she turned back, she looked more troubled than ever. "He blames himself more than anyone."

• • •

The drive to Laredo hadn't changed much—mile after mile of interstate without much to see on either side. They got off to an awkward start, silent and distant, the strangers they really were.

After a while, though, Rafael reached for the radio dial and turned on a Spanish language station. The first song was one Toby used to play over and over when they went anywhere, a young man asking his mother how to know if it was love when he found someone.

"You don't like Ramon Ayala?" he asked curiously.

"I can listen. I'm not crazy about Norteño—too much accordion. I like steel guitar and twang better."

"You and my parents both! Tell you what." He fished around in the console without taking his eyes off the road and handed her a remote. "I've got all country in the CD player. You'll probably like most of it, and I'm fine with it, too."

"I'll wait until we're halfway there," she volunteered. "Fair's fair."

"Okay." He checked his side mirror, flipped on his blinker, and pulled out to pass a tanker, glancing at the cab's door as he did, and smiling.

"Yours?"

"The company's," he agreed, nodding. "Business is good."

"Do you ever get attacked, you or your parents? Not everyone's good with fracking."

He glanced her way briefly. "We're not going to have to argue about real issues while we're married, are we?"

She grinned. "Not if we get 'em out of the way now."

"The people of Cotulla have jobs, houses, hope, and prosperity. Most of them love to see those Benton trucks and uniforms."

They fell silent again, and a particularly gory *narcocorrido* blasted out. *Corridos*, traditional Mexican story songs, were fine, but some of the music glorifying the drug trade and violence offended Esme, just as gangsta rap about the same topics did. She could deal with vulgarity herself but she'd worked around kids so long that she just didn't want them exposed. There were no kids in the truck, but she picked up the remote, killed the radio, and turned on the CD player.

He chuckled. "You and I are going to get along great when Justin's with us."

"So why didn't you want to bring me?" she asked, and the smile faded away and she saw his cheek tighten. "If you can tell me."

"I can tell you, Esme. It's not a dark, ugly secret. I come down two or three times a year to bring donations for charitable groups I like to work with. The children's home in Nuevo Laredo that's really an orphanage—many of the children don't have parents at all. Others are removed by courts, just as they are in the States. But they work on donations and never turn anyone down. Then there's Sacred Heart; you know them, of course, since you lived in Laredo." He turned to smile again. "I especially like the shopping trips they take the children on for Christmas. Letting them experience shopping for themselves or others. It's such a good thing."

He turned back to the road, passing another in the unending line of eighteen wheelers headed toward Laredo's busy land port, and continued, "And there are a few others."

"Marie said something about Angel Wings," Esmeralda remembered. "And Angel said something about you having a good heart. Why would you hate letting me see that?"

He huffed indignantly. "You've seen the best of me," he argued. "Did I raise my voice at you when you hooked me?"

"Yes, actually. You shrieked."

"Shrieked?"

"And cussed."

"Oh." He drummed his fingers along as one of the old Brooks and Dunn songs blasted out. "To be honest, Esme, it's always an emotional trip for me. The memories aren't all bad, especially the recent ones, but the ones I have from my childhood are. The area around the bridge? Sometimes it's hard not to be right back there on the street, begging, some of the memories are still so clear."

She hated the sadness in his voice. Her memories weren't great, but she'd never been hungry or alone. Still, she wanted to know more.

"Tell me about it," she urged. "What you can. Were you ever at Sacred Heart, or were you a foster child—what?"

"I suspect things are different now than they were," he said finally. "But you know our families, Esmeralda—relatives, everyone knows everyone. A lot of times, families step in. My mom and dad tried to sort out my history when they adopted me, and they more or less did.

"My birth mom left me with her mother, my maternal grandmother. But she had diabetes, and they say she wound up institutionalized. I lived in her house with cousins and a niece of hers, and sometimes the woman she used to pay to help with chores. No one was really in charge, and some of the adults were addicts, alcoholics. There were a lot of children. Some must have been cousins, but I really don't know."

"And the Bentons found you." She smiled, trying to ease the memories. "That's amazing, when you think about it."

"There's not a day when it doesn't amaze me and make me feel like the luckiest guy alive." He glanced at the mile markers flashing by. "Do you need a bathroom break?"

"No."

"Then if you don't mind, we'll wait until Cotulla. I'm going to pop into our office there and say hi. I haven't been there much since ..."

Since Cody started her career in music, probably. He seemed to have given up a lot of what he wanted to do for his sister. She wasn't sure how she felt about that. Was he so overwhelmed by gratitude to his parents that he wasn't ever his own man? She'd stood up for herself, and it had cost her dearly—but most days, she felt like she'd earned the pride she felt in her decisions and accomplishments.

She just nodded, not wanting to question too much. He didn't owe her any explanations. Remembering that was hard, though. They'd had fun fishing together. Angel's insistence on how he was a good man had stayed with her through the night. And their kiss—she hadn't expected that. The contact had gone from sweet to knee-buckling in seconds. Again, she wondered how on earth they'd keep their relationship platonic.

And if she didn't want to? If she could forget her pride, and the fact that she would be paid a small fortune for what was supposed to be a mere acting job?

The pickup slowed suddenly and she looked up, expecting to see a slow-moving car or truck, but he put the signal on and exited, and she realized that they'd already reached Cotulla.

"We're just making a pit stop," he assured her. "In and out."

"You're the boss."

"Which reminds me, here, we're just ... together. I don't want word about the engagement to hit the company grapevine yet. Everything would fall apart if my parents came back early."

He pulled into a parking spot marked with his name and walked around to open her door, then held out a hand to help her down. She drove a pickup and could get in and out of one in a miniskirt and heels. Strangely, though, his gesture touched her.

"Rafael," she said, as they headed up a walk paved with flagstone, "you love your parents. I'm not questioning that. But you told me about Paulette, and well—I'm just wondering how you can be okay with lying to them."

He faced her, frowning. "I'm not lying," he said. "That's why we're marrying. Legally."

"So, if they ask about why you didn't wait?"

"They know I'm impulsive. Dad will worry, until he sees I thought of a pre-nuptial."

"And if they ask you if you love me?"

"Then I'd have to lie," he admitted quietly. "But I hope we can head that off by pretending when we have to and avoiding them as much as possible."

"Won't that seem strange?" she persisted, stopping outside the door.

"We'll be newlyweds. We can spend hours upstairs or fishing or something. They'll respect our privacy."

But will we be able to keep our hands of each other? She walked into a spacious, well-decorated room. The receptionist looked up and broke into a huge smile. "Rafael!" She came out and hugged him, then turned and hugged Esme before Rafael even introduced them.

"Gwen, a friend of mine, Esmeralda Salinas." He wrapped an arm around the receptionist's shoulders. "Gwen's been with Mom and Dad—I don't know. Twenty years?"

"Almost thirty," the woman corrected, still beaming. She reached up and touched her hair. "And I don't look a day older!"

"No, you don't."

"So, what can I do for you? Drinks? You know your way to the employees' lounge, but come with me, Ms. Salinas. I'll show you around. Do you want to talk to anyone, Rafael?"

"No, I don't have time. If you'll get Esme something, that would be fine."

"You might want to go by your office, Rafael," Gwen suggested. "I'll take Ms. Salinas along after I show her the lounge."

Rafael frowned. "Why would I go to my office, Gwen? We're leaving—"

The receptionist smiled. "Just trust me. And go."

• • •

Rafael smiled and watched Gwen guide Esme in the direction of the lounge. He knew Gwen well, and clearly she wanted him to go to his office. He wondered if she'd remodeled it for him again, or—

He opened the door. "*Carnal!*" He used the old street slang, knowing that the man walking over to hug him and slap him was his brother in every sense of the word. "Marc, I thought you were in Houston."

"I just got in a while ago. And I have a flight out in a few hours."

"Is something wrong?" Usually, Marc arrived to check out problems—employee malfeasance, insurance or regulatory problems. He'd heard people in Benton Energy Resources groan when they saw Marc Dryer appear. The cheekier ones made crosses with their fingers as protection against the Dryer curse.

"No. Your dad and mom loved the story about the Cotulla team that made the national news. You saw it?"

"Sure."

"So?"

"So for once, I'm the bearer of good news. Bonuses all around and a contribution to the library."

Rafael slapped him on the back. "Good deal, buddy." He grinned, then saw Esmeralda pause at the door.

"Is she?" Marc's question was so low he barely heard it, but he nodded.

"Esmeralda, Marc Dryer." He walked over and closed the door. "Marc, Esme has agreed to marry me."

"Congratulations." Marc grinned. "If I were Rafael, I'd make damn sure it was permanent."

"Thank you." But she shot a killing glance at Rafael. "Does everybody here know?"

"I had to tell Marc. He's been involved with the situation in Truth, trying to find out more about some of the people who were there the night Cody died. And he's my best man. If he weren't there with me, my dad and mom would see through everything."

"Just for the record, Esmeralda, I told him the idea was crazy. But his folks really are stubborn about their beliefs. They've been trying to marry me off since my freshman year in college. You'll see when you meet them."

"I guess. Still it's kind of hard having perfect strangers knowing you married for money, Marc."

"I can see that." He nodded. "But you shouldn't take it as marrying for money."

"No? So how should I take it?"

"As a well-paid summer job that lets you live in a country home, with nice folks and no stress."

"That will sound better on my next résumé." She smiled at Marc. "Nice to meet you."

He leaned over and kissed her on the cheek. "Likewise. Don't take any guff from my bro." Then he slapped Rafael on the back again. "I'm gone. You'd better pull this off, or you're toast."

"I know." He walked to the door with Marc, who stepped out in the corridor before adding, "And don't you dare hurt the girl."

"Ready to leave?" Rafael asked, and Esme nodded.

"Sure. But I think I like Marc more than you, even though he's a little hyper."

"He's a pain. But we love him," Rafael said easily.

They got back on I-35 and Rafael glanced at the dashboard. "We'll grab a bite somewhere in Laredo, unload, and then," he stopped to glance in his mirror before passing another semi, "let's take your folks out to dinner if they don't have plans."

Chapter Twelve

She didn't want Rafael to meet her family. Her mother and father would be bad enough with their pointed glances and embarrassing questions. But she couldn't, wouldn't, let her brother Beto meet him. She'd visited her parents since leaving home—out of duty, and maybe the faintest remnants of love for the two people who had brought her into the world—but she knew they were petty and greedy. At least toward her. She should have asked Rafael what he expected of her family before she signed. With so little time before his parents came, she'd really thought they'd just stay in Truth. Not once had she considered that he'd want to meet her family. She'd have to think of some way to limit the damage knowing her family would do to them both. Her mother and father she could handle for the brief time he would know them. But Beto … she'd never forgotten the gossip, the slurs, and lies he'd used against her from childhood on.

Nor had she forgotten the time she'd been home from college during her freshman year at college. Her parents were out visiting friends, and he'd come home from some friend's party drunk. She'd looked up to see him in the door, leering at her. She'd already changed for bed and was sitting there in pajamas.

He made some obscene comments and she'd gotten up to shut the door, never imagining that he'd touch her. Instead of letting her get the door closed, he'd stuck his foot in, then shouldered it open again. He'd reached for her, jerking her to him, fondling her, trying to tear her clothing off. Fear and fury had given her the strength to fight him off and shove him out into the hall. She'd locked the door and collapsed in a heap of the floor, crying hysterically. Her own brother had tried to rape her, and she sat there shaking until her mother and father came home.

Her mother hadn't believed her. She'd sided with Beto, and so had her father. They'd blamed her, blamed the fact that he was drunk. She'd gone home since then as infrequently as possible, and when she went home, she stayed in a motel. She'd never spent another night under their roof again.

He was looking at her curiously when she didn't answer.

"I really want to meet them," he said. "I know you said you weren't close, but surely we're going to invite them to the wedding."

"I don't think so."

"Why?"

"Look, Rafael—do you prefer Rafa or Rafael?"

"Nice try. Most of my friends call me Rafa, but call me whatever you're comfortable with. Why don't you want your parents at the marriage? Wouldn't that help patch things up, if one of their problems was—well, that you and Toby weren't married?"

"You don't know them. Look, you had the pre-nuptial written so you can't be manipulated and robbed blind, right?"

"Sounds harsh, but yes."

"You don't have any protection from them."

"Are you sure you're not misjudging old problems?" He reached over and found her hand, giving it a squeeze. "Esme, I just find it hard to believe that your parents are such creeps. I mean, kids usually grow up like their parents. Don't you think? I mean, professionally, wouldn't you agree?"

"Maybe generally. But not always, Rafael. You have to know that."

"Not going with Rafa?" he teased. "Not formal enough?"

"No. Not distant enough, either." She turned her head and pretended to be interested in the buildings that had sprung up on the outskirts of Laredo in her absence.

"Tell you what. Let's get these things unloaded so we don't have to worry, and then we'll have lunch and the first fight of our engagement."

In spite of herself, she laughed at that. By the time they'd taken the collected items to the various organizations, she had to admit she was ready for lunch. They wound up at Taco Palenque, the only Laredo mainstay they both loved.

Standing by the high counter to order, the smells made it hard to concentrate on all the reasons why she shouldn't let Rafael meet her parents. A faint sensation of guilt crowded in. For all her mother's failings, she missed her now and then. They'd come here for most Mothers' Days, and after she'd won the district science fair the year before she'd met Toby. And she and Toby had come here on the anniversary of their first date. They'd only been able to order a single taco each, but she'd never enjoyed fajita more …

Rafael and the cashier were looking at her, apparently waiting for her order. She ordered the fajita plate, and filled their glasses while they waited for their order. It took a few minutes, but they finally found a table near the doors that led to the tables outside that were often occupied by teenagers or families with young children.

"Anything you'd like to do this afternoon? You could shop for a wedding dress. And we don't have the ring."

"We don't need all that," Esme protested. "Rafael—"

"We discussed this, remember? I told you the job included expenses. We need a dress and the ring. And those are job expenses."

"You're not planning on a formal wedding, are you?"

"No. But I want to do better than T-shirts."

"We can go into San Antonio. When is this wedding going to happen?"

He shrugged. "Today's Friday … how about a week from tomorrow?"

"A week?"

"Two weeks is too long. We could choose a weekday, but who gets married on a weekday? Besides, your parents might not be able to get away if it's not a weekend." He smiled at her, but it was a smile that told her he was in charge of her wedding details. "This marriage is about family, so it wouldn't make sense to leave yours out."

"Okay." Esme inhaled deeply. "A week from tomorrow." She pushed her plate away. "Let me call my parents and see if they're home."

Don't be home. Be in the hair salon. Be across in Nuevo Laredo. Just don't be home.

Her mother answered on the second ring.

They exchanged the usual stilted greetings before Esme said, "Mom, I'm in Laredo. Do you think we could drop by the house and visit?"

There was a long pause on the other end, broken by a heavy sigh. "I suppose it's some man? I guess you can come by. We'll be home anyway."

"Maybe in a couple of hours?"

Her mother agreed and hung up. Esme knew that she'd drag out a broom and mop and clean the living room, dust, and complain constantly about the extra work to her husband. Her dad would sit in his favorite chair watching whatever games were on TV and making occasional grunting sounds of agreement.

"Well, that didn't sound too bad from this end."

"No? Wait until the part where I tell them I'm marrying you in a week."

"What's the worst that could happen?"

"My mom will demand a million explanations, want to know things about you that I don't know and probably never will—"

"My parents will put me through all that, just later on. And they'll be worse, because it will be after the fact. Are we ready?"

She nodded, watched him place too much money on the table as a tip, and pull her chair out. "That's different, though," she said, standing and following him. "You're lying to your parents for a good reason, if there is such a thing, and you were honest with me. I'm just flat out lying to my parents."

They stepped out into sunshine that made them blink.

"I'm sorry," he told her. "To be honest, I didn't think about how my fiancée—about how you—might feel. My only concern was keeping Mom and Dad in the dark about … everything." He opened the truck door and waited for her to climb up. "Pretty selfish of me, huh?"

Selfish? She wouldn't mind waitressing again for the tips she'd seen him leave. He was willing to pay a fortune for his parents' and nephew's happiness. Apart from the snarled death threat she'd heard, he seemed perfect. That worried her: there weren't any perfect people, only people who thought they were perfect.

He went around and got in, turning the truck on. "We've got a couple of hours to kill. Any ideas?"

The sunlight streaming in through his window haloed him. His lips were slightly pursed, and the reddish cast the sun gave his dark hair and the sparks in his eyes made him almost irresistible. Oh, she had ideas. She was just under contract not to jump the man's bones. Regretfully, she shook her head.

He backed out and stopped, waiting for the traffic to give him a break, and apparently debating whether to turn left or right.

"Show me where you lived." The idea came abruptly, and Esme saw him flinch when she asked, but she wanted to know. "Fair's fair. You're going to my parents' house."

He didn't look happy, but signaled a left and headed toward the oldest part of Laredo. Esme catalogued the changes as they drove. Some of the import places were still there, with their colorful Mexican curios displayed on the sidewalk and behind chain link fences—pots, piñatas, ceramics, and metal animals of every kind. There were new tattoo shops, the usual franchises, and old motels apparently under new management. Home, but not really …

They drove downtown, fighting the usual congestion, finally turning onto Zaragoza Street and passing historic San Agustin Cathedral, the plaza in front of it, the luxurious La Posada Hotel on the left. "The other kids and I used to come hang out here sometimes when we knew mass was over. We always thought everyone who'd been inside listening to the sermon would be generous with us."

"Did it work?"

He shook his head. "Not always."

He continued down the street until he hit San Bernardo again and pointed at *Puente de La Americas*, Laredo's first bridge, which still swarmed with cars and pedestrians going into and coming out of Nuevo Laredo, Mexico. "We also used to go panhandle on the bridge—got in scuffles sometimes with the Mexican kids—but mostly it was peaceful."

"I used to go across a lot. I'd buy gum or a paper, but I was terrified of hitting someone. Kids would just rush out—"

"I was terrified of the bridge," he admitted. "But at the time, *mi tío*—or at least some guy who claimed he was everyone's uncle— made us go every day."

She sat in silence, trying to imagine Rafael in shabby clothes, avoiding the traffic and trying to eke out a few cents—money which she bet he and the other kids didn't get to keep.

"I imagine kids can't get onto the bridge anymore from this side," Rafael went on, manipulating the tight, one-way streets filled with parked cars and thronged with shoppers from Mexico in search of values in the thrift stores. He finally came to a corner, where he paused a moment, indicating the decrepit houses on one side of the street, across from a weed-covered lot with trash. "That third house down ... that was where I stayed mostly. Eventually I wound up at the shelter, but not until right before my mom and dad adopted me."

She felt sickened by the scene, although she knew there were neighborhoods everywhere that looked the same. She'd known about it when she lived in Laredo, but still remembered feeling ashamed of her parents' house when friends came over. Compared to Rafael's beginning, she'd lived in luxury. How shallow she'd been—was she still? She'd agreed to marry a man for money, something she thought once she would never have done.

She glanced at Rafael. He looked pained, eyes mirthless, his lips pressed tightly together. The console separated them, or she would have flung herself next to him and hugged him.

"Funny isn't it—it really isn't any different than when I lived there."

She had no words, so she said nothing about the structure with missing boards, an open place near the roof, a porch that had collapsed on one side.

"I don't see anyone," she said finally, hopefully. "Maybe—"

"I imagine we'd see kids if we came after school or in the evening. I'm willing to bet people still live there."

She wanted to change the subject and managed to reach far enough over to lay her hand on his arm, squeezing gently. "I'd really love to see where you attacked the Cadillac."

"Actually, it was right over there." He pointed to the lot, halfway down. "I saw the car from the porch over there. Some of the kids at the house, and one of the women who was there at the time—we called everyone 'tía,' even though I was already old enough to know why she was there and that we weren't related—started trash talking '*los ricos.*' Talk about anger toward folks with money! It got ugly. I got mad."

He turned to her. "You need to know that about me, Esme. Anger used to govern most of what I did. I can't believe how often I destroyed something even after I was out of here, just because I'd give in to my rage."

"So, why were you angry at the car? Just the fact that it was so expensive?

"No." He seemed ready to refuse to explain, and she saw moisture form in his eyes before he turned away. "There was a little girl … we called her *Pioja*—"

"You called her 'louse'—that's awful!" The counselor persona kicked in, outraged that a little girl had apparently been ridiculed by—she controlled her own outrage. The little girl had been ridiculed by children who didn't know better. Who'd been just as abused and neglected as the little girl had been herself.

He went on, tonelessly. "We rarely went to school. We'd never heard of child predators, and we made the little money we made talking to strangers. Someone had seen her out in the street late one night and … she and I had made stupid, nine-year-old pacts about how we'd marry when we grew up. She … didn't grow up."

His voice quavered slightly and he swallowed hard. Without thinking, she unbuckled her seat belt and scooted closer, running her hand over his cheek. "I'm so sorry," she whispered, even knowing the words could never help.

Behind them, a horn blared. Few cars apparently used this street, but Rafael pulled through the stop and parked at the edge of the lot. When the car passed, he put the truck in reverse and backed up until he could turn and head back toward the streets that would get them out of the desolation.

"When I saw that Cadillac, all gold and shiny, I just lost it. *Todos dijeron*—everyone said that some rich guy probably took Pioja. I grabbed an old hammer and ran across the street. Put dents all over it, broke the driver's side window—I did a lot of damage for a kid. And then the Bentons came out of a house down the block, apparently a house where Pioja should have been, but her parents …" He took a shuddering breath. "They were addicts. Didn't want her and had three other kids anyway."

"What did they do about the car?"

"The police came. I never knew who called them, the Bentons or someone who lived around there or what. They insisted the car wasn't the problem and demanded CPS come. Wouldn't leave until the police went over to where I lived and started making arrests and calling for medical help and social workers.

"I didn't know who they were then, of course, but my dad asked what he'd done to me, and said I should save fights for the ones who hurt others. My mom scolded me pretty harshly, for her, for endangering myself. Asked if I knew what would have happened if I'd cut an artery. Then she hugged me and asked if I'd like to go get food. They talked to the police, took me to McDonald's, and started making arrangements that day to provide for me."

Tears streamed down Esme's face unchecked. How did children survive the situations they were so often placed in? She'd seen horrible circumstances in her line of work, even in Rose Creek, but Rafael's story was unimaginable.

He saw her tears and tried to blot them, but Laredo's downtown streets were narrow and full of parked cars, and when a car swerved from the curb to cut him off, he cursed and jammed on the brakes.

"There are tissues in the console. And much as I appreciate the company, you'd better put your seat belt on again."

Esme dried her face and threw the tissue in the bag he had hung from the glove compartment. She wanted to smile at the incongruity of the fabulously appointed pick-up and a plastic bag from a local grocery store hanging by a corner from the compartment door.

But she had a final question she needed to ask about the loss of his friend, sensing that the change from penniless street urchin to successful heir couldn't have been easy. "Did you ever find out who killed your friend?" She couldn't use the nickname *Pioja*, would not insult any child with the name of a blood-sucking, socially embarrassing parasite.

"Years later, I found out that her name was Laura," he told her. "Her stepfather was in prison until recently ... died there for what he did to that poor little girl." He drew a ragged breath. "I also found out that my mom and dad had gone there after they heard about the murder to offer to pay for her burial and hire investigators to track down her killer if the police had any difficulties."

"Oh, my god," she murmured.

He managed a short laugh. "Do you see why I would do anything—anything—for those people? And why I cannot let them down again?"

"But you were a kid. You thought you were defending ... or ..." she couldn't remember the English verb for seeking vengeance, and switched to Spanish, "*vengando a* Laura. How can that be letting them down, if they didn't know you?"

"No, but then there was Paulette. And Cody." He wiped a hand over his face, roughly, and stopped at a light. "Think we can swing by your parents' a little early? Maybe we can find a nice place for dinner, if they'd like. I do need to head back to Truth tonight."

"We're not far. I guess we might as well." She gave him directions that would take him to the Heights area, where beautiful old homes in lushly landscaped yards had been the "in place," the residential area of doctors, politicians, and the very wealthy.

"So we take Clark Street?" he asked, and she nodded.

"We can see how badly worn the *guacamayas* are," she said gravely, using the Spanish name for the red and blue macaws decorating boulders along the busy street. The artwork had been painted originally by high school students and came under scrutiny off and on, with supporters defending the birds as an integral part of Laredo, and detractors labeling the faded painting a major eyesore.

They drove down the broad, tree-lined street, both glancing instinctively at the former Martin mansion, now purchased by someone new and completely changed from its simple lines and beautiful front yard. Wrought iron circled the formerly unfenced property and benches and statues cluttered the yard.

"Signs of the time that those fences are there?" he asked, and she shrugged.

"Probably."

A few blocks later they parked on the curb of a corner lot. Esmeralda looked out the window at the plain brick building, low to the ground, with little in the way of landscaping. The grass was mostly gone, the victim of heat and lack of care, and she might have been more embarrassed than she was if she hadn't just heard Rafael tell her his story.

They walked up to the door together and Esme found herself clutching Rafael's arm for moral support, which she thought was ridiculous because this was her house, not his. He didn't seem to mind, smiling down at her reassuringly and tucking his arm in closer so that her arm was pressed into the solid warmth of his torso.

Just before she reached the door, she saw the flutter of a curtain off to the side. Her mother, undoubtedly, who had already noted the truck, Rafael's casually expensive clothes, and his good looks, and reported them dutifully to her father.

"Smile," he whispered as the door swung open.

Chapter Thirteen

Esmeralda had expected the worst of her family, and they hadn't disappointed. Her mother and father sat down stiffly and tried to make conversation, but her mother's look of suspicion never changed, nor did her father's constant channel surfing to find sports games.

Her mother called her into the kitchen, supposedly to take tea out to everyone, but really to ask the question that Esme had known would come.

"Did he get you pregnant?" her mother hissed, the minute they reached the refrigerator and were somewhat out of sight of the living room.

"No. I'm not pregnant." She snatched the tea pitcher and filled a glass, not volunteering any additional information.

"Call me Adriana," her mother ordered when Rafael called her "Mrs. Salinas."

"Ernie," her father put in gruffly, then went back to his game.

Just when Esme counted herself lucky that Beto wasn't there, he walked in, smelling of beer and cigarette smoke. Her mother introduced him to Rafael in glowing terms, and he perched on the edge of the sofa and interrogated him.

"So, Benton. That's not a Hispanic name. Anglo, right?"

Almost before Rafael could explain he was adopted, Beto started on the pick-up, about how expensive it was, how nice it must have to be money.

And when Rafael invited him to join them for dinner, and his mother said she thought maybe he'd like to go with them to a reasonably priced chain that had started in Laredo, Beto was indignant.

"My sister's getting married! Is that the best you can do, bro?"

After protests and complaints and an argument that had given her a headache, Beto had convinced Rafael to try the Tack Room, a well-known, high-end restaurant on Zaragoza Street. Part of La Posada, the restaurant served quail and similar delicacies, and featured steaks named after classic horse races like the Belmont and Preakness.

Her mother and father sat across the table looking around furtively at the wait staff and elegantly dressed customers, many women sporting expensive jewelry. Beto kept gulping down wine the waiter brought and whispering crude observations until Esme managed to kick him under the table. He glared at her, but perhaps because Rafael was sitting so close to her, an arm loosely along the back of her chair, he didn't say anything.

"So, what do you do, Beto?" Rafael asked, conversationally.

Beto flushed and huffed. "I'm between jobs. No one's hiring right now."

"He was manager at a big auto parts store," her mother interceded. "They decided to make some cuts, and you know how Laredo is." She nodded. "They let him go because they could hire someone for less."

Esmeralda could feel Rafael's tension through the micrometers separating his skin from hers. Clearly he found Beto as insufferable as she did, and he didn't know the half of it.

The strained atmosphere lightened a little with the arrival of the appetizers. Beto had demanded bacon-wrapped shrimp, a local version of crab cake, and panchos with tenderloin. He reached immediately to serve himself, but Esme plucked the platter away, hissing a little at the burn, and offered them to her mother first. Out of the corner of her eye, she saw Rafael smile and pass another tray to her father.

"So, as we mentioned back at your house, Esme and I have decided we want to marry next week," Rafael said, while they waited for the steaks to come out. "We'd love to have you there.

It'll be a simple wedding at my place, but I want Esme to have her family with her."

Esme doesn't want them there, though. Rafael had claimed to have anger management problems, but he was as cool as a cucumber while fury bubbled through her. She hadn't thought she could think less of her brother, but the way he was behaving was inexcusable. And her parents had brought him up like this, selfish and demanding and never accountable for any of his actions. Disgust filled her. Maybe Rafael would have second thoughts about having her as his wife. She wouldn't blame him.

The entrance of the waiter with their steaks cut off her train of thought. She let go of the resentment and worry and waited until everyone was served.

"Dig in, folks," Rafael invited.

"Good," Beto grunted. "Thought you might be one of those jerks who'd make us pray."

Rafael sent him a scathing look, but said nothing.

"That was uncalled for, Beto," her mother chided, and her father nodded, but was already busy on the sizzling meat.

"We'll try to go," Adriana said eventually, addressing herself to Rafael. "It's kind of hard for us to get away."

"My car's in the shop and theirs is pretty old," Beto offered.

"It's not that old," their father protested. "I'm older than it is. Just don't like to travel much anymore."

"What if I had a car drive down from the Cotulla location and take you up? We'll be sure you have transportation while you're there."

"If the wedding's on Saturday, we probably should go up early," Beto said immediately. "I mean, don't fancy weddings have rehearsal dinners and stuff?"

"We're not going to, but just let Esme know when and we'll make arrangements," Rafael promised, but to her parents. He never even glanced at Beto.

A little later, the group wandered out, crossing the almost empty street to the bright lights edging San Augustin Plaza. The cathedral towered over the plaza, lights soft around it. The plaza still had strollers, many of them from out of town, some who came to the cathedral regularly.

"Still one of the prettiest places in town," Rafael murmured, as Esme waited to climb into the truck until her family was settled.

She looked at him with some surprise, since she'd learned how he'd spent his childhood here, but he shrugged.

"Beauty just is. The cathedral was never to blame for anything."

Back at her parents', Rafael firmly refused an invitation to go in for coffee or a drink, insisting they needed to get back to Truth as early as possible. Esmeralda climbed into the cab, hoping to hurry the process along. Her mother and father went inside, but Beto stayed planted where he was on the other side of the truck. She saw him say something to Rafael, adding an exaggerated wink, and held her breath as Rafael turned away suddenly from the truck, stepping close to him and leaning into him. Whatever he said had Beto moving away, face contorted with anger, but his movements also indicating nervousness.

"What happened?" she asked as they swung out onto a street heading east toward the interstate accesses.

"Nothing," Rafael muttered. "Just forget it, Esmeralda."

Embarrassed as usual by her family, Esme turned away and leaned against the back of the seat, letting the darkness and light play out as the truck streaked along.

Eventually, Rafael seemed to notice her silence and withdrawal. "He was drunk, Esme. Why let him get to you?"

"He got to you, didn't he?" Esme demanded. "I did warn you about my family."

"I'm not marrying—hiring—your family. Nothing they can do to me can hurt me. I just hate that you all don't seem to have a great relationship." He smiled as she turned on the CD player. "How did you pull off a day at school without music?" he asked.

She laughed. "Miniscule MP3 players during lunch, planning, and restroom breaks. No one in Rose Creek knows I live for my country music."

He laughed. "I find that really hard to believe. Anybody who has seen you at Tía's would know. Speaking of which, how's your relationship with her coming?"

She frowned. "None of your business, and fine." Not true, but she didn't want to discuss it with Rafael, when he seemed to be such a central part of everything to do with her aunt, good or bad.

The lights of Laredo receded and darkness prevailed, although Esmeralda knew they'd run into the always daylight-bright Border Patrol checkpoint any time. She preferred the darkness, liked the peace it provided. And the intimacy with Rafael.

"What do you have against my aunt? I mean, you said that she helped destroy Cody, but your sister was a grown woman." She saw his face tighten, and the corners of his mouth turn down. "I don't want to hurt you, but it involves Tía as well as Cody. How did they meet? I saw a picture of you, Cody, and my aunt. You could swear Cody was her daughter."

"They did seem to have some strange bond. I never understood what Cody saw in her. She had the best mom in the world."

"Was Cody adopted?"

"I suppose you need to know some of the story," he admitted unhappily. "Wouldn't seem real that we could be together and not talk about her. Mom and Dad tried for years to have children and couldn't. They adopted me, but as all the procedures to aid in conception improved, somehow they had Cody."

"Were you jealous? You were—"

"Twelve. And no, surprisingly, I wasn't. Maybe a little afraid when I misbehaved that I might get sent away somewhere, even though Mom and Dad never threatened me or said that I would.

I think maybe I wasn't jealous because I already had so much more than I'd ever had that I didn't mind sharing. And even though I'd never had parents, really, I'd never been alone before I was adopted. I'd been used to having kids around, so I was overjoyed when Cody came along."

"Was she always into music?"

"Not the way you are, no. But she could always sing. I thought when some friends heard her in middle school and she got a lot of attention, it really changed her. She suddenly wanted to sing." After a moment's silence, he said, "Let's stop at Cotulla, just there at the Big Wells exit. I need to stretch and get gas."

"Would you like me to drive? I can."

"If you hauled a horse trailer through the hills, you sure can." He shot her a grin as he slowed to exit. "Cody wouldn't let me move her horses. She paid a guy who used to drive the Clydesdales to do it."

"Wow. She had horses?"

"Still does. Well … they're Justin's now, I guess." He pulled up to a pump and turned off the truck, stretching and smothering a yawn with his arm. "Long day. Do you need anything?"

"Well, we're here, so …" She slipped out of the cab and went inside, immediately spotting the restroom sign. When she came out, Rafael was walking up and down selecting junk food. "Chips, chocolate—what's your vice?" he asked. "They also have chicken legs, but they looked a little overcooked."

"You have room to eat again?" she asked immediately.

"Maybe not eat, eat. But snack, probably."

She got a bottle of water, which he promptly took away and paid for, then smiled and handed her the bag. "Make yourself useful."

She smacked him on the arm with the bag. "Careful. I might still change my mind about wanting to work for you if all I'm going to do is carry bags. It insults my intelligence."

When they were on the road again, she asked about the information he'd tossed out. "Where are her horses?"

"They're both at Witches Haven. I never thought to show you the stable. That rock fence that sits back from the house? The stable's behind that."

"One more question about Cody?" she pressed.

He sighed but didn't refuse. "Last one."

"Why do you say you're responsible?"

"Because I was just like Mom and Dad, but worse—I could never say no to her, either, and I kept thinking I could get through to her. I let them think I was controlling the situation. And I introduced her to the bastard who hurt her the most. He worked for me. I hired him in spite of the fact our human resources manager said not to."

She tilted her head. "Why?"

Lights flashing by from the oncoming traffic across the median showed the anguish in his face. "I liked him. I knew he'd been in trouble, but I wanted him to have another chance."

"Like you got?"

"Yes."

She stretched and shifted. There was so much more she'd like to know, but she'd told him she wouldn't ask. *Tonight*. She closed her eyes, thinking she'd just relax and forget the stress of the trip and the emotional turmoil of the past several days. The music from the CD faded away and then was gone.

• • •

She was asleep, her face in profile, almost angelic when light fared momentarily over her face and then dissipated in the darkness. Damn, she was beautiful. He wondered again how he thought marrying her was a good idea. For Justin, undoubtedly, and she might have as good a chance as anyone of seeming to be the perfect wife in front of his parents. She was smart and tough, and they'd like that. But he wasn't ready to risk commitment yet. He'd promised himself—and her—a safe, non-physical relationship. No sex. No making love. Right now, tempted as he was to pull into the next rest area and wake her with kisses, he couldn't imagine having her in and out of his bedroom without breaking all the rules. She'd suggested that might happen.

He swerved at the thought, without meaning to, and the tires thumped along the lane dividers meant to wake up sleepy drivers. He glanced at her, but she hadn't been startled into awareness. He sighed with relief. A few more miles and he could say goodnight. There were no residents to impress tonight, so he could skip the kiss. Definitely safer that way. She hadn't minded, though.

What had he let himself in for? He was especially glad that her family would be gone by the time his parents arrived. They'd be hurt he hadn't waited to marry, but he could explain that away. How did you explain Esme's family to two adults who regularly gave the shirts off their backs and the cash in their pockets to anyone who needed a hand up? Esme's stories of her youth and her lost love made him hurt for her, and he could see the lack of warmth her parents showed to her, to each other. Sad.

And the brother. Anger bubbled through him as he thought about Beto, clearly his parents' pride and joy. How could they show her so clearly that she didn't exist on the same plane he did? He found it hard to believe it was all about Toby. Hadn't they changed at all? He'd almost ended the evening by smashing his fist in Beto's ugly mouth. As he'd been going around the truck to get in, Beto had inched in closer. "Be sure you get her good tonight, Bro. She owes you."

He'd turned enough that he hoped his back and shoulders shielded him, and pressed a finger into Beto's throat. "Don't you ever insult Esmeralda again," he warned, pushing the finger in until Beto coughed. "I grew up on the streets," he added, and while that wasn't entirely true, Beto seemed to accept him at face value.

It was already Saturday—12:02 AM—when he turned into the drive up to Witches Haven. A week and hours from now he and Esmeralda would legally be married. He drew in a deep breath and wondered how he'd make it through next Saturday, let alone survive his parents arriving.

The dogs were outside on the porch when he pulled up and stopped. He frowned. Marie knew she was supposed to get them in before dark when he wasn't there. They liked to run and they were big. He knew they'd never hurt anyone, but goat ranchers in the area had been known to shoot large dogs that were running loose.

Esme stirred, then suddenly sat up, startled and disoriented. "What ... oh, we're here?" He noticed she didn't say "home." She'd probably need to practice that one, in case she ever found herself alone with his parents. He'd planned a number of diversions, but he couldn't fill every minute of her time. She opened her door and slid out, and the Danes raced toward them, barking joyfully. Good thing there were no immediate neighbors, or he'd probably be reported by annoyed neighbors.

"Sorry I fell asleep," Esme apologized. "I'd better get home."

"You can't leave this late," he argued. "Shouldn't drive the curves when you're not wide awake."

She yawned so widely and suddenly she only partially covered her mouth. "Oops. Maybe I'm not wide awake. But I'm perfectly able to drive. And I can't stay."

"Why?"

"Tía will be upset. She'll think that we ... that I ..."

"Spent the night together?" he volunteered. "Isn't she the one who sent you here?"

"She wanted me to apply for the job. I'd never forgive her if I thought she assumed that meant I'd sleep with you, Rafael Benton."

He frowned. "You might as well get used to being here," he said after a minute. "We don't have a lot of time. And if you're here in the morning, I'll have time to show you the stable and Cody's horses."

"I haven't even seen my horse in what seems like weeks," she reminded him. "I'd stay to see the horses, but I don't have clothes to stay overnight."

"Maybe Marie—"

"Don't you dare suggest I borrow something from that woman!" Esme hissed. "She hates me! And I don't like her much, either."

"Maybe if you gave each other a chance," Rafael suggested. "I really need the two of you to get along."

"We'll get along. We won't wear each other's clothing."

She glared at him and he glared back. Finally she shrugged. "I'm wide awake. I'm going home. What time do I have to be here to see Cody's horses?"

"Try to come before eight. I need to drive in to San Antonio. I'm flying to Houston, but I'll be back Monday."

"So is this wedding you say we're holding a week from today going to plan itself, Rafael?"

"Good night, Esme. Be careful." He collared the Danes and led them toward the house, not looking back.

Chapter Fourteen

Cody Benton hadn't minded spending money. She'd been born into money, she'd made money, and at least where her horses were concerned, she'd gone all out. The stable was low and sturdy, with six stalls along a wide aisle. Thermostats along the wall provided temperature control and decorator lights dotted the ceiling, banishing any shadows or gloominess. The stalls were spacious, and only two of them were occupied. The occupants were beauties, too, and probably cost a fortune themselves. A palomino quarter horse looked up and nickered at them. In the other stall, a tall gray gelding watched them, ears up, expression alert but not friendly.

"The palomino's name is Treasure, and she's an AQHA champion," Rafael told Esme. "Cody didn't show her, but she bought her after she got the points she needed. The gelding is a Dutch Warmblood. I understand that he comes from a line that has competed very successfully in Olympic events."

"Impressive. They're beautiful. Do you ride?"

"Not often. I rode occasionally with Cody if she asked me to, but the time just wasn't there. She had an agent who booked her tours and appearances, but my parents had asked me to monitor arrangements and try to keep her away from certain people and places—like trying to stop a tidal wave with one hand." He shrugged. "I usually lost when we disagreed, and toward the end … she didn't make time for her horses either."

"Are you planning on keeping them?"

He reached in the open door to pat the mare, but the gelding moved back in his stall, clearly suspicious of them. "Probably. I couldn't stand letting something happen to them." He smiled. "I'm trying to find a pony for Justin. Cody talked about very little else when she first found out she was pregnant. How cute ponies were and how every kid should have one."

"This is such a beautiful place, and you even have riding trails. I wish I'd found a little better place for Domatrix."

"Bring her here," he offered. "Seriously, why not? We have the room. "

"It's tempting. But then I'd have to move her again in a few weeks. And anyway, I can't do that to the Petersons. I'm not sure they have an income other than what they're getting from boarding her."

"Hmmm." He took a couple of steps down the corridor, considering. "But think of how perfectly it would work into the plan."

"Now you want my horse involved in this scheme?"

"We both agree that this has to be a platonic relationship, right? I mean, everyone knows the worst thing you can do is have an affair with an employee, right?"

She didn't answer. She'd seen a couple of affairs at schools that had turned out with happily ever afters. Besides, he was too close to her, close enough that she could smell his cologne. Close enough that she wanted to reach out and trail a finger across his lips, silencing all his talk about not making love to each other for the next two months.

"Uh ... sure," she said, when he looked confused over the lack of an answer.

"So if you have Domatrix here, you can ride every day. For hours. Less time together, less temptation."

"And wouldn't your parents find that a little odd, us avoiding each other?"

"Maybe. But Cody was horse crazy as a kid. Mom might just think you were like her about horses, only longer. Although since I haven't seen them or Justin that much lately, I guess it would defeat the purpose. But I still think you should bring her. No offense to the Petersons, who seem very nice, but she'd be safer here."

Esme couldn't argue with that. She just couldn't bring herself to tell the Petersons.

"Rafael!" Marie called from the far end of the stable. "You told me to be sure you left by nine! You'll be late." Belatedly, she added, "Good morning, Esmeralda."

"Good morning."

"Knew I'd be late, and I've been up since five." Rafael sighed. "Listen, don't worry. My flight is early Monday. We'll get the marriage license and a ring then, okay? Unless you want me to bring one from Houston."

Talking about rings so early in the morning seemed a little surreal. She couldn't tell him she didn't want a ring in front of Marie, who supposedly didn't know their engagement wasn't real, so she just nodded. "Have a good trip," she said, then smiled. "Tell Justin I look forward to meeting him." That was true. She hadn't had a personal conversation with a child since school ended.

He nodded, said goodbye to both of them, and hurried off, leaving them alone.

"See you around," Esme said, but Marie held out a hand in a placating gesture.

"Wait, please." She looked embarrassed, but forced a smile. "Esmeralda, Rafael told me my job depended on treating you the right way."

"I didn't ask him to."

"No, I know." She rubbed her hands together nervously. "I don't know why I behaved that way, and I promise I'll do better. And I wanted to ask a favor."

"Okay." Esme waited, trying not to tap her foot on the ground.

"My parents are semi-invalid," Marie confided. "Luckily, I make enough here that I can pay for help when I need to work late. Mostly I rush straight home, but tonight I really would like to go out."

"Okay," Esme repeated, hoping she wouldn't be asked to stay with two people she didn't know and whose daughter she didn't really like.

Marie blushed. Bright red, for no apparent reason.

"There's this guy," she added.

Oh.

"He's a country singer—Esmeralda, you have to see him! He's gorgeous, and he's got this voice …"

"What's his name?"

"You might not have heard of him. He's just breaking in. He's playing at the Silver Dollar tonight. That's …"

"I know. The place next to the Silver Boot and Booty and down the street from my aunt's."

"Anyway, Bounty Collins is playing there!" Marie almost squealed with excitement.

"Who?"

"You haven't heard of him?" Her face fell. "You will soon. He's been in Nashville but he's making one last trip through Texas before he goes back for good."

"Okay. And the favor?"

"Go with me tonight. I'll buy you a drink or—whatever. We can grab dinner if you want. We can get to know each other."

Esme considered the invitation. She didn't think she could be friends with Marie. But if Marie was infatuated with some up and coming local singer, so much the better. Marie couldn't moon over Rafael if she were mooning over someone named Bounty Collins. So she smiled. "My aunt won't like me going there instead of Tía's, but I'll tell her I was checking out the competition. What time do you want to be there?"

"Nine. Would you like a burger or something first?"

"No, I'll just meet you there, Marie. I need to run some errands first."

"Thanks," Marie repeated, her whole face glowing. "I'll walk you back to your car. Did you know that Bounty writes songs, too?" She chattered on all the way back to the drive, and Esmeralda just sat in the quiet of the truck for a long moment before she turned it on, relishing the silence. She could only hope that Marie's adulation for Bounty would strike her speechless while they were at the Silver Dollar. She wouldn't be able to stay sane if she were subjected to such prattle.

Chapter Fifteen

Esme walked carefully over the floor of the Silver Dollar, aware that a number of male heads turned her way and the room was crowded enough that she might bump into someone if she weren't careful. She finally spotted Marie at a table not too far away from the stage and waved. Marie beamed at her and jiggled in her chair, full of excitement.

Esme sat down at the table with a smile, amused at the transformation. Sober and professional in their former meetings, Marie looked years younger and years happier in her skin-tight mini-dress and stilettos. "You really like this guy Collins?" she asked, sitting down with Marie.

"I met Bounty last week! I actually met him. Can you believe he told me to come tonight?" Marie gushed. "What do you want to drink?"

Esme ordered a margarita and sat back, listening to the laughter and noise around her and thinking about Rafael. Would he have objected to her coming here? Surely not. She tried to focus on what Marie was saying, but every other word seemed to be Bounty, so the gist was, the girl was in love.

A burst of applause and Marie's mouse-like squeak of excitement accompanied the bar owner, a former country singer himself, as he announced the appearance of "country's next big star, Bounty Collins." Applause and a few whistles greeted the introduction.

Esme turned her attention to the singer who walked out. Spangled, fitted western shirt and jeans with embroidered boots and a white cowboy hat. Blue-eyed and blond—the man she'd seen walk by the window that night she and Rafael had eaten at Rosita's and she'd gone to Tía's afterwards. The singer flaunted a bit of swagger and plenty of good looks. Good for Marie if she'd already met the guy. She probably hadn't had much time for herself with the demands of taking care of invalid parents and earning a living.

Bounty strummed his guitar and sang a few bars of an Alan Jackson song, then introduced his band members. He played well enough, and his voice was okay. But the presence wasn't there. He covered songs listlessly at times, and Esme didn't think he showed any genius with a couple of songs he had written. Before his first break, she was ready to leave and head for Tía's. Or home. Leaving Marie alone so quickly seemed rude, so Esme stayed, hoping that she'd be able to sound convincing if she had to compliment Marie's crush.

While Bounty encouraged everyone to support the bar and have another round while the band took a break, Marie reached over and grasped her hand, squeezing it tightly. "Do you think he'll come over … look … he is!"

Esme reached over to pat Marie's hand, hoping that the woman wouldn't pass out.

Bounty walked up, and this time he tipped his hat and nodded. "Marie, you look beautiful," he told her, leaning over and pecking her cheek. "Thank you for coming to see me again. I know you told me it's hard."

Then he turned to Esmeralda. "Well, hello, gorgeous!" He leaned over and kissed her nearer the corner of her lips than her cheek, then pulled out a chair and straddled it. "Marie," he said over his shoulder, "thank you, thank you!" Then he turned back to Esmeralda. "When and where?"

Esme saw Marie's face freeze, then turn scarlet. Embarrassment and anger, probably, and she couldn't blame the other woman a bit.

She pushed her chair back. "Thanks for the compliments, Cowboy, but I'm engaged."

She saw Bounty glance at her finger. "The first ring wasn't expensive enough," she explained. "Marie, I've got to run now.

Bounty, if it hadn't been for Marie, I wouldn't have had the pleasure. Better take care of your number one fan!" She waggled her fingers and walked out, furious at the way the singer had behaved with Marie. Now how would she mend fences with Rafael's assistant?

She glanced back at them, and could tell they were arguing about something. That seemed odd. Did Marie have enough of a claim that she could reproach him over coming on to another woman? A country honkytonk probably wasn't the best place to find a man who wasn't a player. She frowned. She was sure Marie had said first that she didn't know the man, that she just wanted a chance to meet him—and then Marie had mentioned that she already knew him. Maybe she'd just misunderstood. What possible reason would Marie have had to lie? Mentally shrugging it off, she decided to drop in to Tía's.

She opened the door to see a trio of regular customers belting out "Whose Bed Have Your Boots Been Under" and doing Shania Twain a huge injustice. The poor woman would want at least an apology if she ever saw this. She waved at them as she walked over to claim a stool, looking around and seeing neither her aunt nor Angel.

"Where's everyone, Tom?"

He didn't answer, turning around to set three full beer mugs in front of their owners, then wiped his forehead with a bar towel and tossed it aside.

"We don't even have that many customers and I can't buy a break." He peered at her. "Hey, can you serve drinks as well as you sing?"

"Oh, no." Esme smiled at him. "Speaking of drinks, can I have a glass of water with lemon?"

"Wimping out?" He brought her the water before turning back to take an order from the waitress who came in some Saturdays.

"Yeah, but I only slept an hour or two last night. My aunt and Angel are both gone?"

"Tía didn't come in again today. Angel called and talked to her, then she started feeling bad and ..." Tom shrugged. "I told her to go home, but she insisted she'd be back in a bit. She's a hard worker and one good woman to have around."

Tom's tone expressed sincere admiration, and maybe a hint of something more. The idea of Angel and Tom being in love amused her, although probably they'd chosen their prospective romantic partners badly. Her smile faded away. She'd chosen hers for money. Not exactly, but certainly Truth would think so. If not now, when Rafael and she just turned and walked away from each other.

"You look glum," Tom noted. "Hey, that's not the look for a woman in love to be wearing."

"You heard?"

Tom hooted. "If anyone in Truth hears, everyone hears. That's why it's called Truth." He gave her a wink and turned to wait on new customers, and she climbed down from the stool, carrying her water, and wound up at a table by the window again.

The boisterous trio who had been singing up on the stage without benefit of Tom's help suddenly came rushing over. "We wrote you in! Come on, girl!"

"Night off. Besides, I'm a married woman now."

"Engaged," one of them protested.

"And that's the same thing. I'm spoken for, guys. Go away!"

"Aw, hell, Miss Esme. We're not disrespectin' you or your man. We just can't hit those high notes like ol' Billy Ray."

"What's he got to ... oh, no. I will not—not—do 'Achy Breaky Heart.'"

They didn't listen, just caught her hand while the customers around who had heard her sing before started chanting, "Esme, Esme, Esme!"

"Someone will get my table—"

"I'll watch it," one of the clerks at the local grocery store said, grinning. She waved at the three other women with them, and they left their husbands to take over Esme's table.

"One, and I finish my drink and go home."

Out of the corner of her eye, Esme saw Angel, wan and preoccupied, come in and whisper something to Tom, then give him a gentle shove toward the karaoke machine. A few seconds into the song, Esme admitted to herself that she loved moving with the song while she sang, stomping and shaking and hitting the notes the men had complained about without any trouble. She almost gave in to the shouts for an encore, but when she glanced at the bar, Angel looked worse than before, and Tom had gone back to serving drinks to some much thirstier customers.

"Angel, are you all right?" she asked, and the older woman nodded. "Don't worry. I think I just let my sugar and pressure get messed up. I'll be fine. Once the crowd thins out, I'll leave."

"Have you heard from Tía?"

"She answered the phone at the house but just hung up on me." Angel took a glass Tom handed her and took a sip, wrinkling her nose. "These kids don't know how to make lemonade," she muttered. "He's more likely to kill me than cure me."

"I think I'll head home," Esme said reluctantly. Facing her aunt tonight wasn't something she wanted to do, but she hadn't seen her all day. Hadn't her aunt even wondered how the trip to Laredo with Rafael had gone? Or how her own sister was doing? The old hurts started winding their way up to strangle her heart and mind again, but she wouldn't let them. More than ever, she'd make a go of her summer job. She could do it to help Tía and salve her own soul. Eventually, maybe she'd even try to understand her mother.

She walked over to finish her water.

"Hello, gorgeous," Bounty Collins said, so close that his hot breath brushed past her ear.

The glass fell out of her hand, spilling its contents all over the laminated table top.

"Oh, man, I'm sorry." Bounty stepped around her and swiped ineffectually at the ice and water spreading out to the edge. The ladies who had moved when Esme came back leaped up with handfuls of tissue and paper towel they dragged from their purses, and Tom came rushing over with a towel.

With everyone working on the table, Esme turned indignantly to Bounty. "How dare you? What made you think you could come in here to my aunt's place and fall all over me when you treated Marie like you did?"

"Calm down, calm down." He pulled a chair back. "Sit down for a little." He smiled and nodded at everyone and thanked them, and they wandered back to tables. "Look, pretty woman, Marie's sweet, but she's just someone I met. She knows I'm not interested in her. Now you …"

Anger pulsed through her, and she fought an impulse to slap him just for Marie's sake. But she'd attracted enough attention. She fought back the urge to grin when she thought of Rafael, off in Houston, probably thinking she was home alone, asleep.

"You have five minutes," she muttered, and sat down. "And you owe me water with a lemon twist." He stalked over to the bar and came back with a beer and her water; watching him walk towards her, she could see why Marie was in love and a number of women in the club were all eyes. He was nearly as tall as Rafael, with muscled arms and a chest that stretched the denim of his shirt. Not long ago, she realized, he would have been her dream man, a fantasy to chase. If he led others on and discarded them, well—their loss. Tonight he just repulsed her.

"What did you want, cowboy?"

Before he could answer, Tom suddenly came up to the table. "Excuse me a minute, Esme. But, look dude, you know you're not supposed to be here. So when you finish your chat, go."

"Tía would be glad to see me," he told Tom. Then he turned his back on the bartender. "Look, Esmeralda, I'm sorry I was rude. You know how it is, the adrenaline, the crowd—and you gotta admit, you're a knockout."

She shook her head. "Give it up. An ass is an ass. I doubt you treat anyone better than poor Marie. And besides, I'm engaged."

"I don't see a ring," Bounty noted.

"You don't have to."

He stood to go. "Okay. But I hope you'll close your eyes and see me instead of him."

Did he hear himself? "You're pathetic," Esmeralda told him. "Leave."

He frowned and plucked his hat off the neighboring table. "See you around."

She finished her replacement glass of water, said goodbye to the couples at the next table, and went over to the bar. Angel looked better, and declined an offer to let Esme take her home. "He didn't kill me with his lemonade, so I'll be fine," Angel muttered, and Esme grinned.

"Tom, I'm taking off, but I just wondered—why did you run Bounty Collins off?" Esme asked.

Tom and Angel exchanged glances, and then Angel shrugged her thin shoulders.

"There's hell to pay anyway if anyone took pictures with their phones," Angel pointed out, talking to Tom and not Esmeralda

After a minute, Tom nodded, and turned back to her.

"You didn't need to do it for me," Esme prodded. "I can handle my own problems."

"Not that one you can't. Not if your fiancé finds out."

"What? Now I have to give a damn if Rafael thinks I'm having fun at my aunt's club?"

"It isn't that." Tom fidgeted, clearly nervous. Finally he put down his ever present towel and faced her squarely.

"The thing is," he said, "Bounty Collins isn't allowed in here because that's not his real name. His name is Doug Harper, and Rafael thinks he killed Cody."

Chapter Sixteen

Rafael's phone buzzed, indicating he'd received a message, and then buzzed again and again. Puzzled, he eased himself up and away from where Justin had fallen asleep in the middle of his bed. He'd lain there beside his nephew for the past two hours, knowing he should carry him back to his own room, put him down properly, but not wanting to wake him.

So many texts in such a short time had become unusual on Saturdays. When he'd been really working at things that mattered, before Cody's death, weekdays and weekends all ran together. Now, even weekdays weren't always busy.

Momentary hope flared. Had Esme texted him with some question or other? He'd felt so connected to her on their Laredo trip. The hurtful memories had been cleansed by sharing them. At least, he felt that way. Then again, he no longer had to deal with anyone from his pre-Benton past. She still had all of her past pain except Toby, and he suspected that she held some necessary dream that Toby and she could have made it.

He managed to get to his phone without waking the toddler. The first message was from the owner of the feed store, who kept Cody's horses supplied with whatever he thought they needed. "Congrats on ur engagement," the message said. When the picture finished loading, he felt his chest constrict. His breath caught. Whoever caught the shot caught Esme as she twirled, her short skirt flipping up, showing thighs that … Heart pounding again, he flipped to the next. A whole freaking video of "Achy Breaky Heart." Line dancing was supposed to take place in steak houses among waitresses in boots and jeans. Not in flirty little skirts with tops that didn't cover much of anything.

He couldn't imagine complaining to her, though. Maybe after they married he could convince her that she couldn't be out like that when his folks came. How would they ever believe a woman that wild, that sexy, had decided to settle down? He wasn't jealous of the three drunk guys; she wasn't paying attention to them. But the music seemed to own her, move her of its own accord … good thing she wasn't into tangos.

Two more shots were stills of the same dance, one of them so blurry that he deleted it on the spot.

When he went to the next picture, sent with no message from a number he didn't recognize, he froze again. But this time it wasn't from the rush of desire for a fiancée he'd never really make love to, a physical reaction to the most sensual woman he'd ever seen.

Cold fury hammered him in the chest and he sat down on the edge of the bed so hard that Justin stirred and mumbled. He reached over to pat him, in spite of the blind rage threatening to push him over the edge. What the hell was Doug Harper doing pressed up against Esmeralda, his mouth all but wedged to her ear?

•••

Esmeralda woke up late on Sunday, disoriented and feeling that she'd done something terrible. She just couldn't remember what. As her senses cleared, she remembered Tom's angry orders to Bounty to leave and Angel's worried remarks about cell phone pictures. She'd been talking to the man Rafael hated most in the world, and she hadn't even known.

No point in worrying. She'd go into San Antonio and look for a dress for her wedding. The sooner she and Rafael married, the sooner they could get on with the charade and be done. That thought didn't ease her mind, so she focused on planning out the entire day. Shopping and lunch in San Antonio. Alone. She couldn't find any more headaches off on her own, could she?

Then she'd go riding. The Hill Country was beautiful, and she could take a little hot weather. She'd come from Laredo, after all, where spring temperatures often topped a hundred. She and Domatrix could use the exercise.

After she dressed, she picked up her phone to find a number of messages. The first one was from Lillie Mae. Surprised, she opened the message. "Girl, you oughta know this picture is out there. Rafa won't be happy." And there she was in the Silver Dollar, with Doug Harper grinding his mouth against her cheek, almost getting her right on the lips.

Lillie Mae was warning her, not scolding her. But if Lillie Mae had somehow seen it, could Rafael have gotten it? She had no idea who had taken it. Surely not Marie who'd been shocked, hurt, embarrassed—she wouldn't have had the time or motive. The place had been full of people she didn't know, and everyone these days took pictures of everything. So who did it didn't much matter. But where had the picture gone, besides to Lillie Mae? What if someone who knew Marie sent it to both Marie and herself? Girls night out, they might have decided, not knowing that Bounty was destroying Marie right in front of their eyes.

Oh, God. What if Tía got the shot, too?

She didn't know what to do. Call Rafael and ask him straight out if he'd seen the picture? Ask Lillie Mae how she first heard? She smiled grimly. One thing she wouldn't do would be to ask the cantankerous woman what to do about the whole mess. She'd gotten her head bitten off once too often already.

Nothing she could do made sense. The woman she'd been once would have gone out to demolish her foes, whoever they were, even if they were just small town gossips. The woman engaged to be married—the woman in a lot of trouble—deleted the picture and went shopping.

•••

Hours later, she thought she had a grip again. No one else had called or texted, so maybe only Lillie Mae had seen the picture. Rafael didn't strike her as the kind of man to sit and do nothing if he thought he were being played for a fool, so surely he would have had the balls to call her and ask. She tamped down the little voice in her head that pointed out the old Esmeralda would have called him.

She'd found a beautiful dress, a silvery sheath with wispy lace sleeves that made her think of fairy wings. A fantasy dress for a make-believe wedding—perfect. And the price had been reasonable. If Rafael wanted to give her a ring she'd give back to him at the end of the summer she couldn't stop him, but she could afford her own clothes.

Rushing, because she didn't know how she'd spend her days once she married Rafael, she threw on riding clothes and hurried down the stairs. She almost pulled off her escape, grabbing a bottle of water and sprinting for the door, just in case anyone should appear, and—

"Not so fast, *sobrina*!" Tina's voice froze her steps. She'd never heard her aunt call her "niece" in Spanish before, and the word held a sinister tone the way she said it.

She inhaled, forced her hands not to knot into fists, and turned. "Good afternoon, Tía. I hadn't seen you." She made herself smile. "I bought a dress for the wedding. I think you might like it."

"I'm sure you're concerned about what I like," her aunt spat. Esme stared at her, surprised. And worried. She didn't smell alcohol on her aunt's breath and Tina's eyes looked clearer than she'd seen them recently. And yet she seemed furious, ready to attack her own niece. For the life of her, Esmeralda couldn't understand the changes she saw in the woman. The woman she'd idolized for so many years evaporated into a harder, more insulting version of her mother.

"Did you have fun last night?" Tía hissed. "Get all hot and bothered slumming in that hellhole that calls itself a bar? Oh, and you didn't just go out whoring around, you took Rafael's little spy just to make sure he'd find out about everything."

"You know what? I'm done trying, Tina. I don't owe you explanations, and I don't want the apologies you owe me. I'll move out tomorrow."

She left, careful not to look back or let the door slam. She was on the bottom step before tears traced a slow course down her cheeks. She didn't bother wiping them away, just climbed in the truck and drove away.

Irving Peterson was repairing the fence when she arrived, with Connie standing by to offer assistance. As she parked, both turned to wave at her, friendly as always.

"Hi, honey," Connie called, bending over to pick up some wire cutters and hand them to Irving. "Come to visit the horse, or us?"

"All of you." Esme smiled. "How are you doing?"

"We're doin' fine," Irving assured, and the two of them exchanged glances. "I guess we can tell you."

"She probably already knows," Connie retorted, giving Esme a quick hug. "Why, I bet you thought of it."

"What did I think of?"

"Yesterday, Mr. Benton called us."

"Rafael called you?"

"From Houston," Irving said, with satisfaction. "Our kids don't even call us from Houston."

His wife elbowed him. "You'll make her think we raised 'em bad," she protested. "The kids call us," she told Esme. "When they can."

Esme smiled. "I don't call my parents as often as I should. So I'm sure you did a great job raising yours. But why did Rafael call?"

"He offered Connie and me jobs," Irving explained. "Sort of."

"Really?" He seemed to have a habit of hiring people for unlikely jobs. What did he want the Petersons to do?

"Since you and him are getting married, I figured it had to be okay just to listen," Irving was saying, and his wife looped her arm through his, apparently to offer moral support. "Never thought I'd be willin' to listen to a man who lived in Witches Haven."

"And now we'll be workin' there!" Connie chortled, squeezing his arm. "I told the man not to judge, didn't I?"

"Yes, I remember. That's wonderful! What will you be doing?"

"Well, his folks will be visiting, and Cody's little boy—poor thing." Connie's face filled with sorrow. "Cody was like those clouds before a storm—shiny and all edged with fire and gold—then dark as death. But her little boy doesn't have to be like that. I'm glad his grandpa and grandma have him. And Rafael."

"Anyway, Rafael wanted me to help out with the horses and the yard," Irving took over for his wife. "And he asked Connie if she'd like to work in the house." Irving looked a little embarrassed over that, and his wife shook her finger at him.

"I sold worms and catfish bait! I think I can run a vacuum cleaner and duster, old man! And I'm proud that at my age I can still do for myself and others!"

"It's wonderful," Esmeralda said sincerely. "I'm really happy for you both."

"Well there's somethin' else," Irving admitted. "There's a problem with your horse."

"Is Domatrix okay?" she asked fearfully.

"She's fine. We put her up to work on the fence. But Rafael wanted you to move her. Said it made sense if we were there, she should be. And since you're marrying him …"

It did make sense, and he'd already suggested it to her. The problem was how easily he'd made sure she would take his suggestion. By hiring the Petersons, she didn't have a choice. If she didn't move her, her mare would be alone and unwatched. A suggestion became an order just that easily.

"Of course it makes sense," she assured them. "We'll make whatever arrangements we need to when he comes home. I'm going out for a while. If I don't see you when I come back, take care. And congratulations."

She left them standing there, arms looped around each other, and headed off at an easy trot, wanting to put some distance between her and the world. She rode up one of the lower hills behind the Petersons, stopping at the point where the cedar cover broke into a small, flat area. There were a couple of flat rocks there that would make perfect places to sit—unless of course there were scorpions or rattlesnakes. She finally decided she'd rather not take a chance and lifted her reins, ready to ride on.

Suddenly Domatrix's head came up and she twisted her head and looked around. Esmeralda turned too, and caught her breath in surprise as she saw Rafael come cantering up the hill after her, the tall gray gelding's strides eating up the terrain.

She patted her mare on the neck to steady her and waited until he drew up alongside her for him to tell her why he had come back to Truth a day early.

"I got pictures," he said, without preamble. "Seems the whole town of Truth has my private phone number."

She raised an eyebrow. "Kind of scary to be in a town where that happens. Why would you get pictures?"

"Probably because whoever sent them thought I should know that my future wife was burning the town down."

"Your temporary wife," she reminded him. He'd said pictures, so there were more than the one Lillie Mae sent her. She wondered if all of them were of Bounty coming on to her or if he had pictures of Marie and she together. Maybe even pictures of her dancing at Tía's. It was creepy to think someone had followed her around with a camera, though. Even worse if she hadn't noticed.

"Someone sent Lillie Mae a picture," she added. "For the life of me, I don't know why some old lady gets all the town dirt first."

"Your choice of words is dead on," he muttered. "All the town dirt."

She bit her lip until it hurt and looked away. "Your choice of words is insulting."

She thought he might just turn and ride off, but instead he swung off and dropped the reins. "Let's sit over there and talk, Esme." He indicated the flat outcropping of rock. "We're going to have a lot to do tomorrow without anything hanging over our heads."

"I had decided not to sit there," she admitted, but got off Domatrix anyway, dropping the reins and hoping the mare remembered her training and wouldn't wander off. "Scorpions and snakes."

He grinned slightly. "Have you quit taking risks, Esme?"

She snorted. "That'll be the day." She climbed up on the rock and scraped her feet around hoping to dislodge any unseen residents. He followed her up, and when she looked back, he had his cell phone out.

"These," he said, handing it to her.

She glanced at the photos. The video of her impromptu dance made her smile. "I'm not apologizing for these," she told him. "I had a blast."

"So I saw."

"We're going to be married for a few weeks, Rafael. You've made that clear. You're not going to control my life. You hired me. You haven't bought me."

"Are my mom and dad going to buy we're happily married if you spend your nights dancing with drunks?"

"They weren't that drunk, and it was one dance. I didn't spend the night there."

"No, I know." He moved on to another picture. "You spent half the night with Doug Harper slobbering over you."

"Two things. I don't like your tone of voice, and how the hell did I know someone named Bounty Collins was Doug Harper?"

"Everyone in Truth knows. He changed his name legally right before Cody died."

"I was not in Truth. I did not know." She started to add that Marie had conveniently not mentioned that to her, but stopped herself. This was between the two of them. Marie must have thought she would know.

"So, did you go to the Silver Dollar just to see him?" he asked.

She walked to the edge of the rock and stared out into the tree-covered distance. "Yes. But I didn't know who he was."

He rubbed his face. He looked tired and she wondered if he'd stayed up all night raging over the photos.

"Can we sit?" she asked. "Before I see something scary and don't want to?"

He nodded and came over to join her, sliding down and resting his feet on the smaller rock below and reaching his hand to her. She took it and let him steady her as she, too, eased down to the hard surface.

"I didn't know you wore boots," she observed. "Nice."

He ignored that, and pocketed the cell phone. "Can we make this work, Esmeralda?"

She thought about that. After her aunt's new attack, which didn't even seem driven by alcohol, just viciousness, she didn't know that there was any reason to. Except that she wanted it to work.

The realization struck her hard. She wanted to marry Rafael Benton. She scooted away a few inches, unable to think logically with most of his body in contact with hers.

"Do you still think you should?"

"Now more than ever. And there's not a lot of time." He half-turned, and a lizard they hadn't seen skittered off the lower rock

"I hope nothing else does that." Esme leaned over to look again. "I don't mind lizards. They're okay. But snakes … " She reluctantly turned to listen to Rafael. "Why is time running out?"

"Nana Ellen's old." He circled a hand in the air. "I mean, of course she is, and my parents are, but I never think about their age. Sometimes it seems that our lives together just started. I lost a lot of years. To have Ellen tell me she was retiring at the end of the summer and then find out my parents had hired two nannies to help watch Justin came as a shock."

"I can see how it would. But I still don't know—"

"My mom's scared that a court wouldn't want to leave Justin with them if he won't be watched by family members."

"But you're plenty young enough. And responsible. How can they think …"

"They've known me in all my worst moments, maybe. You haven't. Yet."

"Yet?" When he didn't answer, she sighed. "I know it can't be easy to talk about her, but Cody and my aunt have a history. You and she do. And I'm on the outside. How can you expect me to know anybody, do anything, when you keep everything hidden away?"

"What is there to tell you that I haven't? I was assigned to protect her. I didn't. She died."

"Why do you blame Bounty Collins if your sister was a grown woman and chose the destruction she did?"

"After I introduced Harper to Cody, she wanted to spend all her time with him. At first, it looked like a relationship that might work in spite of the fact that she was already becoming well-known and he was just starting out.

"He went on the road as her assistant, someone who could sit in with the band in a pinch—and Cody liked him, so I stepped aside and pretended they were just friends. But Cody's life started to fall apart. Drinking, dating one loser after another, canceling performances …"

"Having Justin?" Esme put in.

"Yes," Rafael agreed. "Except that Justin was a blessing, not a curse like all the rest. Cody loved him so much. At first, he was enough to help her hang on. My parents were upset that Cody refused to tell who fathered Justin. She insisted she didn't know. They kept telling Cody and me that Justin was why marriage mattered—for him, and for all the Justins of the world. I don't think an hour went by that my parents wouldn't bring up that 'm' word. Cody got ballistic about the situation, and Harper got scared. Kept saying that he was leaving, and none of us tried to stop him."

Unbidden and unwelcome, Toby's memory needled her. He'd gotten scared, too, scared of making her life miserable with her parents and brother constantly attacking him. He'd left, and she'd tried to keep him from joining the Army for her sake.

"Then Harper signed over at the Silver Dollar and became a permanent fixture there," Rafael continued. "When Cody was between road trips or appearances, she'd wind up over there too, just to be close to Harper. Your aunt was furious. She kept telling Cody that she'd betrayed her by hanging out with the competition. We never could figure out why Tía thought Cody owed her. The only tie between them was that Cody happened to stop in Truth on her first tour, and enjoyed singing karaoke and visiting the club.

"To appease your aunt, Cody started insisting that Harper be allowed to sing at Tía's, too, and have access to the club when and if he wanted."

"I wonder how Cody got into my aunt's good graces so easily." Esmeralda shifted on the hard rock, wishing she had somewhere softer to sit.

"I don't know, but after Harper showed up, so did the drugs. Cody might have dabbled before, but with Harper around she just plain went over the edge. Before she died, we'd put a restraining order on Harper. We were keeping him away from her, and she seemed to be doing really well. My parents had been awarded custody of Justin, but Cody wanted to win him back. We were all praying that she would." His boot heel began tapping the rock with frustration. "We thought Harper had left town. I was keeping Cody busy at Witches Haven, listening to songs, planning a new tour, riding every day. Marc called and asked me to fly up to Houston for a day. There didn't seem any harm in it."

He fell silent for a long time. Birds squabbling in the trees around them and a single engine plane flying over them took the place of conversation. "I was in Houston and Marie called, saying that your aunt had stopped by and Cody left the house with her, even though she wasn't supposed to. Marc and I got Dad's pilot to fly us to Truth. We were there within two hours and just minutes too late. According to investigators, Doug Hooper, your aunt, and Cody were all upstairs when Cody overdosed. She was alive when I got here, but barely."

"Rafael, nothing you've told me sounds like any of it was your fault. None of it."

"Maybe." He pushed himself up, rubbing his butt and then holding out a hand. "Can't take it any longer."

She caught it and pulled herself up, but she didn't let go of his hand. "Your parents must have been devastated. They'd had so much trouble having her."

"Yeah. Things were …" He eased his hands out of hers and turned away. She suspected he was fighting back tears.

"My mother took it harder than any of us. She had to be hospitalized for a couple of days. The first time she saw me after it happened, she asked why I hadn't been there. She said she wouldn't be surprised if subconsciously I hadn't envied Cody because she was their real daughter."

"What?" Outrage burned through her. These were the parents he wanted to please? She would have gone on, but he faced her again and reached out to cup her face in his hands.

"Ssssh. Don't. She didn't mean it, Esmeralda. It's like a wound between us that doesn't heal, because it hurts so much. She can't forgive herself for saying it, and I can't help thinking I could have done more to save my sister." His voice was ragged.

"But to say something like that—"

"It's all right. Really. But your aunt and Doug—Esmeralda, I'd never ask you to leave your family. Your aunt is what she is, and I don't like her, but I can't tell you to stay away from her. But I have to ask—tell you—that I can't handle seeing you with Harper. Under any circumstances."

"Look, Rafa, I didn't know who he was. I thought he was a creep when I met him, and I won't see him again."

"That easy?" Rafael teased, and she nodded.

"Just that easy," she agreed. "I can't stand the man. Lucky you."

"Anything else I should know?"

"I'm running away from home." She stood on tiptoes, placed her hands on his shoulders, and brushed his lips with hers, then danced quickly away as he reached for her. "Need a roommate?"

Chapter Seventeen

Esmeralda packed the last of her toiletries into their case and picked it up, looking around the room carefully. She didn't think she'd forgotten anything. Sadness weighed on her as she turned off the switch and carried the bag downstairs. She'd really wanted a better outcome with Tina, but she'd reacted with her usual decisiveness, leaving no wiggle room. Tina was in her bedroom, pretending not to know anything. When Esmeralda first started carrying her things out, Tina had wheedled and begged, but Esme didn't change her mind about leaving.

She tried to soften her departure, pointing out that she would have left after the wedding anyway. She took some of the blame, claiming that she could be proud and stubborn, "just like you, Tía."

Andy came in, friendlier than he had been during her whole brief stay. "So sorry to lose you," he told her, relieving her of the small case. "But you'll be so comfortable at the devil's place—and you're marrying him anyway."

Esme ignored him, but paused as Angel came down the stairs, her face weary and worried. "I'll miss you. Will I see you around?" Angel asked.

"Of course. I don't know if I'll be welcome in Tía's, but you'll know where to find me." She hugged Angel. "Thanks for sticking with Tía. I don't know if she realizes how alone she is without you." She kissed Angel on the cheek. "Take care."

Angel left, picking her purse up on the way, en route, undoubtedly, to stir up menudo for the early crowd at Tía's.

Esmeralda looked around a final time, letting the pain register. She'd walked out the door to escape her mother and father. Now, she'd do the same, closing off the very different relationship she'd hoped for with her aunt. She'd never had trouble sharing a few hours or nights with a man. But she'd never stayed, except with Toby, and she'd been a stupid, starry-eyed teenager then. Toby had wanted her up until he stepped on the bus to leave Texas. Family? They'd never made her feel loved enough to stay.

"So you're really going?" Tina asked, pausing in the hall between the kitchen door and the living area. "Hard to believe you came here begging to stay and now you're gone without a second thought."

Calm. Stay calm. "Tía, I'm sorry I imposed on you. I hope someday you'll understand how much I wanted to know you."

"But not love me? No matter. You've got your little gold box, Esmeralda. I hope you enjoy your payday. Others would."

Esme walked over to her aunt, and this time the alcohol on her breath and clinging around her like cheap perfume was overwhelming. "Tina, you need help. Won't you see someone?"

"I don't need help, I need money. Do you think I drink because I have to? I just want out. Out of this bottomless well that leaves me penniless because no one's got money anymore. I won't need alcohol a minute after I pay off the loan I took out from ... the loan I took out."

"I accepted this position as Rafael's wife largely because I thought I might be able to help you. The money is still yours."

"And why would you do that?" Tía asked, her voice slurred.

Esme shrugged. "Because I don't sell myself, Tía. I bought my own wedding dress. I'll take as little as I can until the charade is over, and then you'll have your money. And I'll have my freedom."

"Freedom for what? To show your money-maker all over Truth, Texas?" Tía's voice was acid. "You oughta take Rafael Benton for every penny you can. You think he cares about you, even as an employee? Hah! He let his own sister die of heartbreak because he wouldn't let her marry Doug. How sick is that, a brother being put at his sister's door to keep her lover away because he wasn't good enough? Sound familiar, *sobrina*?"

"Goodbye, Tina."

"Go! Go ahead and run to that arrogant bastard. But ask him—no, ask Marie, so you'll get an honest answer—ask her if they cut a check for me. A ten-thousand-dollar check in my name, because I did what he couldn't do. I got him the perfect little summer playmate!"

Esme stared at her aunt in shock, then wheeled and raced out of the kitchen. Outside the heat and the shame slammed her, and she stopped and retched until her legs shook. She took Cattle Guard Road for the last time, stopping indecisively at the highway. She could turn left and head into Truth. She could turn right and go to Witches Haven, where Rafael was waiting for her. She could turn right and drive on, beyond Witches Haven to the interstate and not stop until she hit Rose Creek. She turned right and headed home.

• • •

Esmeralda turned in front of the mirror and looked at the too thin woman modeling a dress that looked pretty and meant nothing. Empty. Like a model at a photo shoot, she'd taken a job. She'd do it to the best of her ability.

Tears stung her eyes and she blotted them with a lace handkerchief—the something borrowed and blue, Lillie Mae explained in a scribbled note she sent upstairs along with the handkerchief.

She walked over and glanced out the window. So many people were scattered around, ruining the landscaping. Her mother and father were center front, conversing with the justice of the peace who'd driven out to administer the vows. Her eyes narrowed. She didn't see Beto anywhere. God help him if he ruined the wedding.

She flinched at the thought that the wedding could be ruined. How did you ruin a summer job? If anyone could, though, it would be the Salinas family. Her parents and brother had been in the house since Wednesday, interfering, sponging, taking advantage of every moment of hospitality and luxury they could. She'd stayed away from them, mostly, not even feeling guilty as Connie and Rafael tried to please them. Watching Rafael reassured her that at least he had his anger issues under control. If he could stand Beto, then she was perfectly safe.

A knock on the door startled her. She opened it and Marc stepped into the room, smiling. "You look amazing!" Then he turned his head a little, studying her from different angles, and frowned. "Although I bet that dress didn't fit so loosely when you bought it. How long ago?"

"A week."

"Ha! I knew it. You've lost weight since I met you in Cotulla. My guess is you're a little worried about this job. But I'm convinced you can help Rafael. He's been so different since Cody died. He blames himself for letting his parents down, and he actually thinks he can make them feel better like this." Marc caught one of her hands and gave it a comforting squeeze. "You know, Rafa's staying here in Truth. He's decided he's ready to quit globetrotting."

"I've heard that."

Marc smiled gently. "You stood this town on its ear from what I've heard. Knocking a town on its ass and showing it you're not afraid is a good way to go in."

"I can see why Nana Ellen calls you '*los cuates*.' You behave like twins. Marc, if I asked you something, would you be honest?"

"If it's not about me, sure."

"What kind of woman do you think I am—really? I'm marrying a man for money. For maybe two months."

"No." He shook his head slowly. "You're taking a temporary job to bring happiness to two people Rafa and I both love. You're making Rafael forget some of his pain over Cody by making it easier for him to try to win custody of a kid he loves. Why would anyone look down on that, Esme?" He glanced at his watch. "Almost time, my cold-footed bride." He made it to the door, then added, "You know what I'd do if I were you, though? I mean, if the temporary part bothers you?"

"Stand him up at the altar?" Esme asked hopefully and he laughed.

"Nope, just turn it into a permanent position. You know it's yours if you want it." He closed the door between them, and she could hear him whistling all the way down the stairs.

•••

Rafael reluctantly handed Justin back to Nana Ellen when she came again to reclaim the toddler, pointing out that the wedding ceremony was minutes away. He wished he'd stayed on the back porch a few more minutes, watching his nephew play with Chief and Luc. The two dogs were banished to the screened area until the wedding guests left, and Justin was enamored. They kept turning mournful eyes on him as Justin hugged them and chattered at them, but clearly they didn't know what to make of the baby.

Rafael glanced at his watch and wondered if Esmeralda was up there, worrying too much. She'd moved in a week ago, and though he had insisted she take his bedroom, so that she could get comfortable there, he'd barely seen her. The couch in his study hid a pullout bed, but on most nights, he'd simply crashed on the sofa itself.

The spacious upstairs would have held a small army, and he and Esme had their own space—until guests arrived. On Wednesday, Esmeralda's parents and brother came in, claiming they wanted to help with preparations. They made themselves completely at home, taking over two of the bedrooms and expecting to be waited on, fed, and entertained constantly. He steered clear of Beto when he could, and noticed that Esme rarely spoke to any of them, a situation that worried him.

Then Nana Ellen arrived with Justin, an assistant nanny named Veronica, and half the nursery items from the Houston house. Esme seemed taken with Justin and in awe of Nana Ellen, who even with her advanced age could bark out orders and organize with the best of them. Luckily, the woman who had spent many years chasing after him seemed to like Esmeralda, too, so he had one less problem there.

Marie, on the other hand, had become sullen and withdrawn. He wasn't sure why, since he'd explained the whole situation. He'd tried to be positive and professional to his assistant, but when he'd heard her make a snide remark to Beto about Esmeralda, he dressed her down and warned her that he wouldn't tolerate indiscretion or insults directed at his fiancée. She was off Saturdays, and he hadn't seen her at Witches Haven the entire day.

A hand on his shoulder startled him.

"Ready?" Marc asked. "We should go to the gazebo, because—wow!"

Rafael's breath caught a little as Esmeralda paused on the top stair. The dress she'd chosen flowed over her body in a liquid silver stream. Sequins glittered and created tiny rainbows that danced around her in a celebration of color and sparkle. She looked down at him, though, and didn't smile, and his heart sank a little. Again he wondered why she'd seemed sure of her decision when she'd kissed him that day on the rock, and so withdrawn since she'd moved in after leaving her aunt.

"You're not supposed to be here," she told them, as she reached the bottom of the staircase. "Go away."

"We're going," Marc assured her. "Look, if it doesn't work out, I'm free—"

Rafael glared at him. "Don't, Marc," he growled. "Not even joking, okay?"

"Someone twisted his tail awfully early today." Marc walked over and kissed Esmeralda on the cheek. "Go get married," he told her. "Your presence is needed outside, Rafael. The groom doesn't walk the bride down the aisle."

"I'll be there in a minute. Are you okay, Esme?"

She laughed, but the apprehension in her face was clear. "Sure. My mom's been telling me all morning how I'd better not screw up this one shot in my life, my brother's plastered, and the aunt I came to Truth to live with hates me."

He wasn't sure what he could say. He wanted to say "and your fiancé loves you," but he couldn't. He didn't love her. And if the breathlessness he felt around her, the constant dread that he'd wake up and the summer would be over, argued that he might, maybe, love her after all, he refused to accept that. He wasn't really her fiancé; he was her boss. He reminded himself of that sternly. She didn't look ready to face any new dilemmas, and he didn't push her to tell him what was wrong.

But he had to touch her. He caught her hands and squeezed them. "You're incredibly beautiful, Esmeralda." He lifted her left hand and kissed it. The diamond and emerald ring on her finger added its own sparkle. "This moment feels real," he murmured and meant it.

"They told me to come walk Esme out," her father announced gruffly from behind him, and he nodded.

"Go ahead," he said, reluctantly letting her hands slip from his.

He rushed to get to the gazebo ahead of the bride, taking his place with Marc, and listening as the music began and guests clapped. Smiles greeted Esmeralda as she made her way toward him, and the sun on her dress was almost blinding. Lillie Mae, leaning a little on the back of her chair, caught her arm and halted the procession, and he saw Esme lean in to listen. He didn't know what the old woman said, but Esme turned bright red, and she wasn't easy to embarrass.

By the time the ceremony started, he suddenly realized it didn't feel like a job. It felt like marrying a woman he could easily love.

* * *

The knock on the door startled her. Rafael? This was his room, and a husband didn't knock on his wife's door on their wedding night. Besides, he'd been using the study entrance all week, only coming through the master bedroom to rummage for clothing or take a shower. The first day or two he hadn't even showered here, and she assumed that he'd used the guest room baths.

He stepped in and collapsed back against the door dramatically. "Please don't make me go out there again!"

"You brought it all on yourself."

"Justin's asleep, and only Marc and your family are still here. Well, plus two nannies. I broke Luc and Chief out of the porch, and they took over the study. Maybe they'll dissuade Beto from walking in every five minutes."

"When is everyone leaving?"

"Marc's flying to Houston tomorrow and then he leaves for New Orleans. Poor guy. Never a moment's rest."

"You sound like you care," Esmeralda snorted. "And my family?"

"Your mother and father are leaving tomorrow. Beto asked if he could stay."

"No! I knew he'd try to pull something like this! He ..."

"He asked me for the room he's in now until he 'finds something' and a thousand dollars."

Her anger morphed into shame. "God, Rafael, I am so sorry. I—you didn't agree to anything, did you?" A thousand dollars? She thought suddenly of Paulette, and how Rafael admitted to letting her use him. At least he had thought he loved her. He had thought of her as a fiancée—not the drunk, vulgar brother of a woman who would be gone in eight weeks.

"I explained that with my mother and father coming home, and bringing their old high school friends with them, there wouldn't be room."

"Are they bringing friends?"

"Not that I know of. I wanted to let him down easy. So he asked for me to pay for a room for a month while he looked for work, and a thousand dollars to help him get a leg up. Don't worry about it, Esme. We can't help who we're related to. I told him I could pay for one of the long-term cabins at River Court and loan him a hundred bucks. Then I told him he could have had five thousand dollars and the room, except he treats you like dirt and I won't take that crap from anyone."

"He must have loved that."

"Yeah. But he took it really well, especially since he knows what I told him after that—that I'd punch him in the face and press extortion charges against him if I saw him again tonight." He tilted his head, listening to the Lady Antebellum mix she'd been playing all afternoon. "Seems like I've heard some of those already," he said.

She went over and turned them off, knowing that songs about needing someone and good times and not needing anyone were sentiments she couldn't share with Rafael. Then she turned to the dresser and absently began to brush her hair, hoping he'd leave.

He sighed and walked over to sit on the edge of the bed. She wished he hadn't.

As if he read her mind, he patted the comforter. "When I used to think about how I'd spend my wedding night, this never occurred to me. Come sit down." He laughed. "Since that's probably the closest together we'll ever be in this bed."

"No." She put her brush down, and for a moment, she watched him in the mirror, remembering that first time she'd seen him.

"Refusing a dare, Esmeralda?" he chided.

She turned and leaned against the solid wood for support. "Rafael, you've asked me all week if something's been bothering me. It has."

"But you wouldn't talk to me. We need to change that, Esme. Okay, out with whatever it is."

"I'd started thinking, when we talked that day on those rocks, when you took my word about how I met Doug, when I started really thinking about you," she hesitated, but wanted him to know. "I thought today—tonight—might be different. I was going to ask you to drop the hands-off promise." She saw his eyes widen a little and thought he might have taken a deep breath. She knew she had his attention. "And if you said no to breaking the unwritten contract—well, I figured I could get you into that bed if I wanted to."

"But … that's not where you're going now, is it?" he asked softly.

"No. Rafael, why did you lie? Well, I guess you were honest in the first interview. When you said you wanted to buy me." Her voice trembled a little as emotion swamped her and the day's stress made her feel nauseous.

"I don't know what you mean," he protested. "What—"

"Why didn't you tell me you gave Tía ten thousand dollars for me? Why didn't you tell me I didn't have a choice?"

He was silent so long she thought he wouldn't answer. Then he pushed himself up off the bed with an oath that startled her and came across the room so quickly she couldn't move. Or run. He gripped both her arms near the elbows and gave them a slight shake.

"You listen to me, Esmeralda Salinas Benton." The emphasis on her new last name was unmistakable. "I do not buy women. I spoke stupidly that day, and I apologized. And as for buying you, I would have cut out the middle man and gone straight to you if I were interested in buying you." He dropped her arms and folded his arms across his chest, still furious. "You're acting insulted, but I'm the one who should be."

She couldn't stand so close to him with his anger so apparent. She walked to the far side of the room and opened the door to the balcony. "My aunt was having a meltdown the day I left. I didn't want to believe her, but she told me to ask Marie. I did. She wouldn't exactly say yes, but she also didn't say no—just mumbled that a husband wouldn't buy a wife, so maybe I should ask you."

"Have you ever used an online dating service, Esmeralda?"

His question was so unexpected that she couldn't understand it. When she did, it made her angrier.

"Don't you patronize me! If I pay a few bucks for an introduction that is not like some money-out-his-nose jerk paying my aunt to be sure I wind up with him."

"No?" She could see Rafael let go of the anger, see his face become the reasonable, unemotional mask he must have perfected over the years. "You pay a finder's fee, don't you? You don't guarantee you'll fall in bed with any guy you might meet, do you?"

"But …"

"Esmeralda, one of the reasons I didn't tell you is that I wasn't happy about it either. I accused your aunt of pimping—because I was outraged that she wanted money just to mention the job to you. But she insisted it was nothing more than the fee companies pay employment agencies to find qualified candidates for important positions. And nothing—nothing—is more important than the position of wife."

Why did he make everything rotten sound better?

"Lillie Mae knew. And who else?"

"Jade Brockton. He's the owner of—"

"The Silver Boot and Booty. Lillie Mae told me. Did they get finders fees?"

Rafael ran a hand over his face. "I wish you'd just let it go, Esme. Has it ever occurred to you that I don't want to tell you the things you don't want to hear? That I'm afraid the truth will hurt you? No, they didn't get a penny. They were offended I'd asked, but since your aunt had insisted—well, I wanted to be fair."

"I wonder if she had your job in mind when she told me to stay."

"What do you mean?"

"When I told Tina—I am not going to call her tía anymore unless I'm speaking Spanish—that I'd come to take her up on her invitation and move in with her, she wasn't happy at all."

"That's more or less the impression I got," he agreed.

"You ... how do you know?"

"I was in her office waiting for her. You can watch the whole floor through the glass. She seemed angry, and you looked ... wounded." She started to protest, but he held up a hand. "You asked," he reminded her, gently.

"Yeah." She suddenly felt too tired of all the pain coming from and leading back to her family to deal with someone, even if his intentions were good. So she stretched and walked over to the door connecting the study and bedroom. "Rafael, this is your room and all, but ..."

"I should scram?"

"Please?"

He nodded. "Scramming," he agreed. "But Esme, if you need anything—or just want something—come tell me, okay?" Then he grinned. "Especially if it's just kicking your family's collective asses." He stopped in front of her, leaned over, and kissed her softly. "Don't let them hurt you."

She bit back a sob and managed a carefree snort. "Why should I let marriage change anything now?"

"Esme, I mean it. Don't joke about what hurts you so much. If I can do anything to help you with them—anything—I will."

"Okay." She lifted her hand and touched his cheek. "Thanks." She nudged his arm. "Out you go. Oh, and Rafael … don't knock on my door. I don't think husbands knock on their wives' doors." She grinned at him. "It's not manly."

He laughed and then closed the door softly between them. She heard the lock click.

"You, on the other hand," he told her through the wood, "are welcome to knock."

She laughed, too, and wished that she really could.

•••

Easy living would kill her. Esmeralda stretched her legs out on the couch and smiled at Justin, playing on the floor between the two huge Danes. Rafael had flown to Houston, but promised to be back in time to take her to dinner. In the six days since the wedding, she mostly had eaten and listened to music. Nana Ellen let her play with Rafael's cherubic nephew, but she always hovered about, maintaining the chain of custody. The inactivity was killing her, even though she had managed to ride every day this week, a new lifetime best.

She was surprised that she missed Rafael. He usually was hard at work in his study, and she'd be with the horses or walking the grounds for hours at a time. Frequently, though, she sat in the study when he was there, to read or watch a baseball game. The presence of another person was comforting, and when she'd let herself daydream about Rafael while he sat there unawares, keyboarding away, well—the time was well spent.

"Time for me to take him," Nana Ellen declared, coming in to swoop him up. She pressed kisses on his bare feet and he giggled and squirmed, making both of them laugh. Motion near the door made Esme's head swivel. Marie stood there, her face hard, clearly not ready to be friends anymore.

"Good morning, Marie."

"Good morning, Ms. Salinas," Marie responded, with even more of a sneer than before the Bounty Collins incident.

Because Marie's hostility annoyed her, Esme smiled back. "It's Mrs. Benton, now," she reminded the other woman. "If you don't mind."

Marie frowned. "I do mind. You married Rafael, you tried to pick up Bounty—and you got me suspended."

Marie had been gone? Thinking back, Esme had to admit to herself that she hadn't seen her around and really hadn't cared.

"I don't know how I could have done that."

"I sent Lillie Mae the picture of you and Bounty," Marie explained indignantly. "I thought the town needed to know who you were."

"And who am I? Besides Rafael's wife?"

"His wife!" Marie's snort was derisive. "We both know you're not that, don't we? I'm his assistant. I wrote the check to your aunt. There's nothing about you I don't know, Esmeralda."

"Why did you ask me out, feeling the way you do?"

"I thought I might be wrong. But I wasn't. I came in here to see Justin. He looks like his daddy, don't you think?"

"I don't know his daddy," Esme pointed out.

"Sure you do. Bounty Collins is his daddy. They look just alike. He wanted to start custody proceedings, but I told him he should wait."

"Why should he—if he really believes he's Justin's dad?" Esmeralda demanded, worried.

"Because," Marie said, gleefully, "you'll be gone in two months. All Rafael's crazy plans will go down the toilet. If Justin's dad is a happy, married man and Rafael's a vengeance seeking madman— guess who'll get custody?"

"I didn't know Doug was married."

"Oh, he isn't." Marie smiled and held up her hand, showing an engagement ring. "We're getting married two weeks from now.

My life will be starting out with Bounty and his son—and your job will be winding down. 'Bye now, honey."

Her former elementary school colleagues in Rose Creek always warned each other not to think that a day couldn't get worse. A bad day could always get worse. When Esme saw Beto's name and number on her cell phone, she wanted to hurl the device against the wall and just get a new one. With a private number.

Instead, she clicked the call on and waited for the day to get worse.

"Hey, sis," Beto slurred. "Guess where I am."

"I don't care where you are. Why are you calling?"

"Well, a friend and I were talking, and he thinks maybe I'm being selfish. Maybe I shouldn't have kept it to myself all those years."

Esme's heart hammered. Was he going to apologize for that incident so long ago? Maybe he felt driven to confess to their mother that she hadn't lied. "What are you talking about, Beto?"

"Look, sis, here's the thing. I'm in a bit of a fix. But I got something really important to tell you. Come to Tía's and talk to me. Oh, and I need the rent money for one more month. Because after that, I'm gonna be payin' my own way. Forever." He hung up on his end.

She stared at the phone, knowing that she'd probably be either disappointed or infuriated. Knowing, too, that she didn't have a choice.

Sighing, she went upstairs for her purse and checkbook.

•••

Esmeralda didn't see her aunt anywhere, but Tom greeted her warmly and Angel hugged her as if she were a lost child returning home safely. Then she pointed wordlessly to a corner booth in the back, where Beto sat, facing the wall.

"He's had too much," Tom muttered, keeping his voice low. "But we have orders from Tía that he's to get what he wants on her tab."

"And this from the woman who needed me to bail her out financially," Esme noted, pain stabbing her again at the thought of her aunt.

Esme walked over and gasped in shock when he turned around. He'd been in a fight and she'd bet he'd lost. Both eyes were swollen, the right eye looking much worse than the left, and his lips were swollen and cut.

"What the hell did you do now?" she demanded.

"How do you know it wasn't your husband? He threatened me, did'ja know?" He squinted at her. "No, don't go." His words were hard to understand, partly because of his injuries, and partly because of the almost empty pitcher of beer on his table.

"Sit down." He grinned lewdly and waggled his eyebrows. "If you can."

"What did you want?" she demanded, not sitting.

He extracted a piece of paper from his pocket with clumsy fingers and waved at the bench again. "Gotta sit," he insisted. "We got a lot to talk about, baby sister."

Reluctantly, she slid in, and he handed her the paper. She looked at it. Bounty's name and a scrawled phone number. She positioned her fingers to rip it in half, but with surprising speed, Beto recovered it.

"You need to call him. It's about the kid."

"Justin?" Alarm gripped her. "What about Justin?"

Beto shrugged. "Why should I give a damn about the brat? I don't know nothing. I can't find a job anywhere. I need a month's rent."

With unsteady fingers she wrote a check and handed it to him. He handed her the paper again. "He'll only talk to you. He got a deal in Nashville, so he's leavin' again. He don't know whether or not he's ready to fight for Justin. He wants you to call him, so you can talk to Rafa. He thinks maybe you all can work it out and not hurt the kid. I told him you were reasonable. Practical." He snorted, filling the air between them with the fumes of alcohol and stale tobacco. "I also told him you are hot. And always have been. If you know what I mean." He laughed lewdly. "He said he'd figgered that out by himself. Play your cards right, Esme, and you could get the best of both worlds. If you know what I'm saying."

Esme refused to recoil from his vile innuendos, concentrating instead on Justin. On helping Rafael keep his nephew forever, even—she swallowed hard—even when she left Witches Haven. She forced herself to find that voice of reason that Beto had mentioned. "Nobody even knows if he's Justin's father. He doesn't have a right—"

Beto reached for the pitcher and held it out. "Want a little?" When she shook her head, he chugged from the pitcher, beer running out of his misshapen mouth. "Maybe. Maybe not. I don't much care, one way or the other. Just doing a favor."

She looked at the paper and put it in her wallet. She'd tell Rafael. He could decide whether or not to talk to Doug. Then she stood to go.

"I thought you might have changed," she told Beto. "I can't believe I'm letting you blackmail me. You, my own brother."

Beto made a big show of looking from side to side before shrugging and crossing his arms over his chest. "Ain't no brother of yours here, honey. For you to be my sister, you'd have to be the daughter of Adriana Martinez Salinas and Ernesto Salinas."

She couldn't speak, clutched at what he was saying without quite grasping it.

"Oh, and sweetie, that little lie you tell?" His voice dropped as he spoke, and the hair on her arms stood up. "Wouldn't have been a big deal if I got in your pants like all those other kids did. No big deal, doing it with a cousin."

She jerked her head, trying to shake it, to deny the filth and anger of the garbage he was hurling at her. But deep inside, something already screamed. "Why are we cousins?"

"Because Tina's your mother. Why do you think Mom and Dad hated you always being there, taking everything from them and me? They adopted you out of pity, because Tina didn't want you. And you know what? She don't even know who your dad is. Or care neither."

The words hammered into her. She took a few steps towards the door and the bright sunshine outside. Somewhere between his table and the door, blackness claimed her.

• • •

Somewhere in the darkness she heard jumbled voices, voices she didn't know. She turned her head, trying to escape the light trying to call her back. Over the nose and pain, she suddenly heard Rafael's voice.

"Esmeralda? Esme!" The panic in his voice registered, and she managed to open her eyes, but the pain was still there, throbbing through her head.

"What happened?" she asked.

"You fainted. Why? Angel saw you talking to your brother. She said he'd been hurt—was he that bad? Do you need us to find him and take him to the hospital? Tom said he left right after you fell. We don't know what happened."

As warmth enveloped her, she realized that she was cradled in Rafael's arms. He was sitting on the floor, and Angel and Tom were standing near her. Behind them she could see other denim-clad legs, so clearly they were still in the bar. With that realization, memory of the confrontation with Beto flooded back, and she pushed against Rafael's restraining arms.

"Let me up," she demanded. "I have to … Rafael, let me up."

Somehow he got his feet under him and managed to lift her up as he stood, not putting her down in spite of her struggles.

"We're going into San Antonio for X-rays."

"No! I have to go. Tía's ..."

"She's here," Angel soothed. "Upstairs, in her office. She came a few minutes ago, but I guess she saw that a crowd of us was already here."

Rafael set her down, but didn't release her completely. "Calm down," he ordered. "You're not going upstairs until we know you're all right and we're sure that your aunt won't make matters worse."

"There isn't any way anything could be worse," Esmeralda said, her voice sounding childlike to her own ears. She stiffened her body and inched away from Rafael. "I'll be back." They were watching her with such worry that she searched briefly for words to make them feel better, but couldn't think of any. So she just walked away to the stairwell at the back of the club.

Tina was sitting at her desk making out a deposit slip when Esmeralda shoved the door open. She jerked, and muttered something as a bill floated to the floor, then pushed everything to one side.

"I thought I locked the door. This is my private office." Then she frowned and waved at the chair in front of her desk. "Sit down before you faint again." She chuckled. "Everyone down there probably thinks you're already pregnant. What a hoot that is, right?"

Esme sat carefully, holding on to the arms of the chair. She would not fall in front of this heartless ... in front of her mother.

"Spit it out, girl, I have to work."

"Beto said that he and I are cousins. He said that you're my mother."

"No. Adriana is your mother. She and Ernesto adopted you."

"Why ... why didn't you ever tell me?"

"Because I didn't want you. And I'm sorry, but I still don't! I was fifteen and pregnant. I only had two options, and Adriana had been married five years already. They only had Beto. They decided to help me by adopting you." She pushed herself out of the chair and went to the window. Trying to heal sorrow or guilt she didn't want Esme to see?

Esmeralda wasn't surprised though, when Tina turned back, her eyes dry and her face expressionless. "Look, I tried to get along with you when you came. I mean, a niece is family, but you're not as clingy or annoying as I thought you'd be. We could have been friends—we can be friends. Just not family. I'm not a woman who wanted children all those years ago. And I'm still not."

"Once you said that Cody was the daughter you never had, remember? And all the time, you had me—"

"You'd understand if you ever met Cody." Her aunt—her mother—turned back to look out at the imposing picture. "You should be grateful to me," Tía continued, after a few minutes of silence. "You had a roof over your head and food on the table. Now you'll have more money than you'll know what to do with." She went back to the window, turning partially toward the club, but still watching Esme with cold eyes. "The money you'll get for showing Rafael Benton a good time is all yours. Someone made it very clear I wouldn't see any of it. And that means our good friend Andy will be calling some folks in Chicago. Telling them I can't pay—ever." She smiled mirthlessly. "We might not see each other again. Goodbye, darling."

Esme made it downstairs on shaky legs and pride, but she knew she couldn't drive.

"Everything's fine," she lied to all the worried faces around her. "Rafael, could you drive me home? I'm a little light-headed."

He didn't answer, just put an arm around her shoulder and used the other to shield her from everyone else as he guided her outside. He buckled her in and hurried around to the driver's side, but by the time she had climbed in, the tears had come and she didn't try to stop them.

He didn't press her, just drove, sending occasional glances her way. Without a word, he helped her out as soon as they got there, and escorted her up to his room. He pressed her down on the bed, picked up the phone, asked about Justin, and said to call him if they needed him. Then he came back, sat down beside her, and wrapped his arms around her, rocking her as if she were a baby.

"What in the world did Beto and Tía do?"

She shook her head and turned enough that she could wrap her arms around his chest and cling to his strength. When she thought she could control herself enough to regain some dignity, she answered him. "She's not my aunt."

He drew back a little, caught a corner of the sheet, and blotted her tears. "What do you mean? Aren't she and your mom sisters? Stepsisters—is that it?"

"No. She's my mother. She had me at fifteen. She gave me up for adoption. She didn't want me then, and she doesn't want me now."

"Damn Beto!" He leaped to his feet. "Why would he tell you … you can't believe him. He's not right."

"He told me. And then …" She drew a shaky breath and met his eyes squarely. "And then Tina told me the same thing. She made it clear that I wasn't Cody—the daughter she never had."

He collapsed beside her again, stunned. "I—I don't know what to say. You don't think it's just—they're both drunks."

"She wasn't drunk. And it makes sense, really. My parents—I guess I should say my aunt and uncle—took care of me because they thought they had to. I've been an imposition all my damn life! And nobody but Toby ever really wanted me, either."

• • •

I want you. But you wouldn't believe me right now. Rafael buried his face in her hair, kissing her scalp, rocking her again, and eventually she went limp in his arms. He settled her on the bed, slipped off her heels, and covered her. Then he locked the door, took off his own shoes, and stretched out beside her to watch her.

She slept restlessly, rolling and tossing and occasionally kicking him with a foot. He tried to move when she did so that he wouldn't wake her up. He didn't think he could bear to see her face so destroyed by the unexpected news.

Anger percolated through him, the old, killing anger he'd only partially admitted to Esmeralda. He hadn't wanted to frighten her. As hurt as she was, if she knew what he wished he could do to her brother and mother, she would be terrified. He'd have to remind her tomorrow, though, that Tía wasn't her mother. She was merely a woman who'd brought a baby into the world and walked away— much like his own birth mother.

He'd have to put it better than that. He'd hurt her if he made it sound as if she shouldn't let the revelation disturb her. Yes, she'd seen the house he'd lived in, without parents. With friends who were there one day and then gone. She'd had a roof over her head, food, and protection. In some ways, only the labels for kinship had changed.

He thought back to her angry words about Tía's feelings for Cody. Dammit, how much evil could one person let go on an unsuspecting world? He'd almost lashed out at Esme, for blaming another of Tía's victims. Almost.

His phone vibrated on the bedside table, the light going on. Alarmed, he saw that the call was from his mother. He looked at the time and realized it was earlier than he thought. Not 10:00 P.M. yet.

She had texted, and he knew he wouldn't wake Esme if he answered. But when he read the actual message, he couldn't believe she didn't hear his yelp of dismay.

"Honey, we'll be home tomorrow. Someone sent us this. Congratulations!" Attached to the message was a picture. Their wedding picture.

He propped himself on an elbow to look at Esme. She still slept soundly, but the pain had faded away. How could he expect her to be able to function tomorrow, when she was shattered? Then again, if anyone could, Esme Salinas could. Esme Salinas Benton, rather. With a slight smile he turned around and went back to sleep.

...

Esme stirred, feeling rested and uncomfortably warm. She was covered, she realized, surprised, and tossed the bedspread aside. She'd fallen asleep in her street clothes—a denim dress she often wore. Why hadn't she changed? She rolled over, and bumped into the long, hard wall Rafael's body formed. He cut the bed in half. She didn't remember—and then she did. His comforting words. Rocking her to sleep. She just didn't remember the part where he lay down beside her and drifted off.

She slipped out of bed. Rafael continued sleeping, an arm thrown over his face, his cell phone near his hand. She retrieved the phone and put it on the night table, wondering if he usually slept with it. Then she removed her clothes and slid back under the covers.

She was tired of the pain, tired of not having anyone. He hadn't wanted a physical relationship. She needed one. At least for tonight. Tomorrow they could go back to their hands off relationship.

"Rafael," she whispered. He stirred, but didn't wake. She inched closer, snuggled into him. He mumbled and moved a hand. She could see the shock when he woke, feeling her bare skin against his hand. He blinked and would have drawn away, but she shifted, pressing her knee against his legs, leaning forward to kiss him.

"We weren't going to do this," he mumbled, and she shushed him by kissing him again. She trailed her fingers up his arms.

"Don't make me beg," Esme whispered.

"Never." She caught the hem of his tee and began tugging it off. He maneuvered to help her. She started with his jeans, but he gently removed her hands. "We can't," he repeated. "You're reacting to what happened—"

"And you're reacting to me," she whispered, moving her hands over him, then replacing her roaming hands with her mouth. He moaned, but caught her hair and tugged her head up.

"I don't have protection. We agreed that if we knew we didn't have it, we wouldn't."

"I'm good," she whispered, and lowered her head again. When he called her name hoarsely, she straddled him, crying out as she felt him inside her. Then they both began to move, urgency building until he pinned her hips and thrust higher and harder, and she threw her head back and moaned with her own climax. He pulled her back to him, wrapping her in his arms.

"Esme?"

"Hmm?"

She could hear the smile in his voice. "You're right. You are good."

She let her eyes drift shut, trying to remember when she'd said that. When she did, her heart thudded painfully and she went still. She had lied to him, implied that she was using protection when she wasn't. She couldn't think beyond giving in to the fire and burning away the pain.

She pretended she'd fallen asleep. Manipulating him one more time, because she couldn't bear to disappoint him. She loved him too much.

Chapter Eighteen

The smell of coffee woke her up. She turned to see Rafael there, looking apprehensive.

"Time to get up, Esme."

"Why?" She turned a little and stretched, exposing herself as the sheets fell away.

"Damn, don't do that!" He grabbed the bedspread and flipped it over her again.

Why didn't he want…? Fear gripped her. Nobody wanted her. Had she driven Rafael away by disregarding his hands off policy?

"Don't think I wouldn't like to, but we need to reevaluate the situation," he said, sounding like a businessman more than a lover. Like a boss rather than a husband. "Esme, someone sent my parents our wedding photo. They're in San Antonio on the way here—maybe half an hour away."

"You're kidding, right?" But she was already out of bed, searching for a robe.

"I'll wait for you in the study," he murmured, and walked away from her.

• • •

Chris and Alice Benton were nicer than she imagined two people could be, even when she'd heard they were special. They greeted everyone with hugs and kisses, and Mrs. Benton wouldn't let Esmeralda go.

"Don't you dare call me Mrs. Anything," she scolded. "You're family, so you have a choice. You may call me Alice."

Rafael's father shot his wife an amused look. "You only gave her one name, Alice," he reminded her. "What's the other choice?"

"Well, on second thought, there's no other choice."

Esme laughed and nodded. "I'll call you Chris," she said to his dad.

Surprisingly, neither interrogated her. When they found out she was from Laredo, they commented on how much they liked her hometown. When he commented on the color of Esme's hair, Chris touched his wife's white hair and said, "Believe it or not, this was red, too."

The four of them crawled around the floor looking for Justin's toys when he tossed them, and Chris made a huge fuss over Chief and Luc. "Haven't seen 'em for what—two years?"

"At least," Rafael said easily. "Hard to believe I've been here in Truth that long already.

"Well, boy, you've got a home in Houston when you want it." He smiled at Esme. "You, too, Mrs. Benton," he told her, his blue eyes dancing.

"We're probably staying here, Dad," Rafael ventured, his tone gentle. "The place grows on you."

He snorted. "If you say so."

"Any more problems with claimants?" Rafael asked, and his father shook his head. "No. Things quieted down when the probate news got old. The main concern's still good old Doug."

The two elder Bentons excused themselves a short while later, claiming jet lag and old age—a malady, according to Alice , that could cause severe bouts of wanting-to-sleep-itis.

"I have that and I'm not old." Esme grinned.

On their way out, Alice stopped to hug and kiss Esme. "As sudden as it was, I'm so glad y'all married," she admitted. "I don't begrudge anyone their freedom, and I know it's not what it used to be—but it's worked for us."

"And my parents," Esme concurred, not really lying. They were still together. But then she realized that they weren't her parents at all, and had to fight to keep from losing her composure again.

Rafael was suddenly there beside her, looping an arm around her shoulder, and squeezing her. "We'll see you later, then," he told them. "Go ahead and get some sleep. We'll have to show you Esme's horse later. She's keeping the others good company."

"Sounds good," Chris said approvingly, then winked. "And maybe Alice and I can join Esmeralda in a little karaoke. She's going to be a good influence on you, son. Get you right with country music again."

Alice chuckled and tugged on his arm. "Old man wasn't supposed to ask you about that video yet," she added over her shoulder. "We don't know who sent it to us, but we loved your version." Almost as if they'd rehearsed it, the two broke into the chorus of "Achy Breaky Heart" as they disappeared down the hall.

Esmeralda watched them go. "What am I going to do? I can't deal with all this right now. Your parents, my parents—I can't deal with any of this."

"Esme … you don't want to hear this, but what really changed? You have Adriana and Ernesto. You never really had Tía anyway."

"But I always felt I should have been with her. Always. I just never knew why."

"Don't let it weigh on you. You've gone through worse."

"Much."

"Then?"

"I hate logic. I'm going riding, Rafael." She didn't invite him, and he didn't ask her.

• • •

The evenings were perfect for sitting outside and chatting, but Rafael and Chris went inside early to look online at a property they were interested in purchasing in Louisiana.

"You and Rafael married very quickly," Alice said, and Esme breathed a little prayer. She didn't want to say something so wrong that Alice, clearly a smart woman who knew her son, would be suspicious.

"I know. I've always been … impetuous. At least, I've been told that I am." She hesitated. "Alice, how long did you know Mr. Benton before you knew you were in love with him?"

"Honestly? "

Esme nodded. "Yes. Please."

"A day." Alice smiled at her surprise. "And mind you, we had nothing. I worked as a clerk, he worked sweeping an auto mechanic's yard out. My dad would've tanned my hide, so I didn't tell him, but the day I met Chris, I told my momma I was in love and wanted to marry him. We got married when I turned seventeen, and we've been together almost forty years."

"I … I turned Rafael down at first," Esme admitted, being partially truthful. "But he's persuasive. We'll have to hope it turns out as it should."

"Hope won't do it, girl. You have to work at it. We all do. But Rafael's worth a lot of effort, and I'd say so if he weren't my son."

"You truly love him as much … as much as Cody?" she asked.

Alice flinched.

"I'm sorry," Esme said softly. "But I recently found out I was adopted. I never knew. I just … I guess I just wonder how it should be. When it works."

"Rafael is my son," Alice replied without hesitation. "I hurt him when Cody died, and I know it. I said some awful things about him being jealous of Cody. I'll spend the rest of my life being sure he knows I couldn't love him more even if I had given birth to him."

"Thank you."

Alice stood, yawning. "I've got that darned old sleeping disease again." She grinned. Then she laid a hand on Esme's head. "Just remember, if someone hurts you with their words, the words might be different tomorrow. Don't cut yourself off from family. Good night."

...

Rafael paced back and forth in his study. Memories of Esmeralda waking him up to make love teased him. Worry over her emotional state tormented him. What if she regretted making love on the night she found out she was adopted? That was the night she found out that her mother knew her, had always known her, but had never wanted her. What if he couldn't resist the urge to leave his study and return to her room, this time being the one to tease and touch, to taste … He stopped himself. He preferred to be in control. He hadn't been in control since he and Esme had made love. He couldn't let all the problems overwhelm him.

His mom and dad had received a certified letter from Doug Harper stating that he intended to sue for custody. His fists clenched. The man who had helped destroy his sister couldn't take her baby away.

"Are you all right, Rafael?" Esmeralda stood in the doorway a slight line creasing her forehead. "You've been moving around in there like a caged animal."

"I'm fine," he muttered. "Okay, maybe not. Harper says he's going to sue for custody."

"You've got the lawyers and money," Esme pointed out.

"But what if he's got the blood?" Then he looked at her. "Are you going out?"

"Yes, I'm going to Beauty In Truth." She laughed at his blank look. "The beauty salon. It's right next to the restaurant."

"I knew that," he faked, and she winked.

"Sure you did. I'll be back."

"I hope so," he called after her. "Esme." The name slid out like a plea. He didn't want the summer to end, but it was flying by. Watching her walk away was scary, and she was just going to a beauty salon. What in the world would he feel when she walked away for good?

She'd never stay. Not when she still thought he'd just hired her to placate his parents. How would he convince her that he loved her? If she left, he'd be that child without anyone again, angry and scared.

She'd been withdrawn since the night they'd made love. Or maybe the morning after, when he'd announced that his parents were on the way. Which lie worried her more—that they could go back to not wanting each other, or that she loved him?

Either way, they were lies he'd asked her to live—for money he didn't even think she wanted.

Suddenly he knew what he had to do. He glanced at his watch. His mom and dad were probably in the den downstairs, catching up on news and sharing their morning coffee.

He found them there. Totally predictable. He smiled as they looked up, two loving people who had saved him from self-destruction. He owed them so much. He closed the door and leaned against it.

"There's something you need to know," he told them. Pain stabbed him as he added, "I've lied to you."

His parents looked at each other, then at him. After a moment, his mother got out of the overstuffed armchair and walked to the daybed, patting the spot beside her. "Come sit with me," she invited.

He wanted to stand, hold himself away from their pain and censure, then the forgiveness they always gave, no matter how little he deserved it.

But if his mother asked for something, he'd do it. He walked over and sat down, turning enough that he could face both of them. "It's about Esme and me," he said.

Chris set his coffee mug down on the desk and pulled off his reading glasses. "This can't be another Paulette thing," he muttered. "You all signed an agreement."

Beside him, his mother straightened. "Christopher Justin Benton, you apologize to Rafa right now! How dare you compare that ... that thing to Esmeralda!"

"But—"

"Even a fool as blind as you can see this is not a Paulette kind of thing!" Alice's anger vibrated in her voice, but then faded as she turned and hugged Rafael impulsively. "I'm afraid, though," she said, not addressing his father any longer, "that this is a broken heart kind of thing." She squeezed his arm. "Am I right?"

Emotion overcame him, and he couldn't speak, so he just wrapped his arms around her and hugged her gently.

Across the room, Chris Benton sighed and reached for his glasses again. He put them on, stood, and came over to rest one hand on Alice's shoulder and another on Rafael's.

"Tell us what you need us to do," he said.

• • •

Esmeralda flipped open her wallet, looking for the bill she'd tucked in to pay for her trim and manicure. As she pulled the money out, a slip of paper fell out. She recognized it as she picked it up, but checked anyway. Doug Harper's phone number.

She found she still couldn't discard it, or tear it in pieces. Maybe Rafael would like the number. He could talk to Doug, make him think about Justin. Rafael wouldn't understand why she had the number. He'd wonder why she'd been willing to accept it from Beto. The fact that Beto had Bounty's phone number raised her own suspicions, too, but Beto was out of the picture now. The temptation to do something for Rafael—something that would move him the way he moved her—burned inside her. She could just call and see what he wanted. She could do something to help the Bentons and their cherished little boy.

A voice she didn't recognize answered the phone, but then Doug Harper came on. He introduced himself as Bounty, but she refused to address him by that name after his disgusting behavior and his legal threats.

"What did you want from me?" she demanded, and he immediately started with the innuendo.

"Well, what do you think I wanted?" he drawled.

"Don't call again."

"Don't hang up," he said quickly. "Please. I'm sorry. I can help you."

"I don't need help. And I don't need a man, either, Doug. I have one."

"Look, I think Justin is mine. And I want him. But I have a record deal now. I've been offered a tour as an opening act. I may not be the best choice to raise him."

"So leave him where he is," she said. "He's happy, Doug. He's a happy little boy with grandparents and an uncle who love him."

"I … I don't know. If I don't claim him now, later they might say I never showed any interest. I think I have to try now." He paused. After a long silence, he sighed into the phone. "Look, meet me at the Silver Dollar. Tomorrow. I want to do the right thing."

"Not from what I heard," Esme reminded him.

"Esmeralda, did your parents ever hate one of your boyfriends?"

"They hated all of them, but especially the one I wanted to marry. So what?"

"Did they try to break you up?" She didn't answer, and she could almost imagine him nodding at the silent receiver. "Yeah. Cody loved me, Esme. She wasn't a stupid woman. Her family just wouldn't let her choose. I wasn't good enough."

She could see that happening, except … "You came on to me. I didn't ask for it or enjoy it. You knew I was engaged. Why?"

"I'm a jerk, Esme. I don't deny that. I play a Romeo type in my show. The girls eat it up, and right now I have to draw as many folks as I can. But if you gave me a chance, I think I could leave you with a better impression."

"I have to go," she said. "If I'm in town tomorrow, maybe I'll call."

"I'll be at the Silver Dollar at four for a sound check and rehearsal. Come if you want to."

All the way home, Doug's explanation turned circles in her head. Toby had been such a good kid. Nobody had ever given him a chance. What if the Bentons were just wrong about Doug Harper? Even if he filed for custody, that didn't mean anything except that he really wanted his son. If Justin were his son, of course.

She found Rafael outside, watching Justin try to interest Chief in a game of chase. The dog stayed where he was, even though Justin crowed and jumped up and down and rolled the ball.

"What's up?" he asked, moving over on the canvas-covered sofa.

"Rafael, how well did you know Doug Harper?"

"Very well. I hired him, remember?"

Actually, she'd forgotten that as soon as Doug painted the comparison with Toby. "I just can't help wondering if you all gave him a chance. I mean, I was thinking about Toby. He was a good man.. Really. Or at least, Toby would have been a good man if he'd gotten that far. Rafael, what if you just sat down with Doug and talked to him, man to man?"

"And all this popped into your head for no reason?" he drawled, unconvinced.

She didn't like him questioning her. "I told you, Toby's been on my mind." She thought he flinched at that, but refused to back down. "Talk to him, Rafael."

He stood up and swung Justin into his arms. "We got a letter from his lawyers, Esmeralda. Our lawyers are talking to him. And when lawyers are talking—everyone else stays out of it. Everyone." He stalked out of the room with Justin slung over his shoulder laughing and waving at her.

•••

Doug sat at a front table, waving at customers who acknowledged him. The sign outside said Bounty Collins, but Esme had never met him as Doug. Maybe he hadn't been such a creep in the pre-Bounty days.

He stood when he saw her, giving her an apprehensive smile that made her understand why women liked his looks. He didn't seem at all threatening. They sat down, and she let him order a beer for her.

"So … Rafael told me you've filed for custody."

"My lawyers are handling it. Like I said, it's a tough call."

"But one you made, apparently."

"I could stop it."

"Really?" She sipped her beer and stared at him. He fidgeted. She could still see through him, she realized. Doug and Bounty were the same after all. Her excitement fizzled, and she realized she'd wanted to impress the Bentons by saving the day for Justin. She was becoming the old Esmeralda all over again—manipulative and needy. Wait. *There is no old Esmeralda.* She drained half the bottle. "You could help make that happen, Esmeralda. You could help me."

"I suggested they were wrong about you," she volunteered. "I know that my parents tore Toby apart, for no reason. Maybe if you made it clear you wouldn't take Justin, they'd give you a chance—get to know you."

"They had chances," he said bitterly. "I kept Cody alive, not the other way around. You should see what her life was when she didn't know who her kid's father was." He gave her a smug smile. "Or wouldn't tell. I'd like to tear your do-no-wrong hubby apart with my bare hands. He could have listened to Cody. He could have listened to me. He could have let us be in love—and she might still be alive."

His story echoed in her head, replayed like a song. Or a bad dream. His story was hers. Cody hadn't lived; neither had Toby. She reached for her phone and drew her mug closer. If he gave her five more minutes of truth, five minutes that made him believe he was sincere, she'd call Rafael and force him to come over.

He reached out and laid a hand on hers. "He's still the lucky one, her brother is. Your husband. He's got you. I've got nothing. At best, a kid with no last name who might not ever know who his daddy is."

His words pierced her soul. She didn't know who her father was. Her mother didn't know, either. How dare he talk about a woman he had claimed to love like that? She stood to go.

"Stay a little longer. One more beer. Let me tell you a story about how your husband and I met. Maybe you can remind him …" He got up and walked to the bar, coming back with the promised beverages.

"Here." He handed her one, and took the other. "Cheers."

She nodded curtly, but didn't raise her drink. Her cell phone buzzed suddenly, and she looked. Beto's number. She didn't answer, but when it kept ringing, she started worrying. Maybe her parents—her aunt or uncle—needed her and couldn't call. Maybe—

"Excuse me," she said, standing. "I need to take this." And she wouldn't take it in front of a stranger who knew her brother.

She could hardly hear his voice, and she walked around the room trying to improve her connection. When the number faded from the screen, she closed the phone. "I've got to go."

"But your beer," he protested. "You didn't touch it. I wanted to tell you—"

She didn't sit down, but she lifted it, sipped it, then pushed it away. "Thank you," she said, and left.

Her truck was halfway down the block, but the distance kept seeming to lengthen. She felt sluggish and tired, but she'd slept well the night before. She turned to look behind her. Fear made her skin prickle as she thought she saw Beto move into the shadows of a stone column by one of the buildings. What could Beto be doing still in town? Rafael said he'd given him bus fare home.

She couldn't help the sudden suspicion she felt. Maybe Bounty wanted to break up the marriage early. Maybe Beto wanted to mete out some further damage. They might be two of a kind, out to hurt her, hurt Rafael—hurt Justin. The scandal they could cause by making her appear to be pursuing Bounty, just days after the wedding, might be something they'd do out of sheer hatred. She tried to walk faster, but her legs wouldn't cooperate. Across the street, the door opened as customers came out of Rosita's Restaurant. She didn't know the woman, but the other was the game warden—PJ. Even through the dizziness trying to cripple her, she remembered that game wardens were certified peace officers. She held her arms out a little at her sides trying to keep her balance.

"PJ!" she called, as if he were her new best friend. "PJ, I want to ask you …" His momentary confusion disappeared and he started toward her, smiling, but she saw him looking around carefully, his head moving imperceptibly as he spotted something.

"Are you all right?" he asked.

"Wobbly. I think maybe the beer I was drinking had something in it. I didn't drink much …" She swayed.

"Someone might have been following you," he said softly, motioning towards his companion, who had stopped several yards away.

The woman who had been with him came up, and nodded at Esmeralda, though she looked annoyed. "I feel dizzy," Esme explained, "but …"

"Let's get out of the sun. I'm Reyna." She supported Esme as they climbed up a sloping walk and stopped under an awning.

Behind them, PJ had disappeared, and came out minutes later walking beside Beto.

"He says he's your brother," he told Esme, and she shook her head. "No. He's my cousin."

"We're family," Beto whined. "You owe me—tell the officer the truth. You're my sister!"

"Please," Esme said softly. "Please—can you make him leave? I don't want to drive yet." She knew she sounded shrill. Panicked. But she couldn't help herself. "If I have to be here with him … no. I won't." She tried to move away, but stumbled and stopped.

"Didn't your husband pay for a bus ticket for him?" PJ asked.

When Esme looked surprised, he chuckled.

"Yes, I know," she agreed, weakly and without humor. "This is Truth." She took another faltering step before turning back. PJ and Reyna flanked Beto, effectively keeping him there. She wouldn't run. "What were you and Doug planning, Beto?" she demanded, her dry throat making her voice hoarse. "Were you going after me or Rafa?"

Beto's hate-filled face twisted in a leer. "Prove we were doing anything, cuz. You were working on a little affair with the man your husband hates most in the world. I was just walking down the sidewalk. Stopped to take a leak, and this gorilla grabbed me for no reason. I'll sue," he spat.

She'd never felt so sick, but it wasn't the drink. Her head pounded, but most of the dizziness was gone. The nausea and the weakness threatening to swamp her like a tidal wave, dragging her under and away forever, came from Beto's hatred and contempt.

"Thanks, PJ and Reyna. Everything's gone but a headache." She waved a hand at Beto. "I—I don't know what you can do with him, but I can't be here. I need to go."

"Don't worry about him. You shouldn't drive. Maybe Doc Roberts is in."

"No need." Esmeralda brushed at her hair with her fingers and took a few experimental steps. "See? I can walk again. I have to leave, PJ. I don't want to see him again. Ever."

In the end, she didn't drive home. PJ called Rafael, who insisted on taking her to the clinic to have blood drawn. PJ alerted the sheriff's office, who went off to the Silver Dollar. Everywhere eyes watched her, and conversation buzzed around her. She'd never manage to be free of scandal, even when she was supposed to be the hero. Not only hadn't she talked Doug out of pursuing Justin, she'd bet money someone had overheard the exchange about being Beto's cousin, not sister. Soon her sorry story would be all over town. The mother who didn't want her, but claimed a stranger as a daughter. The woman who'd married for money and couldn't even succeed at that for two months. The one thing Rafael had asked her to do was stay away from Doug, and she'd blown it.

Dejected, she moved one foot after another, doing what she was told. That was easier than thinking. PJ's friend offered to drive Esme's truck home, and Rafael insisted she ride with him.

"Why, Esmeralda? How could you have done the only thing I asked you not to do? Sitting at a bar drinking with that—that bastard." He shook his head. "I expected more of you."

After that, neither of them spoke until they got home.

"There'll be cell phone pictures and gossip," he said, stopping her when she moved to unfasten the seat belt. "There's no getting away from it."

"If there's no getting away from it, then there's no need to talk about it." She pushed his hand away and unbuckled the seat belt. "I'm sorry, though, Rafael. Believe it or not, I thought just once

I'd be the good guy." She smiled faintly. "I'm not up to dinner." She slid out and made her escape, still on unsteady legs.

Rafael never came upstairs. She waited for him, wanting to explain, wanting him to understand that she hadn't done it out of pride or stubbornness. She'd really thought maybe there was something to Doug's claim that the Bentons just couldn't accept his love for Cody. She couldn't quit thinking about Beto's phone call, followed by Doug's insistence that she drink another beer. What could he have wanted? To spite Rafael, maybe? Be caught in some public display with the enemy's new bride? Or had Beto been the ringleader, wanting—God knows what he might have wanted.

She glanced at her clock. Almost two in the morning, and she was alone. They hadn't risked sharing the bed since … since the night they'd risked their hearts and made love. But he'd always been next door. She'd spent hours hoping he'd knock. Or just open the door. He never had, but now, knowing the room next door was empty chilled her.

Early the next morning, she got up and dressed, then went downstairs. The whole family seemed to have disappeared, although Connie greeted her warmly and offered her breakfast.

"Connie, where is everyone?" she asked.

"The Bentons left. They took Justin back to Houston."

"Why?"

"I wish I knew. Broke Rafael's heart, and when they left—he took off somewhere. I don't know where."

"Thanks, Connie."

"Do you really want to know what happened?" Marie asked.

"Yes."

"Your brother tried to press charges against Rafael. He keeps telling the sheriff that Rafael paid to have him beaten up. "

"No one can believe that."

"No. But it harassed Rafael just enough to make him snap. Your brother started mouthing off about you, and Rafael hit him—in front of the deputy who was just about to let him go. They didn't arrest him, but you know a lawyer will get him for everything he can."

"And Justin?"

"The Bentons got worried about all the gossip and talk going around and thought they should take him home."

"This is Truth. There's always gossip."

"Well, not like this. Someone started saying you told Bounty you'd sleep with him if he'd just agree to let the Bentons keep Justin. Said you pretending to be drugged was just part of an act to keep Rafael from going off and killing someone."

"Nobody can believe garbage like that. There were blood tests."

"Look," Marie said with finality. "I don't think half the folks here believe any of the stuff they hear—but they repeat it and spread it and butter it up. Rafael's the joke of the day, with a philandering wife a few days after the wedding.

"And to make it worse—someone let slip that you and Rafael married for money."

"How—who could have known that except you?"

Marie shrugged. "Funny how you can take pictures of documents and share them with a whole town, isn't it? See you."

...

Esme was packed by the time she heard Rafael come up the stairs. He walked into the room, and her heart broke. He looked so tired. And so broken. Losing Justin must be destroying him. Maybe he'd go home to Houston. Nothing could hold him here in this town of lies and bitterness.

"What ...?" He looked at her neat piles of suitcases and boxes.

"I can't stay, Rafael. How can I? I did the one thing you asked me not to do, and Justin's gone. My aunt and brother will keep trying to use me against you until ... they won't stop."

"I can deal with that, Esmeralda."

"You shouldn't have to." She walked over and laid her palm on his cheek. "You kept me from falling apart when I found out who I really am. Thank you." She stepped away, picking up one of the boxes. "I need to leave Domatrix for a while. I don't know where I'm going. But I can't stay here where all the lies will destroy us, Rafael. Marie told me a photo of our contract came out."

"No one but Marie could have done that. That's easy to fix."

"For you, maybe. You fire her, and everything's fine. What do I do the next time I face your parents, Rafa? What? Whether you called it a job or a marriage, I didn't love you when I agreed to marry you. What does that make me?"

"The woman I love."

She blinked away tears.

"No." She shook her head and caught his hands, trying to make him understand. "Rafael, we haven't been together long enough to love each other. And even if we had, I can't let my family harass and push and poke until they break us."

"Toby didn't break, Esmeralda. He went off to find a way to be with you—to be with you always. I want the chance he didn't have."

Esmeralda's throat constricted and she couldn't answer. She just turned again to pick up a bag, but he pulled it out of her hands and tossed it aside.

"You sat with me in Laredo, and I told you about the little girl I lost—the girl who was like my sister. There was this huge hole inside me after I lost *Pioja*. And then I had Cody, and I lost her. Don't walk away, Esme. Don't be the wife I love and lose."

"I'm not sure I'm worth the risk you'd be taking," she whispered.

"Could you love me?"

"I do."

"Then that's worth everything," he murmured and let her pull him close.

About the Author

Leslie P. García grew up here and there, spending much of her childhood in rural Georgia, and virtually all her adult life in deep South Texas. Married and surrounded by children and grandchildren, much of her writing touches on family. A passion for animals, a twenty-year teaching career, and the strange twists and turns that life can take have provided more stories than time to write.

His Temporary Wife is the second in the Texas Heart and Soul series. Watch for Jade Brockton's story in the future.

Leslie loves to hear from readers, and can be reached at all the electronic haunts:

E-mail: *lesliegarcia2000-author@yahoo.com*

Facebook: *www.facebook.com/LeslieP.Garcia*

Twitter: @LesliePGarcia

Please drop by *Return to Rio* for updates, guest posts by exciting authors, and other miscellaneous content!

More from This Author
(From *Wildflower Redemption* by Leslie P. García)

Aaron Estes stood at the window, one hand pulling back the drapes to clear his view. Outside, clouds hovered along the horizon, but he doubted it would rain.

Someone from town—Ross something?—had stopped by earlier and offered to do work. The handyman had scoffed at the chance of rain. "Always cloudy," he'd grumbled. "Never rains."

Aaron had shrugged and told the man politely that he didn't need help. And he didn't—at least, not physical help. Spiritual help, maybe, mental health—the kind of health that comes with peace and contentment. The kind of health he'd probably never find again. He closed his eyes and listened for any sound of six-year-old Chloe waking, but heard only silence. Unwelcome memories tried to push in, and he pressed his lids tighter against his face, unwilling to give in again to the pain.

The memories came anyway: the loud, angry words of a marriage shattering. The cheery morning greeting from the one thing he and Stella still shared—a tiny, precious miracle of motion and light.

Chloe's loud kiss and plaintive complaint when her mother tried to leave without kissing Aaron goodbye hovered near the surface. He could still feel Chloe's huge kiss on his cheeks, hear the petulance in her voice when her mother tried to step around them.

"Mommy, you forgot Daddy's kiss." Stella pecked him on the cheek, and Chloe tugged on her mom's blouse.

"Mommy, don't be silly. Mommies kiss daddies on the mouth."

With lips so tight he could feel her anger, Stella stood on tiptoe and touched her mouth to his. Then he watched as Chloe grabbed her mother's hand, delighted that she was playing mom today, not cop. To Chloe, the world was a game, and everyone in it, players.

He closed his eyes, but the burning didn't go away, so he went back to staring blindly outside. There were no daffodils here, as there were in Alabama, but he heard that just miles north spring came in on carpets of bluebonnets and waves of flaming Indian paintbrush. All the locals raved about the Texas wildflowers. They said he should go see them, but he knew he couldn't.

The scene he'd rushed to just over a year ago crowded in: the hysteria, the cop cars with their flashing red and blue lights; the crumpled body of a child, an injured teacher being wheeled toward an ambulance; and an officer who knew Stella pulling him aside. She'd taken a bullet for a kid, the officer told him. Unfaithful, maybe, arrogant often—but nobody doubted Stella Estes's courage.

The tears rolled down his cheeks and he wiped them away with the back of his hand, trying not to remember that there'd been blood on the daffodils the day the world ended.

•••

Luz Wilkinson tugged on the girth again and nudged Pompom's belly with a knee. "Let it out, girl," she urged. The little pinto sighed heavily and turned around to nose Luz just as the cell phone in her pocket went off. Her horses would have shied at the sudden blast of sound, and the other ponies would have lifted their heads and pricked their ears. Pompom stood there with that complete lack of interest that indicated absolute lack of intelligence.

Frowning over the pony's deficiencies, Luz fished the phone out and hit the button to silence it. She didn't recognize the number. She hoped it wasn't a bill collector, but knew that it probably was.

"Hello?"

"Uh…hi. Is this Eden Acres?"

"Yes." Luz scratched Pompom's ear while she tried to connect a physical image with the deep, masculine voice. She often toyed with visualizing strangers from their phone calls, and almost always was wrong. Silence pricked her into awareness. Perhaps the caller expected someone more enthusiastic, more helpful. Someone who could offer more than one word answers…

"May I help you?" she prodded when he didn't go on.

Another long pause, then came the abrupt questions: "I heard you have therapy horses? And ponies?"

Luz hesitated. Sometimes children from a group foster home came out to ride, and occasionally a counselor who worked with troubled children recommended exposing them to riding. But therapy? She wouldn't go that far.

"We have horses and ponies," she said carefully. "But who told you we have therapy horses?"

"Esmeralda Salinas," the voice said, no longer hesitant.

Luz wrinkled her nose, picturing the elegant redheaded school guidance counselor with her neat suits and perpetual pep. Living in this tiny community, they'd crossed paths several times. They didn't much like each other, but Esmeralda loved horses. That was usually a sterling quality, but this time, Luz's main yardstick for measuring "good folks" didn't hold water, because the counselor struck her as conceited, plastic, and sneaky. Although they avoided each other as much as possible, she boarded the woman's pricey Appaloosa. Undoubtedly Esmeralda would have liked finer stomping grounds for the horse and herself, but no one else boarded horses in this arid, dying community. Very few still owned livestock.

Nevertheless, Luz was surprised that the counselor had referred any male new to town. The director of the children's group home was an elderly woman, and the other referrals were long-time residents, parents in established relationships, but Esmeralda sending a guy her way? He was not single, then, apparently.

"You're Ms. Wilkinson?" Doubt tinged the deep voice. She'd confused the caller. Didn't matter. Confusion was a constant companion these days.

"Yes," she replied. One word again. He could state his business or not. She didn't care.

"Ms. Wilkinson, I need to talk to you about riding lessons for my little girl, Chloe. Or maybe—" Another brief pause, as if he wasn't sure what he wanted. "Maybe even buying a pony. I need advice on what would be best."

He was a client then. She should be happier than she was. She pasted a smile on her face, hoping it would make her voice warmer, more caring. "Great. Advice is what we do best." Quick questions confirmed he knew how to find Eden Acres, and she clicked the phone off and returned it to her pocket. She realized, a little late, that asking the man's name might have been both friendlier and more professional.

"Screw it," she muttered with unusual ire. "Professional never worked for me, anyway. Come on, old lady. Some kid might actually get a pony ride today."

Half an hour later Luz was feeding the menagerie when she heard tires on the gravel drive. She called the motley collection of rescued animals her menagerie, because it took too long to go into the species, circumstances, and problems she dealt with trying to feed and shelter them day to day. Candy, the burro, butted her as she turned away, and the kitten with no name left its feeding dish to run away from some unseen menace, almost tripping her. She wiped her hands on the sides of her jeans and shut the door separating the odd animals from the handful of horses that were both her treasures and bread-earners.

By the time she made it outside, a dark-haired, broad-shouldered man was leaning against an SUV, frowning. He wore long sleeves and a tie, hardly south Texas pony-buying attire. But she wasn't expecting anyone else.

She walked over and held out her hand. "I'm Luz Wilkinson. Welcome to Eden Acres. Are you——?"

"Aaron Estes." He shook her hand briefly, and then cast another look around the premises. Not disapproving, exactly, she thought. It was more a look of disappointment.

"Why don't we go into the office?" she suggested. "It's cooler." And it was well decorated with new paint and shelves of her mother's trophies, recently polished.

They walked into the barn. The half-open stall doors caught his attention. He pointed at one of the horses. "Pretty. Yours?"

"No." She shook her head, and paused to pet the broad blaze of white running down the mare's face. "This is Domatrix. One of my boarders."

"Doma—isn't this Esmeralda's horse?"

"Yes, as a matter of fact." She leaned against the stall door, slanting a glance at him, surprised that Esmeralda had apparently described Domatrix in detail to a man new in town. No wonder Aaron Estes hadn't flinched at the name, even shortened as it seemed to be. Then again...she thought of the tall, regal redhead and the dearth of men in Rose Creek. A man with a daughter likely meant a married man. That would lessen Esmeralda's interest. Wouldn't it? She pushed away from the mare's stall, and he followed the remaining few feet to the office. She waved a hand at the chairs and took her own place behind the small, bare desk.

"So tell me how I can help," she invited.

He looked down for a minute at his hands before looking at her. When he did finally lift his eyes, she could see why Esmeralda had pounced. The man's perfect features and startling green eyes would stop traffic in lots of places, let alone this one-horse, one-eligible-man town.

"My little girl—Chloe—needs a hobby. Something she'll like that's safe."

Luz studied him, perplexed. Somehow the pieces of the big, attractive man across the desk didn't add up. She supposed she was using stereotypes, but he seemed too hesitant and unsure for his own body. Not as if he was uncomfortable in his own skin, maybe, but almost as if he were fearful of something.

She puzzled over the discomfort he seemed to feel, trying to figure out his connection to Esme. He wasn't family; the Rose Creek gossips knew everyone and every relative, no matter how far flung. The counselor had aging parents and a half-brother down in Laredo. A friend? She discarded that. Esmeralda didn't work weekends, and if he were a friend, she would be here. So the relationship had to be professional. Maybe the daughter he'd mentioned was Esmeralda's client?

"'Safe as opposed to bike riding or playing with dolls? Or safe, fun, and a perfect springtime activity—I'm not sure I know what you mean by safe," Luz admitted. "Riding has risks—the same as pretty much everything."

Aaron Estes growled something that sounded profane and hunched forward over the desk, his face tight. "Don't you think I know that?" After a moment, his face muscles eased into smoother lines. His lips twitched, as if they'd known how to smile, but forgotten. "I'm not as weird as I seem. Just a tad nervous and overprotective."

"But you're not in denial," she observed. "That's got to be good." She smiled. "So, tell me about your Chloe."

Pure, absolute love washed across his face. His lips remembered how to smile and he straightened in his chair. "Chloe's my life," he said simply.

Luz returned the smile, but prodded gently for more insight. "How old is she? Does she like horses? Has she ridden before?"

"Six, yes, and no."

Luz blinked, trying to understand the simple, one-word answers. Saw the dimples appear, and then deepen in Aaron Estes' cheeks. She'd always had a weakness for dimples, dammit! Was he one-upping her? "So, is this payback, or do you always keep things so short and simple?"

He actually chuckled. It was a short little rumble of laughter, but a chuckle.

"Payback, definitely. I was nervous enough about calling and you were anything but friendly."

She thought back on her hesitation to answer the phone, how she'd focused on the pinto rather than concentrating on encouraging conversation. He had her pegged, but she didn't care. Wouldn't. She needed customers, but wasn't in the market for relationships of any kind. And professional? She allowed herself a quick mental shrug. She no longer had a profession. She'd been a teacher, and a good one. She'd surrounded herself with kids and poured energy and love into their lives. Then she'd lost it all, including her daughter Lily. Not her daughter, she reminded herself: Brian's daughter, given to her as one more false promise. Now she rescued discarded animals when she could, and was going broke doing it.

So she pounced on something he said. "You were nervous? About asking if we had ponies?" Slight derision might have crept into her words, because he flinched and drew away again.

"Not about ponies." He paused, looking for the right words. "We don't know each other. Esmeralda recommended riding as a form of therapy." He shrugged. "Telling a stranger your kid has problems is hard."

Her cheeks burned with embarrassment. "I owe you an apology—of course it is." She stood up abruptly, annoyed with herself. "Guess it's attack a stranger day—I'm just not sure why. Would you like to look at Rumbles? She would be the pony Chloe would work with first."

"Sure." He got up too, ignoring her apology, and stretched. Outside the office, one of the horses whinnied, and another kicked at the stall. The pungent scents of the stable reminded her it was time to muck stalls—again. Already. Out of the corner of her eyes, she saw his nose wrinkle.

"Do you even like horses?" she asked, curious.

He slanted a glance down at her and shrugged. "Don't know. Haven't been around them. Not really an animal person."

Before Luz could murmur a response, he stopped, turning towards her and holding his hands out in apology. "Not that I don't like them, exactly. I used to travel, and before that—well, I just wasn't raised around them."

"Okay." Luz gave him her own shrug. "So I guess Chloe's mom will be the main go-between here?"

A muscle in his jaw twitched, and the nervous tension he'd shown in the beginning visibly tightened his body. "Chloe's mom," he said through clenched teeth, "is dead."

In the mood for more Crimson Romance?
Check out *Little White Lies* by R.C. Matthews at
CrimsonRomance.com.